ISBN: 9798734233153

Imprint: Independently published

Dragon's Conquest Earrie and Fae

Chapter 1 Honor Ball

High above Ephoreia's clouds a Kingdom of towering stone slept. This floating palace was ruled by a great number of elves.

The elves of the castle appeared similar to a wingless fairy. Each elf bore glowing skin from a great multitude of varying tones. Their skin lit up the palace's walls like torches.

Blank stone reflected peach-pinks, rose-reds, sky-blues, and grass-greens as they danced across the palace's walls like shadows behind a lit flame.

Inside this castle of illuminations, a multitude of stunning elves adorned themselves in fine clothing. Their delicate pieces were handcrafted by halfling servants.

Elves wore light, feathered gowns buttoned with assortments of jewels. Sapphires, rubies, pearls, and many more were clipped along their hems. Some of these elves stood out among the crowd since they wore plated armor to this dance.

Tonight was a special dance, as it was only held every three years. The festivity was called the Ember Knight Honor Ball. A celebration for the royal knights of the ember force.

For such a grand kingdom, there was a mere total of thirty-one Ember Knights participants for the celebration. This number included that of the king himself and his daughter Earrie.

Inside the halls of this exquisite ball, a tradition of blades was upheld. Thirty Ember Knights stood face to face in a lined fashion.

One spare knight stood in front of all of them in their center. He held a large shield with a dragon symbol molded into it, contrary to the others who held swords of iron.

Knights wore their signature Ember Knight armor. Their bodies flashed silver-plated wares with pictures of dragons sleeping printed on their breastplates.

The top half of their backs remained absent revealing bare skin, and their shoulders were cut at the armpit. Small, ankle-high boots with knee-length under mail pinched them tightly as they danced. Naked backs left way for their transformed wings and scales to blossom.

To the left of the king's throne, Fae watched with her cheeks pressed into palms in a sulking fashion. The young princess failed to understand the purpose of pretending to battle.

With a twist of her lips, Fae blew a strand of orange, red hair that blocked her view while attempting to play her part of an ecstatic royal.

The higher-ups she was trying to appease sat to the side of the show behind black lines in rows of white, laced chairs. They clapped and threw their hands in the air to the many sounds of clanking blades.

Swords clashed in tune with a background violinist, and it was clear that this bit was a rehearsed ordeal. The king sat in his pure-golden throne with an enormous smile plastered on his lips. For this wasn't just any ball to the king, his blood was being honored.

Lined closest to the king was a stern-faced Earrie. She was the next princess inline for the throne. Hot-pink hair fell past the backs of her knees as her ends were tied in a knot to maintain its unruly flow. Earrie's skin irradiated a soft pink, and her eyes glowed a lime green that reflected the image of her father's.

Her assigned dullest was none other than Sir Maxwell Penate; The man of her dreams. His parents owned the castle's royal college. This made him a fine, young suitor who would easily qualify to marry the princess, but due to the Ember Knight's code, the two of them choose to conceal their relationship.

Maxwell stood an average elven height of eight-feet tall. His hair was a dark, night blue while his skin and eyes shined moon silver. The princess's dance partner wore his hair shaved above his left ear. He let it hang off to the right of his shoulder just below his chin.

Earrie found his appearance dreamy. Her green eyes stayed in a fixated stare while their blades danced together. Maxwell let out a grin as he failed her many attempts to not blink her eyes in a trance.

Two blades struck to their rehearsed directions. Fae rolled her eyes at their display and positioned her neck to another palm with a growl. Much to her joy, King Richard stood up and clapped. The Ember Knights bowed in a queued fashion as the audience roared and shouted their applause.

When the show ended, halfling servants scurried away and removed separating tape. This led the way for the night to begin.

Many young men perked up for a chance to beg for Fae's hand in the dance. She twirled her ear-length, copper locks while politely declining each one of their offers.

Fae's halfling upbringing made her dance style

stick out of the crowd like a sore thumb. The young princess wanted more than anything to blend with those who mocked her. To prevent any embarrassment, she excused herself to the lady's room.

On her way there, she passed by an array of merchants that were set up to make sales during the ball. They displayed shiny wares on fine tables covered in silk cloths.

Dazzling light struck Fae's eye. A blade crafted to resemble, Nefewra, an ancient sword belonging to the king himself and every highness before him. Though Fae did not know this fine sword, she was drawn in to its beauty.

The young princess held up the blade and attempted a swing with a loud exhale. Her hand slipped accidentally due to its polished grip, and the sword flung through the ballroom floor.

The flying blade caused many to cover their agape mouths. The replica appeared sharp in nature, but it was merely crafted for decoration.

Fae's eyes widened as the fragile piece was snatched midair. "Maybe next time, you should practice your grip before you swing," a voice teased from behind.

The mocker was none other than her sister, Earrie. Maxwell stood behind her and grinned at the scene. Some onlookers joined in and laughed. The royals of Heaven's Castle were always eager to find fault in the young princess.

Earrie eyed the blade. "It's nothing, sister. Just a cheap imitation of Nefewra. It's not even carved right," she said as she returned the decorative sword.

"I'm sorry, princess! We don't know what the real blade looks like as it's been stowed away for many years," the halfling craftsman apologized with a bowed head and shaking hands.

Earrie proceeded to glare at him and spit, "Don't bother crafting such a piece like this again." She glanced down to the sword once more with a disgusted look, "You've put its name to shame!" Earrie flipped her hair and walked off to continue her night.

When the female knight passed her sister, she noticed the embarrassment inside Fae's face. She stopped her steps and made eye contact with Fae. "Don't bother with these guys, Fae, the royals have much better wares," she coughed out in an attempt at an apology.

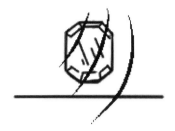

Outside of the ball, a hidden, medical student peaked in. He masked himself behind the courtyard's shrubs. Now, this was not a place for a college simpleton.

Benard snuck in the previous night when security was at low peak, since then, he proceeded to hide in various parts of the castle's courtyard all day. Little by little, the infiltrator inched himself bush to bush like a turtle until he finally made it to a shrub with a window seat.

The boy did not come unprepared for his shenanigans. Benard brought a day's worth of food and water for his little camp out. Even at the risk of being caught and losing his full-ride scholarship to

Penate College, the price of one glance of princess Earrie was worth it in his eyes. Her beauty was renowned throughout the kingdom of Heaven's Castle.

He gazed into the ball with a hanging mouth while he scanned the magnificent scene it beheld. Heaven's Castle's finest young woman danced slow-paced waltzes with young men. Benard dreamed if he could only trade places with one of these men.

His eyes strayed to a short elf on a sprint across the ball. He noticed the royal's distaste for the lady as they scuffed their noses when she passed and folded their arms in repulsion.

Looking up and down when at the commotion, Benard leaned in and pressed his cheeks against the cold window. The medic boy trailed the event to his best ability.

Inside the ball, the copper-haired princess dodged through couples and ducked under tented hands. Halflings servers dropped plates of fresh drinks on sight of the racket.

The young princess couldn't help her dramatics.

Her sister's crudeness caused her tears to fall in public. She needed to escape wandering eyes before word got out of her outburst. The last thing the young princess needed was more negative onlookers.

With a sigh of relief, she reached the bathroom stall. Fae collapsed down on the lip of the toilet with a loud plump. She held both her legs up and sobbed silently into her white, silk dress.

Soon after her escape to the bathroom, Fae's ears twitched up to the sounds of lively girls entering. One of the girls talked about her makeup smearing due to her abundance of laughter. Their thoughtless jokes only made her fingers clench her knees tighter until they burned a bright red.

Breathing heavily, she continued to mask her hiccuping tears. The runaway princess listened to the group of girls for several-excruciating minutes. Her stomach curdled when they touched onto a subject she never heard before.

"To think the poor lass doesn't even know the truth as to why King Richard adopted—" one of the ladies said in a fake-sympathetic voice before her friend interrupted her.

"Shhh—we'll get skinned alive if we talk of that!" the other girl hushed. Fae listened to the sound of a clamping heel.

"I know, but it's so insane to think she's the king's bastard with that stable-halfling Stella!" the previous voice giggled out.

Fae's lips fell open and her heart momentarily stopped at their words. Could this be true?

With sudden understanding, everything made sense to Fae. The inside jokes she'd never felt apart of. The way the royals treated her mother while she was still alive. The fact that Earrie visited her many times back when she was just a stable girl's daughter.

Every question she ever pandered was quelled by this truth. Fae felt like her whole world was crashing down. All the facades hidden behind darkened truths were shattered by that one sentence.

She busted out of her stall with a thump and skidded with haste through the ball. This time, her sprint was in the direction of the courtyard. The young halfling needed fresh air to think.

When she ran into the castle's garden, Fae struck into a young man. Their bodies entangled during their fall.

Benard eyed her with interest. He found her face in the likeness of the princess. This was the same girl who'd captured his eyes a moment beforehand through the glass window.

Fae had yet to make a public debut outside the castle's walls. Few Ephoreians knew who she was. Benard was tied in with the oblivious crowd of Heaven's Castle.

With no exchange of words, the young student no older than age nineteen got up and dusted off his trousers. He bent over and offered a chivalrous hand to Fae.

She looked up and marveled at his red-on-red colors. It was always unique when an elf spotted matching hair and skin tones. Fae offered a shy smile and graciously took his hand.

Inwardly, Benard feared that his sneak-in would be exposed. He vowed to himself to stay calm and act casual.

Fae, on the other hand, feared for the aftermath of her tantrum. Two years of princess training just to be eaten and spit out by the public at her first appearance.

The young princess of age eighteen facepalmed in light of the day's events. Her dad would be furious with her. Even just the idea of facing him made her want to hurl. She would be the talk of the palace for ages.

Benard spun his head around and let out a giggle at her frustrated mannerisms. She blushed a bright-pink on top of her yellow glow, and with a respective bow, the pair parted ways.

The ginger-haired princess continued to run far away from the building that brought her such humiliation. Fae skidded past the college and stone buildings with marble accents. Smooth rocks outlined her steps as she pressed onward. The princess wasn't going to let up until she reached her spot.

After Fae passed through the royal quarter of the palace, she eyed a familiar place. The stench of death lingered in the air, and machinery hummed a sharp tune that rang in Fae's ears.

She reached the not so pleasant part of Heaven's Castle, The Slums, home to the halfling.

Steam factories with clunky parts set the atmosphere of the ghetto. A place where poor, oppressed slaves called home.

The halflings of Heaven's Castle were birthed into this state of poverty. Set to stay there their entire lives. The king ensured this.

Slaves worked in polluted factories to create an abundance of treasuries that resided in Heaven's Castle. They crafted nothing but the finest for the elves. Despite the large coin value of the halfling's many creations, they were only ever paid in scraps of food and old, worn-out rags. On rare occasions, they received low amounts of coin for services but never enough to make a living.

The halflings were hard-working people; They spent most of their short lives creating gemstones and hand-woven silks for unappreciative elves. Their lives were not short by nature but rather an effect of the harsh conditions they lived in.

Heaven's Castle offered refuge to the halflings a millennium ago. Because of this mercy, they'd given up all their rights. Halflings belonged to the elves. Just as their ancestors and their children's children would be. Fae's kind were only seen as working pets for their masters.

Contrary to their hard existence, they had a wholesome community. They found comfort in the simple things of life.

Many halflings learned fine craftsmanship in their younger years, and families were tightly knitted in trusting bonds. Together like a vine, second and third generations lived happily together in small-wooden, deteriorated shacks. Music, along with street dancing, held their people together.

Their hard lives hadn't made them bitter as the halflings lived forever in gratitude because the elves gave them a place to stay away from the suffrage of a broken Ephoreia.

Fae approached her spot. There she gazed at the

stone bench on the edge of the kingdom's boundaries. A viewpoint of Ephoreia.

Without any piercing looks, tears fell freely from her eyes. She sat down and rested her eyes on the dark, blue sky.

Fae gawked at the massive trees. Above their tips, Dragons soared into clouds and dove back in the forest like dolphins riding the blue-green sea.

The magnificent beasts below appeared small in stature, but up close, they stood taller than the highest elf over fifteen-feet high and eight-feet wide. Though Fae had never seen an up-close dragon, textbooks from school filled in the many gaps of distance.

Some time ago, Fae visited Earrie's Ember Knight training camps. The halfling witnessed mock, mechanical dragons in action while Ember Knights trained against stone dragons morphed from the king's very hand. These manikins kept the knights in shape and their reflexes high.

Fae breathed in the beauty of the underworld. She observed snow-painted mountains decked with vast ocean expanses. Ephoreia's continents were shaped like an open book.

Legend says it split in half like a torn-up text after many years of constant war between the two sides of allies.

The princess sighed with a grumble in agitation as she recalled that no one could ever leave the kingdom. The rule existed for everyone's protection; No one ever leaves and no one ever enters. Heaven's Castle remained sealed off from Ephoreia for over a thousand years, never to be opened again.

The tale of how Heaven's Castle rose to the sky stated that long ago a blind, dwarven princess of Mercernip kingdom fell in love with the young, elf prince of old Kinster Kingdom. The two dreamed of creating a refuge to Ephoreia's never-ending war. The dwarven-princess Melah spent most of her life trapped by her father. He used her blindness to take advantage of her and create many deadly weapons of war such as Youretita with his daughter's hands.

Prince Uvler gained rule at the young age of

fourteen when his father King Darelen fell in battle. Uvler sought nothing more than an everlasting peace. Raised by war, the lovers shared an equal desire to end suffering.

The story states that the princess was an Inventor of Ancient. A dwarf who possessed a hereditary, special power that allowed her to manipulate technologies into whatever creation her mind could imagine.

The prince's power came from his possession of the stone ember. Together, the two created a castle above the clouds out of Uvler's stone and Melah's inventions. To this day, the dwarven bloodline of Melah runs in small drops inside of the royal bloodline.

For years, this bench was her favorite spot in the whole kingdom. Back in her days as a low, stable halfling, she would often visit this spot daily, and still, she found herself here for familiar comfort. Ephoreia's landscaping beauty never drew dull in her eyes.

Fae would often come to the brim of Heaven's Castle and spend her days daydreaming. Her mind wandered onto the backs of dragons as she pictured herself smiling holding on tight with flapping hair among mighty winds.

Today was different from those times, for she was not here to hope but to pout. She had no idea who she was anymore. Fae released her hand from under her chin.

The princess felt an emotional numbness brought on by the revealing truth of her birthright. She wanted to cry in peace, but her tears ceased their flow. Soft hiccups escaped her lips, but that was all.

Her mind drifted away to her usual thoughts of dancing in the clouds. No eyes and no standards to be upheld just herself and the open sky.

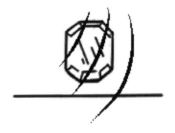

In the ballroom, Earrie noticed Fae's lack of presence. She traced off to the bathroom; A normal hiding spot of her younger sister. When she threw open the door to the room, she knocked on each stall but to no avail. She eyed two guilty-faced women in the corner.

"What did you fools say?" Earrie accused as she folded her arms in annoyance and approached them.

The reluctant woman from before fell to her knees instantly and begged for forgiveness. "My princess! I told her to shut her mouth!" she ratted out her friend without hesitation.

Earrie scoffed, "I hate cowards." She rolled her eyes and tapped her toes. "So again, I ask, what did you say?" Earrie's lack of patience was evident.

The one who originally let out that nasty comment from before raised her head and spoke, "We simply mentioned the rumor." For such a crime, the woman kept her confidence up.

Earrie walked up to face the woman without an inch of space between, "What rumor would that be?"

The eldest princess wasn't fooling anyone. Nearly everyone in Heaven's Castle knew of the rumor even more so the royals.

Many years ago Earrie overheard her mother and father fighting. "Just admit the girl is yours!" she still could remember the desperation in her mother's cracking voice.

Earrie visualized a blurry image of her father nodding his head in admission and relieved the pain she felt in her stomach. She knew even at that age that her misery could not have matched that of her mother's.

As the years went by, she listened to her parents argue the same argument over a hundred times. Each fit, a piece of Earrie's innocence dwindled.

"You still love her! If you ever loved me you wouldn't have done this to me . . . to us!" Clance's cries echoed in her thoughts.

The girl faced Earrie. She cleared her throat and held her head high and said, "We all know that of Stella's seduction of the king eighteen-years ago.

At her comment, Earrie held up her right hand and smacked her square in the face. The girl moaned while others shrieked. After all, since

Earrie was a princess, she didn't have any obligations other than her own and the few her father held her to.

Many times in the past, Earrie acted up, but King Richard always failed to properly punish her. When he viewed her, he saw a Blue Embers Knight. The pride and joy of his kingdom. The king's biased, starry-eyed view of her enabled her to get away with far more than her younger sister Fae.

Earrie paced out of the ballroom. There was one other place she was sure to find Fae. She sprinted through the courtyard and spotted a crouched man behind a bush in her peripheral vision.

With a swipe of her wrist, She grabbed the peep up by his collar. The offender let out a yelp like a kicked puppy. Benard laid frozen under her cold gaze.

Yellow, marble eyes waved to grass green. "Were you here five minutes ago?" Earrie demanded.

"Y-yes, mam," he stuttered his response. The college student looked puzzled and frightened at the same time as he was not fully able to process the reality of this situation.

"A girl, did you see a girl?" Earrie probed.

Benard summoned his strength to respond with a deep inhale, "Why yes, princess, I saw a girl a few years short of you. Sun skin and amber, short hair. She appeared to be half-halfling."

Earrie perked up at his answer, "What direction did you see her last? This is very important."

Benard pointed past the courtyard. The same direction Earrie figured beforehand. She nodded and bolted off.

With a sudden boost of confidence, Benard tapped her shoulder, "If you don't mind, may I help you? Are you searching for this girl?"

Earrie halted in her steps, "Only if you can keep up"—she eyed his lean appearance—"and be of some use to me."

Benard perked up, "I'll do what I can to aid you!"

As they ran through the castle, Earrie made the decision to stop by the abandoned Slum's stables. Stella, Fae's mother, ran them before she died. It wasn't long after the upper class got word of how sick the halflings were that they stopped bringing their horses to the Slums for rest. Instead of doing something to change these horrible conditions or clean out the poor air quality, they simply avoided the area in its entirety.

Benard felt a hungry curiosity in the princess's search. "Who is this woman to you? Has she stolen or committed some crime?" he asked intrusively.

At the implication of Fae doing a crime, Earrie scuffed, "She's my sister. She's hurt and needs me."

Benard frowned. Why had he never heard of a second princess? "Why is she—"

"Running? I embarrassed her in front of everyone. I'm used to . . . showing off . . . When I saw others giving her attention, I made a show out of her," Earrie cut him off.

Benard could tell she was upset at her actions and decided to drop any further questioning.

Earrie stopped when they reached the stables. She pushed open a squeaky door with one, heaving slam.

Inside decaying wood, a shack unveiled itself to be nothing but dust-filled and home to mice. Benard peeked from behind. He looked up to the corners of the room where he viewed drapes of webbing.

"Why would she be here?" Benard asked in a hushed whisper.

Earrie's left eye twitched. She was never the type to be slow to anger.

"Are you going to help or bother me?" she bellowed. At her snap, Benard silenced.

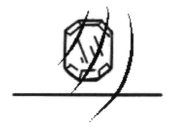

On her bench, Fae sat in silence. She looked to the right and saw a figure emerging in her vision. Her stomach turned. A human male no other than her sister stood outside the barrier.

Fae carried an unknown confusion with her as she stepped towards the barrier. With a press, she felt a bolt of electricity snap at her. The barrier appeared to be in top condition.

"Sir, are you stuck here?" Fae asked, perplexed.

With a sinister sneer, the raven-haired man said, "I'm a simple barrier worker who fell asleep on my shift. Darn, my luck. Well, seems like I've been locked plum out," he smiled as he tipped his head and smacked it in a joking mannerism.

Fae looked at him unsure of his words. She twiddled her thumbs in nerves. The ginger-haired girl felt an ominous feeling when he spoke causing her unease.

The man continued, "Well, I thought for sure I'd be here till morning, but here I am all alone and desperate when a beautiful lad such as yourself shows up. As you can tell, I've never been one for luck. It's almost as if fate has turned my tables this very night. Could you do me a favor and let me inside?" the odd man threw in an alluring wink.

Fae felt some comfort in his words as they seemed to make sense to her. She never heard of any barrier workers before nor had she ever seen anyone outside the restrainer looking inside.

"How could I let you in? I thought for sure no

one ever went outside," Fae asked with innocence.

At her question, the man's thin patience melted away. "Young lad, I'm very dehydrated, and I just need you to give me your permission inside," his impatient tone only caused Fae more weariness.

"Is there no way I could call for help?" She asked. The princess was too scared to allow this strange man entry.

"Please, madam. I only need your permission, so I can quickly return to my home. My wife and younglings must be worried sick over my disappearance."

At the news of his waiting family, Fae felt the pressure to let him in. "I give you permission to enter the barrier," she said.

Her eight simple words would set course to the events that would forever change Heaven's Castle and all of Ephoreia. Fae had no idea what impending tragedy was about to occur.

Chapter 2 The Intruder

At Fae's words, a small, door-like opening appeared in the transparent barrier. At the sight of the opening, all the frustration left the man.

His anger was quickly replaced by hysteria when laughter befell him like the plague. His arm dashed to his gut grabbing it as he stumbled forward in hysterics.

The man flipped back his ear-length hair and walked through the opening. A smile covered his checks, and he crocked, "I knew it! HAHAHA! I just knew you had royal blood! I could smell it!"

He wiped his nose and laughed again.

Fae backed up several-hesitant steps. His unstable emotions froze her steps. What did he mean he could smell it?

"Royal Blood?" Fae mumbled to herself out loud.

"An ignorant one I see. Those with royal blood are the ones with the control over this barrier," he said, while he pet the edge of the barrier. "How should I put it? It's like an inherited, invisible key," the cocky man continued with pride.

He viewed Fae's shocked face. With a tease, he teleported behind her with leopard-like speed and whispered in her ear, "You're a fool—you've done a very foolish thing."

He placed his arms around her shoulders from behind and held up a single strand of her hair. She stood paralyzed as he inhaled the piece. Though Fae didn't move an inch, her body shook in fear.

"W-What did I do?" she asked in utter horror.

He held her tightly. "You've gone and let in your

kingdom's worst nightmare. Given the time of day, I feel a sense of irony."

Fae attempted a squirm to which he squeezed tighter. "Please . . . stop it! You're hurting me!" she cried.

"Well, since you asked so nicely," the man sneered.

He grabbed her wrist from behind and flipped her body into the stone bench. She landed on her stomach while her face remained protected by her forearms.

The raven-haired man wiped his hands in the delight of what he'd done.

"To let someone with your bloodline out here with no knowledge on the barrier . . . You royals and noble elves have become far too comfortable up here asleep in these clouds," the man said.

He turned around and began to walk towards town, "It's time for a change."

Fae felt violated. With the wind knocked out of her, she tried to stand on shaking legs. Her body was sore.

She viewed, in the distance, the mysterious intruder evolving. His body shook, and his clothes ripped off.

Scales grew on his flesh much like the Blue Embers Knights when they transformed. A distinct difference between the two transformations showed its evidence when a long tale emerged from his spine and horns crowned his head, for he was a dragon.

At the sight of the beast, Fae got up and turned her heels to run. Fae promised herself to not look back. She needed to warn her father of the man who tricked her into letting him inside their kingdom. Fae jogged through The Slums until she spotted a recognizable shadow, Earrie.

Above her, a huge coal colored dragon flew in the direction of the palace. Foreign animal-like shrieks bombarded the town. Candles lit and war horns sounded.

The dragon awoke the entire sleeping kingdom. Not everyone inside their kingdom wall's were so vulnerable, for inside the castle gates, the late-night ball held thirty remaining Ember Knights prepared for battle.

Earrie eyed Fae with the dragon overhead and put two and two together.

Above, the dragon called out with a thunderous voice, "Bring me your king! BRING HIM TO ME NOW!"

Benard's knees buckled, "A-A dragon?" he cried.

Earrie wasted no time, the princess reached for her chain necklace and shouted, "Blue Embers, transform me!"

With her call, bat-like, scaled wings emerged from her back. White scales sprouted from her arms and grew until her shoulders, likewise on her legs, yet they halted at her knees. She pet her right hip unsheathing her sword.

With a gaze back to Benard and Fae, Earrie said, "I'm going to"—she made sole eye contact with Fae—"fight. Be safe and get away from the battle."

After her words, she flew into the sky. With summoned wind beneath her toes, she sped to the beast's front.

The dragon in the sky witnessed Earrie and laughed. "Ahh, the Blue Embers Knights. Dragon killers from times past. To think you people in your isolation would have bothered to preserve such a skill."

Earrie ignored him and shouted, "Each strike I make with my blade is for my kingdom!"

She dove inward to his front and swiped her sword. He dodged the strike with slick movement. Out of his mouth, volcanic smut emerged. She breathed deep and shaped the air surrounding her. Wind birthed a tornado around her blade.

With delicacy, Earrie threw back her blade and lifted the twister off in the direction of the dragon. A flap of his wings dispersed her attack. At his nonchalant movements, Earrie knew this would be nothing like the dummies in camp.

"Predictable," he snarled.

Underneath them, the city hustled to different corners of the kingdom. Messenger horses skidded on the stone-paved streets in the direction of the ball.

Earrie spent less time channeling her attacks and placed more emphasis on closing her attack gaps. She concluded very early on that slow, charged attacks served no purpose in an experienced opponent. Her persistent blows took a toll on her stamina.

The beast, on the other hand, did not grow weary. His oncoming attacks were becoming bolder in force. With a double swipe of his paws, Earrie was knocked out of the sky. Her limp body descended like a lightning strike to the ground.

Before she could splatter, the pink-haired princess was caught by strong arms. King Richard held his daughter in similarity to when she was a babe.

"Rest now, you've played your part," Richard said as he eyed around for nearby help.

He spotted Benard standing still, and with no other hand near, he commanded him, "Bring my daughter to safety!" Benard stood in a paralysis of fear until the king yelled at him, "Move your legs, take her and run! NOW!"

At this note, he held onto an unconscious Earrie and sprinted off in the direction of many others who'd fled. He struggled to maintain his grip on Earrie with his untrained arms.

Richard arrived transformed into his embers. His scales were gray, and he met the dragon in the air.

"What would a bug like you want with me?" he spoke condescending.

Many Ember Knights thought of the dragons as overgrown insects. The dragon jumped on him in an impulsive reaction. Richard blocked his claws with his shield of stone.

The dragon made a throwback tease to Richard, "Has the King himself come to save his favorite daughter? Sickening."

The king smiled. "I will hold up my whole kingdom. That includes my family."

The horned beast roared, "I will kill you and your family, steal your throne, and destroy your entire kingdom."

At his threatening remarks, Richard went on the offense. He transformed his shield into a sword and threw it unsuspectingly at the dragon.

With his surprise attack, the dragon's side was punctured. Blood dripped from the dragon's open wound.

"Speak not, filth, you've forgotten your place," he said in satisfaction of his attack. "Dragons FEAR Ember Knights and our mighty power and here you come to my door like a gift wrapped in a bow, Zenith. I will have your head for even thinking of hurting my daughter," Richard said with boldness.

"You speak as though you know me," Zenith remarked.

"Charcoal, black flesh with glowing, red scales and volcanic powers. Yes, history has you recorded for being a merciless killer. You're just a dragon who cares for no one but yourself," King Richard cooed.

They continued to exchange blows in the air. Zenith attempted to pour his lava out on King Richard. In the air, it chunked out too slow to land any damage as its lava attacks were better suited for well planned out traps.

Hot lava seeped down on the town causing havoc and casualties below. The king did his best to block the lava from hurting anyone placing stone run-offs above the homes.

Only a few of the townsfolk hadn't evacuated. Those being mainly the disabled and elderly. Abandoned orphans stood in open streets crying for the help of an absent mother.

On the ground, Fae ran through the streets without direction. Sudden sounds of cutting wind shot behind her. Zenith trialed above her like an awaiting hawk going for its prey. Before her steps failed her, her father came to her aid.

Fae jumped at his touch terrified it might be Zenith. When she realized it was her dad, the young girl sighed a relief.

Richard held onto Fae as he created another massive shield. He carried dwarven blood inside him. This made him far more masculine than the average elf. He stood only six-feet tall, but his bulkiness allowed him to carry a multitude of weight.

Protecting Fae meant staying on the defense during the battle. He needed the other knights to hurry up before Zenith drew the upper hand.

When he heard the news of a dragon, he commanded the twenty-nine Ember Knights under him to prioritize the people and get them loaded on escape pods. "Save as many as you can! Get my people to safety!" Richard remembered the words he'd spoken earlier.

He never dreamed the dragon would be this skilled. That it could not only duel the king but knock out Earrie. One of the most natural skilled Ember Knights the kingdom had ever known. Richard held Fae with one arm and lept into the air.

He had to contain Zenith before he hurt any more civilians. Right as he felt trapped between ensuring his daughter's safety and pursuing Zenith, The Ember Knights showed up.

Richard eyed Maxwell, a green-scaled knight. One he trusted with his life. He was not oblivious, for he knew all along that his daughter, Earrie, was seeing him. He enjoyed Maxwell as a knight and chose to let them have their secrecy.

"Take Fae to the escape pods! Board her with Earrie. This is not your average dragon," the king ordered.

Maxwell didn't hesitate. Following the king's orders, he grabbed Fae and flew in the direction of the pods. He darted into the air like a missile until he spotted the apple of his eye, Earrie.

At the sight of the princess, he descended. She was unconscious. For her to be in such a shape, he could tell inwardly she must have given it her all.

He made eye contact with Benard, "Can you fly an escape pod?"

Benard appeared to be a man of intelligence. It was clear he was not one of manual labor as he possessed soft hands and lean muscles.

"Yes, Sir! I can operate flying machinery," he responded. Maxwell felt like he could trust this man.

He walked up past the line to the closest escape pod. They appeared to be circular balls of machinery. Ticks and clunky old technology powered the balls. The pods were tested every six months to make sure they held up through the years. The pod had a large, glass-window seat up front next to a flashing control panel.

Benard entered the small room first and sat down in the pilot seat. Maxwell helped Fae on second. Lastly, he set Earrie down in.

Without any Ember Knights near, the knight placed his hand on her cheek and lightly kissed her forehead as a gentleman would never kiss a lady on the lips while she's unconscious.

"You be safe. This is just like a vacation to the underworld. We'll see each other again in no time," with a squeeze to her hand, he wished them goodbye and shut the overhead door.

Back in the battle sky, Richard and the other Ember Knights surrounded Zenith. He looked like a cornered dog with thirty, trained dragon-killers surrounding him. The king smirked. He was ready to end this cocky-mouthed dragon. But for all of the knights, nothing could have prepared them for what was to come.

Zenith let out a bubbling giggle as his body started enlarging. Larger, thicker his body increased its size.

He roared out, "Didn't think I'd have to go all out but if you little flies INSIST! HAHA!"

Some knights backed up in horror. He grew half the size of the entire kingdom. Confused looks jumped on their faces. None of them had ever heard of a growing dragon. Surely, his magnitude in size wasn't something they'd trained for.

For the first time, a speckle of fear painted the king's eyes. His noble worries morphed to a selfish one focused solely on his daughter's lives.

"Barrier mode: power off emergency evacuation, fifteen minutes power back on," the king said with certainty.

When The Ember Knights heard the barrier command, they knew what this meant. All who made it to the pods would be sent out to the underworld in hope for survival. His men knew his heart. When the barrier closed, their battle would be a bloodbath. A battle to their deaths and not of pride but for their very lives.

Zenith paid no concern for the barrier opening and closing. He had the utmost confidence that everything was falling into place according to his plan. The Ember Knights were never a threat to him to begin with instead they were his chest pieces. His pawns to be played, for he was the cat and they were his mice.

The next fifteen minutes passed by in what felt like slow motion. Pods were shot into the air like cannon fire while evacuation sirens screamed overhead.

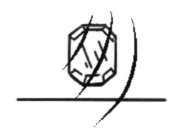

Earrie felt a massive headache. She moaned and set up from her resting stance.

It took the wind knight no time to understand that the castle's escape plan was set in motion, and she was a part of it. Many times in training she'd partaken in practice drills.

Earrie eyed Benard and Fae. Her sister appeared ghost faced. What happened while she was unconscious?

She looked out a window to her side and visualized her father and the other Ember Knights warring against the great dragon.

Her fist pounded on the door. If she could break the glass then perhaps she could fly down and assist the knights. When no cracks appeared in the glass, she continued her persisting knocks.

Panic consumed her thoughts, "LET ME BE WITH MY FATHER! I MUST GO WITH HIM!" Earrie looked around for a response but Fae and Benard remained speechless. "PLEASE! YOU MUST STOP THE POD HE NEEDS ME!" she bellowed out. Her knuckles blistered at the intensity of her attacks.

Before she could swing again, Benard restrained her.

With her wrist in his hands, he yelled, "No, you can't go!"

Earrie stood up infuriated at this boy, "You can't be serious bossing me around! Take me back to dock! This is an order from the princess!"

Benard held tighter and pulled her away from the glass. "I have an order from a power above your own. You will evacuate," he said with glaring, gold eyes.

She pulled her wrist out from his grasp and plumped down angrily. The only one with power above hers would be that of her father. The Ember Knight crossed her legs and pouted while she gazed out the window.

The young sister mirrored Earrie. She sat in a depressed state while she too stared outside.

Fae viewed civilians screaming and running in terror. Ember Knights were smacked out of the air. Buildings were aflame.

All she could do was dwell in her faults. If it

wasn't for her letting this man in the kingdom, everyone would be asleep or enjoying The Honor Ball right now.

People died because of her actions. She couldn't help but think why they had died and not her.

In the cockpit, Benard viewed Heaven's Castle one last time before it disappeared from his sight. He noticed an old couple waving goodbye to departing relatives. His gaze lingered around them to which he saw no other pods. Not everyone made it to the pods before the barrier reappeared.

Benard glanced at the many people who stood there hopeless. He knew they were someone's mom, someone's sister, and someone's child, but it was someone who wasn't him.

He inwardly felt a peace in knowing he'd made it to the pods in time. The not so fortunate souls were dead men walking. A time frame had been stamped to their very heads the moment the barrier closed. With no chance of escape, they held onto loved ones and sang comforting lullabies.

Benard looked down at the panel in front of

him. He recognized the make and model of the pod they were inside. Given the time he'd spent gawking over magazines of the latest technologies of Heaven's Castle, he felt he could do this.

When Maxwell asked Benard if he could operate the pod, he wasn't entirely truthful in his response. He knew a lot of book smarts on the pods, and he had even watched them being repaired before in his college extracurricular activities.

The problem was Benard never actually operated one before. The buttons were lit and labeled with various codes, yet he was ignorant of their purposes.

Benard fumbled with the buttons frantically, and an oxygen mask shot out from above.

Earrie looked frustrated, "Moron, do you even know what you're doing?"

At her comment, Benard tensed. Earrie noticed his physical response. She grabbed onto his shoulder abruptly.

"What are you pressing so many buttons for? Hey, I'm talking to you!" Earrie shouted.

Sweat fell from Benard's red forehead. How was he going to explain his predicament? "Well, you see, princess . . . I don't have experience with the flight. I just happen to know a lot about these machines," he mumbled in hidden admission.

Earrie pulled his shoulder further down making Benard wince. "So you're saying you're useless? Why on Ephoreia are you piloting our ship?" she shrieked into his eardrums.

The princess's temper was beginning to wear down the perfect image Heaven's Castle made her be.

Benard cried out in nervousness, "I have a vague idea how to land this thing. In regards to your second question, I was the last available hand."

Earrie leaned back at his words. Would their journey come to an end this early?

Fae had little reaction to the news of Benard's idiocy. She only shifted views and eyed her upset sister.

"This is all my fault Earrie. All of it. Don't blame him. If you want someone to beat up, I'm at fault," she said in a sad utterance.

Earrie couldn't believe this. They were all accepting an early death without so much as a fight. She reached in front and pushed Benard out of his seat. "If you're not man enough to pilot this ship, I'll figure it out myself," the elder princess grumbled.

She flipped off some switches that seemed to be for emergencies only. With a gaze at the panels, she found one that read 'parachute'. In school, Earrie had once been taught about how they would come out and glide various things to a soft halt until landing. She inhaled, and in an act of faith, she pressed down on the switch.

Chapter 3 Start of a Journey

An immediate thud occurred. Parts of the pod caved in showing heed to white, sharp bones. Benard and Fae reached for each other in panic as if a hug could be their lifeline.

Earrie dropped the wheel when she realized that a beast held them. She screamed in horror.

Her cheeks beamed red at her fear. She was never the type to present herself a coward. Earrie had always masked her fear along with all the other emotions princesses weren't permitted to have.

The group huddled together knowing they had little control of the events to come. When all hope seemed lost, a sudden event that marveled everyone's heads occurred.

Fae fell in the center of the pod, and with a small chime, white lettering danced around her.

The text appeared to be numeric. With a luminescent hue, it twisted and twirled around Fae until her yellow glow was overtaken by a white shine. Her eyes beamed out bright lights. Fae yelled as this newfound power possessed her.

A foreign force morphed the pod as its small width grew long and narrow. The cockpit dissolved into a new creation along with the windows.

Earrie pinned her sword into its foundation to maintain her balance. Benard grabbed hold of her leg. She held Fae in her free arm while the text went in and out of the machine like a darting deer.

Fae's limp body called out in a monotone voice, "Order execute: target close-ranged dragon."

Meanwhile, on the outskirts of the pod, a

plotting dragon dropped the transforming technology. His mouth was not large enough to sustain such a creation. The dragon swiped his claws to pin them into its edges.

Lock-on missiles fired at him successfully stopping him in his tracks. He looked ahead of his flight only to find himself face-first into the peak of a snow-covered mountain. With a fast-paced collision, the dragon caused an avalanche to trample him.

Benard looked up to a closed-eyed Earrie. "My heavens! She's an Inventor of Ancient's past!" the boy called out.

Earrie had a feeling this was the case, but no one had seen or heard of an Inventor being born since Melah. Had this trait been passed down generation after generation hidden only to unveil itself in their time of need?

At the release of the dragon's teeth, the transport fell. Earrie had no idea what to do as the controls were aloof. Benard was just as bewildered.

"Hold on!" Earrie shouted. She canvassed the

open sea beneath them.

Earrie and Benard grabbed onto seats as they braced for impact. With a humongous splash, they descended into towering depths. From the skies to the seas, their adventure was off to a fine start indeed.

With the invention leveled, Earrie sat up and shook her younger sister. Benard stepped slowly with a clear distaste of sea travel. He knelt by the sisters and touched Fae. Both of their attempts failed to awaken the sleeping princess.

Earrie didn't give up hope though as she relentlessly shook Fae. Meanwhile, Benard got up and paced back and forth with his hand on his chin in thought.

The college student walked to the edge of the new creation, and with a sudden epiphany, he understood what this was. They were inside of a warship submarine.

Benard remembered studying them several times in his history classes. They were battleships for underwater warfare.

He found a compass in the front hanger of the

ship. Who was piloting the submarine?

A thought crazed into Benard's head. He stumbled over to Earrie in a burst of excitement, "Princess! I believe your sister is conelveing this underwater boat."

Earrie's stomach twirled at his remark. Was little Fae truly piloting a warship? None of this felt right to her. Just who were the Inventors of Ancient?

With a sudden jolt, the submarine ascended.

"I think she's taking us to dry land," Benard chimed in. He smiled and squeezed the elder princess's shoulders in reassurance.

Earrie felt fed up with this stranger invading her personal space. He was more of a nuisance to her than anything.

She snapped her head around and yelled, "Would you just shut up already! I'm sick of it! All talk and no action!"

Earrie was accustomed to talking to men under her rank like this. Well, truthfully she talked to anyone like this. She never had a way with words. Actions and battles had always been where her voice shined.

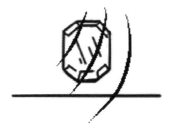

Way above their position inside the center of Heaven's Castle, the battle continued. Zenith displayed another one of his trump cards. He whirled out a multitude of different powers. This technique was unheard of by any dragon or Ember Knight.

Trees sprouted at his beckoning. They shot to the sky and entangled knights. Ice pelts rained down and ripped holes through many of the Ember Knight's wings.

Maxwell fought beside King Richard. He held out his bow and cocked it toward Zenith. The bowed knight was Heaven's Castle's sharpest shooter. His power was paralysis venom. He channeled poison through his arrows.

With a squint of his eyes, Maxwell leaned back mid-air and fired three consecutive shots dipped in venom.

Zenith, preoccupied with his prey, failed to dodge Maxwell's incoming attacks, but the arrows bounced off Zenith's thick scales. Maxwell sighed at his lost opportunity.

The once gaping wound on Zenith's side appeared to be nothing. His injury shaped itself into a sealed penny-size paper cut after he grew enormous.

The Ember knights threw their powers at him but to no avail. This beast was a mighty foe, and he did not come on a whim. He obtained the strength of a hundred dragons along with their powers before he'd even considered stepping his claws into their domain.

Zenith cloaked his true strength the entire match. He barely lifted his claws meanwhile the men around were dying fighting their hearts out.

As the sun rose, the number of Ember Knights dwindled leaving all but six. Maxwell's squad of five and King Richard were all that remained.

Though their chances of living were next to

none, they didn't give up hope. The squad aided the king as he shouted out his mastermind tactics. Knights followed Richard's every order, but this obedience didn't stop what was to come.

An icicle shard struck Maxwell's gut cutting him down to the ground. He laid on top of bodies of fellow knights.

Peering down, he held in the urge to hurl. Maxwell saw open-eyed lifeless piles of mini-mountains with streams of blood underneath them like a waterfall. Blood dripped from body to body into a warm, sticky puddle.

His fingers traced his embers on his chest. The chained necklace was octagon shaped. The jewelry hanging off his neck held all of his powers. It glowed a light blue just like the sky. Some called it Blue Fire, but the majority referred to it as Blue Embers.

Maxwell made up his mind as he was fighting for his final breaths. He would consume his embers. This act was a frowned-upon tactic used only by the most desperate of knights.

With a whisper in his heart, he said goodbye to

his love. Maxwell held up the blue vial and removed its cap. He chugged the contaminants as fast as he could to avoid its burning after effect.

The venom knight wasn't aware why this tactic was forbidden as he heard that it gave them ember powers all the time without getting weak from power usage. This ignorance would soon be wiped from him.

Richard viewed Maxwell from the corner of his eye as his knight swallowed the liquid. He only shook his head, for he knew full well the consequences of ingesting embers.

Maxwell's team was the most experienced knights in all of Heaven's Castle next to Earrie. They'd been born into the system and trained from a young age to be the perfect candidate to carry their family names. Maxwell's knights all had varying powers.

Nothing about their powers stood out too much from the fallen knights as it was their endurance and natural affinity for battling that kept them alive.

Leah beamed her sun power into Zenith's eyes to cause blindness and confusion. Riley jumped through his portals to Maxwell's side.

"Are you okay, captain?" he pestered.

Instead of a usual grunt or nod, he heard laughter. Had Maxwell lost his mind?

Riley stepped back. He sensed something off about Maxwell. Before he could walk any future away, his caption pounced on him like a snake. He snuck his teeth which felt like fangs into Riley's side and shot venom inside his blood.

Arnold witnessed the tragic scene. A man turning against his own mid-battle. He flew behind Maxwell, and with a channel, he placed all his strength into his right arm.

He holstered Maxwell up with a tight squeeze from behind, and flung his caption into a nearby wall.

Arnold glanced at Riley. His body was paralyzed from the venom. Left out in the open, unable to move, Riley would surely be next to perish.

Jenny sent fuming, toxic gas towards Zenith as

she attempted to poison the beast. No matter how big a beast was, Jenny's poison could befall it.

Her powers were almost identical to Maxwell's. It's one of the reasons she'd been assigned early on to his team along with her natural talent for conveying her powers.

Maxwell got up from the wall and wiped some blood off his bottom lip. He let his head fling to the sky and bellowed in laughter.

"Maxwell is no more. That child died. I am Acadash!" emerged from Maxwell's lips.

Even though the voice belonged to Maxwell, the vibrating dialect was of a different speech. He sounded harsher with his words almost crude. The smooth-talking captain was no more.

Zenith giggled along with Acadash. "One of my favorite dragons. Have you come to serve me as your God?" Zenith asked Acadash who possessed Maxwell's body.

Acadash teleported to Riley and shoved her claw-like hand into his heart. "How's this for an answer?" She joked with a smile.

"Very nice. Now finish the rest off and we can

start the game," at Zenith's words Acadash bowed in a playful mannerisms with her left arm dangling like a wave.

Leah focused on beaming Zenith. She failed to react when Acadash jumped behind her. Just like Riley, she was stabbed in the heart. At the removal of Leah's restraints, Zenith swiped his paw and grabbed an all too close Jenny.

"Getting real sick of you!" he yelled. Zenith threw her on the floor and stomped his back leg on her skull crushing it instantly.

Richard wanted to save their lives, but in a battle such as this, there was no place for defending the weak. If you couldn't protect yourself you would be destroyed. With only Arnold and Richard left, Zenith cooed in pride and clapped his paws.

"Two more flies to squash, and we can rest for the evening," Zenith said without remorse. The beast stole many lives today; He was going to need that rest.

Richard decided if he was going to die, he would use his best efforts to ensure he took Maxwell with him. The king feared Maxwell would be used as a pawn for Zenith against his daughter Earrie.

Just in time for him to witness another killing, he changed the direction of his attacks to Maxwell. Acadash inside of Maxwell's body slaughtered Arnold in front of him. She decapitated the man with one foul swipe of Maxwell's backup dagger.

Before Richard could get to Maxwell, Zenith plucked him up like a stray hair. He held the king down while he commanded Acadash to finish him off. He could sense Richard had a fondness for Maxwell and wanted to make every last second miserable for him.

"I did what I could to protect my people. The rest is now in their hands," the king muttered as a rabid Acadash jumped on him. She went for a throat kill just like a lion.

Before Richard passed, he gazed into a distant light, "Stella . . . " he whispered with his final breath.

The king died with a smile glued to his face. A peace fell upon him when he pictured his daughters and Stella, the women whom he loved. He believed that in some distant miracle, Zenith would be subdued, and his kingdom would be together in the clouds again.

Twenty-nine Ember Knights died that night at the hands of Zenith the Tyrant.

Chapter 4 Amnesia?

Zenith threw King Richard's body beneath his feet. With a thought, he transformed back into his human form. Acadash knelt before Zenith to declare her faithfulness.

He marched over to Richard's corpse and tore off his golden crown like a band-aid. The crown bore the most gorgeous jewels in all of Heaven's Castle.

Eyeing the piece in his hands, he noticed the

adornment was too sparkly for his taste and pulled off its diamonds and rubies chunking them into oblivion.

Zenith wasn't finished. He peered over at Richard's corpse and began kicking him. At each preceding attack, Acadash sneered evilly.

She gawked at the display of power. As she thought about Zenith taking down the impenetrable Heaven's Castle in just a few hours, a burning fire in her heart flickered for his power.

With enough strength, she could do anything. Acadash wanted that kind of power for herself, for it could forge the very future.

Zenith peered over to Acadash. "Go and gather the survivors. I'm about to make another move on my board of chess," he commanded her.

With a nod, she flew up and brought every straggler to his mercy. Zenith held up a modified technology that once belonged to humans. He grabbed hold of a squirming young lady and restrained her by the neck.

"I am your God!" he shouted as the victim screamed.

The machinery on his left wrist crawled up to his elbow. The band had many different colored, glass panels. Gears clicked together as they turned like a clock. When he called out the power inside of the overgrown watch, gold-colored electric bolts entrapped the woman.

After the shots made contact with her, he released his right grip. She fell on her head, and her body trembled violently. Suddenly, her arms and legs bulged out with scales.

The woman's head transformed with horns and reptilian-like features. Within a minute, she transformed fully into a miniature dragon about the size of a normal human.

He eyed his new minion with pleasure. "You will serve me till your dying breath," Zenith purred while he patted his new creature with sinister love.

The new dragon opened its mouth and said, "Yes, my Lord Zenith."

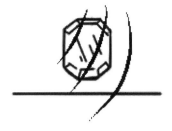

With a halt, the submarine stopped its movement. Benard's cheeks turned green, and he grabbed his stomach wobbling on his toes.

Running to the top of the ship, Benard examined a pointed tube. The object appeared to be a telescope-like machine.

With a bow to his head, Benard peeked through its lenses. His suspensions were correct. The boat was sea level. The inspecting grabbed on to the exit's metallic ladder and placed his toes on its steps.

Benard slid his fingers against heated metal. In a sudden squeal, he peeled back his hand. With gold eyes, he stared at the magnitude of the burn he received.

The sun beat against its metal plates increasing its temperature to a scolding degree. He took off his rubber boots and swindled his hand into their opening. Benard pressed the shoe against the hatch flinging it open. Blaring light marked a fresh beginning for the three escapees.

Inside the ship, Fae awoke. She looked around completely oblivious. The last thing she remembered was a dragon that captured their pod. How did they end up in this metallic, long machinery?

Turning left and right, she noticed the ship's bobbed feel. Fae assumed it was a ship of some sort by the way it flopped back and forth or an expanded form of the escape pod floating in the sea.

Earrie heard Fae's rustles and ran quickly to her side. In an overbearing tone, she explained to her sister that they were in some sort of submarine. She held her sister's hand and placed a stern gaze onto her eyes.

Earrie spoke, "Sister, we think you're . . . an Inventor."

Fae's face scuffed up at the insinuation. She thought back and saw a hazing event. The young girl attempted to sew past the hazy memories of her apparent blackout.

"I had a weird dream. There was a white room. All around me voices taunted, and I felt powerless," Fae confessed as she twiddled her thumbs together in thought.

Earrie blew it off, "You probably thought you died and started dreaming a weird version of the afterlife."

The young sister's lips turned, "Well, if I am an Inventor then there's hope yet that we can finish that dragon."

Earrie respected Fae's hope and shook her head in agreement.

"We will stop him. Mark my words, Fae, he will not get away with what he's done," Earrie vowed, and the two walked towards the exit.

Benard canvassed the outdoors. He heard barking seagulls on the outskirts of the beach. The boy surveyed shells that decked untouched sands. As he cocked his head, he sucked in the fresh air. A strong odor of salt filled his nostrils. Benard wasn't accustomed to such an aroma. For in Heaven's Castle, he'd never been to a beach only seen the enormous, blue color beneath.

Benard listened to clunky footsteps that crawled up the ladder. He bent down and offered a hand to Fae. The action reminded him of when they ran into each other outside of the ball. As she emerged, he noticed how elegant her appearance was.

Bright, yellow skin glowed while it mocked the sun's color. A sudden breeze caught her soft, wavy locks in the wind. Copper strands flew like the waves beneath her.

The boy gazed at the sunrise waving hello behind Fae. She smiled a grin possessing unison beauty with the sunrise.

After she exited, Benard offered Earrie a hand. She scoffed and turned her head up. No boy was going to help her out; She could do it herself.

Earrie placed her hand against the metal to offer her body support as she unloaded. On skin contact, she felt scalding heat, but to avoid giving Benard the satisfaction of helping her, she ignored it and got up quickly.

The group was close enough to the shore that they could walk to it. Benard couldn't help but be amazed at the scene before him. Trees towered up to rival mountain lengths. Animals rustled among the bushes, and seaweed tickled his toes.

Fae ran through the seashore with childlike playfulness. She spun around with her hands out and bent over splashing water.

"Isn't this wonderful?" Fae squealed out in enthusiasm.

Earrie stood firm and composed as she walked through the ocean. The knight couldn't help but inwardly enjoy the refreshing atmosphere.

The princess hid a faint smile beneath tight lips while she released her hair from its low pin. The eldest princess viewed the walk to shore as an opportunity to fix its sagging tail. She replaced her hairband as high up as she could against the force of gravity that pulled against it. Her hot pink strands bounced in the open sun while she tightened it one last time to ensure its placement

Unlike Fae, Earrie always kept her hair length

73

past her hips. She portrayed only a few feminine stereotypes being a trained knight. Earrie adored her long locks, and she couldn't ever see herself losing her length.

None of them slept the previous night, so they unanimously agreed to set up a beach camp during the early morning.

Fae brought together some berries and fresh leaves. She cooked fish on the campfire and fashioned up cod salad for the group. The halfling placed the food on smooth flat rocks that she found among a nearby river stream that connected to the ocean.

Earrie gave thanks by gobbling her food. Benard, on the other hand, ate each bite slowly drooling down his side cheek.

He couldn't help but think about how delicious Fae's cooking was. He thought it was amazing how much she managed to create something so magnificent with such little options. He viewed it as a useful skill to have.

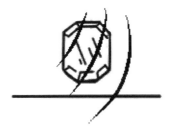

A young man no older than seventeen woke up underneath a blanket of snow. He scratched his head and surveyed his surroundings. Burning snow coated his body. The white substance caused him to react to his instincts. With an unknown urgency, the man ran down from the white mountain tops.

The man had no idea who he was or where he was. He inhaled deeply and twitched his nose while it seemed to direct him to a distant smell. He viewed above massive, tall trees a smoke trail that flew into the sky.

Something odd clouded his view. Three orange tethers floated in the air and linked to the scent. With an airborne reach, he attempted to grab on to the strings. The wanderer felt a stir, and his instincts seemed to heighten with his newfound connection to the cord.

At his connecting touch, he suddenly inhaled

cooked meat. Voices tickled his pitched ears. They sounded far away yet felt so close to him. Running down the mountain, he went in the direction of stimulating sensations.

His feet punched in holes under his toes as he ran down the slope. With a spontaneous slip, he fell and skidded down the hill. Peeking rocks split tears in his back causing him to groan in agony.

Just as they were about to finish their meals, loud steps approached them. Benard and Fae ducked behind a large piece of driftwood they were sitting on. Earrie, on the other hand, unsheathed her sword and walked slowly over to the offending racket.

She whisked her blade in the nearby bushes. The noise seemed to halt in its tracks. Had an animal come to steal their food?

Earrie heard a shriek from Fae and darted around. Before her, a six-foot tall muscular man stood.

His hair appeared to match Earrie's length. Brown in color his strands blended in his eyes.

The princess stepped back when she noticed his lack of clothes.

"Sir! Where are your clothes?" Earrie questioned frantically as she threw her hands over her eyes to shield them.

The young faced man no older than her glanced at Earrie puzzled. "Clothes?" he asked unsure.

Benard glared at him. Was this some pervert? Fae turned around. Earrie grabbed a broken palm branch and chucked it at the man.

"Cover yourself! You're in the presence of a lady!" she shouted.

The man still looked bewildered. Fae reached to her side and pulled off a brown shawl over her raised arms and threw it to Benard.

"Here, help this man out," she said.

Benard grumbled and took the long shall. It had no openings besides the neck. With some tugging, the cloth clothed the man like a skirt. Earrie sighed in relief.

"Are you humans so barbaric that you don't clothe yourselves?" the eldest princess questioned.

The man looked lost. With chocolate, puppy eyes he asked innocently, "Please, tell me where I am, who I am?"

Fae turned around and eyed Benard and Earrie.

"What do you mean? Are you saying you don't remember anything?" Earrie asked.

The interrogation continued over the next hour as she drilled him like one of her knights for answers.

The man told them that he had no memories, and he said that the only real thing he remembered was his speech. Benard thought back to the many medical lessons he received in college until a brain illness called amnesia struck his mind like a bell.

"I believe this man has amnesia," Benard informed the group.

"Amnesia?" Earrie pondered.

"Well, sometimes when people get hurt in their heads, they lose their memories. Other times a traumatic event happens, and they blank out things. In some cases, people have growths in their skulls that cause damage. In this case . . . he appears to have lost all of them," Benard explained.

Fae looked over to the man as he sat on driftwood by the crackling fire and warmed his hands. She brewed up some bone broth with leftovers and pieced together a flavorful meal.

Fae passed him some fish stew and motioned for him to eat. He inhaled the dish with his mouth watering.

"So what made you come here to our camp in the first place?" the cook questioned.

The two were alone. Benard and Earrie had fallen asleep in their respective tents as both were exhausted from the previous day's events.

Fae felt restless after that long, forced nap, so she kept their new acquaintance company.

He looked embarrassed at her and smiled. "My stomach hurt, and I smelled a delicious aroma," he told her with honesty.

Fae smiled, "Are you enjoying it?" she asked, curious of the man's taste.

He nodded and smiled, "To think, you guys would feed me and take me in for the night. I have never met anyone so kind hearted."

The man moved his head up towards the sky and scratched behind his ears. "Though, I couldn't tell you truthfully if I ever even met anyone before," he joked.

Fae giggled at his blunt humor and hunched back into the decaying log. When she noticed a dry feeling in her eyes, she bid him goodnight. Despite the fact it was broad daylight, she decided she would take a rest after all.

Before she left Fae looked at the man, "Since you have no name, I'm going to call you pup."

He looked amused, "Pup, a young dog?" Though he had no memory of himself or his location, he seemed to have enough in his brain to carry on conversations.

"You came to us like a lost pup looking for scraps. You were cold and necked with no owner to claim you," she teased.

He placed his head into his bowl. While slurping the rest of his meal, he said, "Goodnight, Fae."

"Goodnight, Pup."

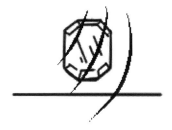

A couple of hours later Earrie woke. She only needed a short time to recharge her energy. With sleepy eyes, the pink-haired princess stumbled out of her leafy tent. Earrie placed her hand like a visor above her forehead waltzing outside.

She witnessed a fire off in the distance; It didn't appear too far off in range. Earrie decided to transform and check it out. The knight assumed it would be fellow pod escapees.

With a leap into the air, she flew overhead the tall trees of Ephoreia's shore. When Earrie approached the smoke, she flew in.

Fifteen elves with recognizable clothing sat around a bright flame. She waved and walked up to them with a friendly demeanor.

Without saying anything, the elves appeared all around her. She blinked her eyes. Earrie felt off at the snickers that escaped their lips.

She attempted to jump back into the sky to escape this feeling of entrapment. The elves tackled her like a pack of wolves. Earrie let out a high pitch squeal as she attempted to kick them off.

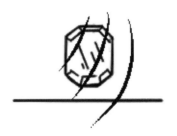

The mysterious man from the beach perked up his ears to the distant scream. He recognized the voice to be that of Earrie's.

Without so much as a hesitation, he got up and bolted towards the oncoming yelps. Running at lightning speed, his leg's pushed him past inhuman intervals. An instinct to aid this woman overtook him like a wild beast.

Without trying, his body bubbled into the transformation of a dragon. He sprung acoss blocking branches while diving throughout the woods in the direction of princess Earrie.

Earrie summoned a gust of wind over her that

successfully threw the dogs off her while jumping in the air.

The elves transformed into small-sized dragons right before her eyes only aiding their overwhelming attacks.

An electric shock collided with her causing her to lose flight. The princess fell between an opening of trees. With no branches to soften her fall, she swiped up a typhoon of air to her rescue.

Earrie was a trained Ember Knight but not so talented she could take on more than a dozen dragons at once.

The ground beneath her transmuted into mud, and she viewed one of the strange beasts laughing at her.

Wet earth beneath her sucked in her body. She panicked as the wind failed to lift her out of the heavy substance.

Just as the princess's hope dwindled, a glimmer of protection arrived to her aid.

Her rescuer appeared to be a tall, orange-scaled dragon similar in size to the dragon who attacked

Heaven's Castle. With the pluck of his claws, he propelled Earrie out of the gutter and into the air.

While the lady skidded in flight, mud blew off her trapped hands. She glided in the direction of the camp. Earrie needed to get back to ensure her sister's safety. The pink-haired knight wasn't about to change fate by attempting to take on all of these beasts at once.

The dragon glanced at the minions. He pounced on them and swatted them around like flies.

Grabbing hold of one, he slurped its blood in a growl. Upon drinking the dragon's blood, he was filled with full-body healing, rejuvenation. At one drop of the blood, the beast remembered himself.

His name was Elvador. He was the dragon who had placed the group's pod in his mouth. When the orange dragon crashed into the mountain peak beforehand, he injured his head. It wasn't until that drop of blood that his memory was repaired.

He eyed the surviving mini beasts. He guessed the small dragons were Zenith's doing. Elvador decided to finish the beasts off before he would return to camp.

Elvador thought back to how he ended up here. With his memories all scattered around, he felt it was time to place them correctly.

Right before he found their pod, he heard some chaos. When he visualized the commotion, he turned on his dragon tracker abilities. The beast followed an orange tether that brought him to that of royal blood. It was clear to him that royal-blooded elves were inside of the pod.

The many years of his life that Elvador spent tracking down Zenith all led up to this one moment. Royal elves had the power to bring down the barrier that Zenith clothed himself in. Not too long beforehand, Elvador had been right on his tail ready to finally attack the beast.

As the dragon spotted the royals, he knew he would have to get the key that resided in them. That was before, he dropped it and flew headfirst into a mountain.

As he made it back to camp, Elvador heard Earrie telling everyone what happened.

He listened in to ensure that she didn't know

who he was. The brown-haired man found comfort in the fact that they didn't know that he was a dragon.

Many elves hated dragons, especially Ember Knights. After all of their kingdom's propaganda, he felt it better to keep his true self hidden. Elvador didn't know if he could trust any of them.

At the time of his arrival, Fae perked up. She noticed him walking through the woods and ran to greet him.

With a friendly hug, she declared, "When Earrie told us of a camp of dragons I thought"—she let go and eyed him—"the worse . . . Where were you?"

Elvador gulped. This was his chance to make his impression and not screw up.

"I heard a noise in the woods . . . I went to check on it but got lost," he said, stumbling to make up a lie. It was hard to be dishonest to Fae's green, trusting eyes.

"Well, you should be glad you didn't find anything. There's dozens of beasts in the woods!" Earrie exclaimed, from behind.

Benard was the only member of the group to

have a bad feeling about this man. He found the time frame all too convenient in light of the events.

With growing suspicion, Benard asked, "If you were lost, how did you return?" The dragon dropped his innocent act at Benard's questioning.

"I found footprints over there that led to here. Must have been Earrie's," he answered.

Benard, still on edge declared, "They weren't. They were mine. After you left, I went to scavenge medical herbs. Earrie came back another way."

Elvador hid a glare. This elf was onto him.

Now that his memories were back, he noticed that Benard bore a striking resemblance to a fallen friend he once knew, Elliot. It was hard to view Benard without feeling a pain in his chest of his past comrade.

After the reunion, the group chatted about where their next destination would be.

"We need to figure out how that dragon was able to increase in size and what the technologies it bore on its hands were," Earrie said as they discussed their foe.

"Those technologies are the source of his power. I just feel it," Fae said.

When she thought back to the events, she remembered his arms had been covered in odd technology. If anything was giving this dragon amplified abilities, his technology would be the culprit.

The others nodded their heads in agreement. Elvador wasn't aware that Zenith was able to grow half the size of a kingdom. Maybe it was best that he didn't get the chance to fight him after all. Through a multitude of years of chasing this man, he never heard of Zenith possessing the power of growth.

He decided he needed to stay with the group and find out more about Zenith's assault on their kingdom before making any more moves.

"We head south," Benard said.

The medic boy ripped off a piece of Ephoreia from a book of maps he retrieved out of his leg pocket.

The day Benard planned his intrusion to the

honor ball, he brought many educational textbooks about Ephoreia's underworld to help him pass the time. The student never would have thought they would come in as useful as they were now.

Earrie and Fae together asked, "Why?" Benard pointed to a town on his map.

"The town is called Mercernip. This is where the Inventors originated from. I've heard stories that machines run their town," Benard said.

Elvador agreed with the plan. If anyone could tell them about the technology Zenith possessed, it would be them. He continued to play the part of an amnesiac as he carefully maintained his cover.

On their walk southwards, Fae stood next to Elvador. She found him very intriguing. He gave off a humorous demeanor, and he was built strong for a human. He seemed naturally intelligent. This was despite the fact he possessed no memories or so Fae thought.

Earrie headed the trail as she was used to fronting. Benard took this time to be next to her.

He realized that he viewed her without biased lenses, unlike his perfect-image of the girl beforehand. The medic boy now comprehended that she had faults just like every other girl. This understanding didn't change his feelings if anything they only made him more crazy about her knowing she had spice.

"Why are you staring at me, moron?" Earrie questioned with a glare at a dazed Benard.

He blushed and moved his head forward. "I just spaced out is all," he muttered.

Earrie glared, "Well, could you space out in some other direction? It's distracting."

Benard felt embarrassed. He tried to keep his eyes off her, but they kept fighting their way back to her.

In the background, Fae giggled at her sister's attitude. Elvador felt a sense of peace around Fae.

She seemed to be an average elf, but inside she held a pure heart. Fae held no desire to do anyone harm.

The dragon thought Fae's appearance was above average though. A look fitting for a princess. He didn't know nothing of Fae's past, just that she was one of the princesses of Heaven's Castle.

Elvador favored her orange, flamed hair; It reminded him of his scales when he transformed. The color gave him a sense of familiarity.

Fae's long, pointed ears stood out framing a round face. She wore a white, short dress. Not ideal for their traveling conditions, but the outfit suited her. The princess was dressed for a ball after all.

He observed her height. It was not at all in the standard of the elves he remembered from times past, but Earrie was also rather short for an elf. He wondered why Benard was so much taller than them, but he didn't bother to ask.

Fae found herself falling into her childlike antics again when she sang a tune.

"The elves who rule all call us tools. We are nothing but mere workers, for the lurkers. We bang and bang while wondering, who made those old factories sing?" She hummed in a broken voice.

Elvador questioned himself, What kind of song

is this?

Her elder sister listened, and with a heart drop, she slowed her steps.

Ever since Earrie learned that Fae was her sister, her heart held a special spot for the halflings. Many times over the years, she asked her father to change their conditions. But due to her mother queen Clance's hatred of the halflings, he never went through on his word.

After a long day of walking the group decided to make camp. Benard and Elvador competed to set up the tents. Meanwhile, Fae set up dinner, and with a whetstone, Earrie sharpened her blade.

Elvador bit his lips and rolled his eyes whenever they mentioned Zenith. None of them knew Zenith's name, so they all referred to him as the dragon who attacked their kingdom. He desired to tell them everything about the tyrant, but it meant blowing his cover.

Zenith was the most powerful in all of Ephoreia; He was the evil dragon who'd taken hold of all the kingdoms in the land. Though he didn't do this with some goal to change the world or even make himself the leader of it, he did it in spite.

Zenith hated Ephoreia. His hatred spewed from a bitterness that never left him from over a thousand years ago. That concoction of darkness only threw him further into the depths of disparity as it simmered all those years.

Nothing was ever enough for Zenith, but no one was able to stop his demands and tyranny.

Some hours after their supper, all four of their heads fell fast asleep. Their peaceful snores were almost as though the fate of the world didn't rest on their shoulders.

Chapter 5 Stable Girl and the King

Around several decades ago, a young lady encountered a boy. This was a strange meeting of predestined fate that would change the course of history forever.

One evening Prince Richard brought in his horse after a long day of training. His father King Howard was not very pleased with his late-night activities. He thought back to the last time he got caught coming home late.

"You're engaged to be wed, Richie! You haven't got the time to be out fooling around late at night. The last thing you need is a bad reputation," he remembered his father's scolding while he walked his horse to the stables.

Richard laughed back at his joking response, "Maybe the royals will call me the Midnight Rebel, haha!"

Ever since his antics began, his father kept close tabs on him. Every store he entered and every person he spoke to was monitored. If he wasn't going to protect his name, his pa would do it for him.

The prince decided it would be best to leave his horse in the Slums' stables for the night. He'd chosen this route to avoid his father's attention.

After he dropped his horse off, he planned to sneak into his room through an adjacent window he'd left slightly cracked open.

Even though the young prince trained many years longer than his fellow knights, he still hadn't received his embers. This was because of the tradition upheld by the royal bloodline; Each new kind would inherit the stone embers when his predecessor passed. The same embers King Uvler possessed when creating their castle long ago.

Richard crept into The Slums. He wore a robe that cloaked his face with a mask to protect his royal identity. He hid himself not because of what people would say, but he feared the over protective nature of his father and what new rules he may enforce if caught.

Richard noticed a lit lantern at the slum stable. He relaxed his composure and stopped his worries that they may have been asleep.

When he closed in, the prince tapped on the door with a shy knock. A young, halfling woman with ginger, red hair opened.

She smiled faintly and let out a rehearsed murmur, "Sir, I will take your horse. It's four-coin a night, and eight for grooming."

Eyeing him up, she noticed he was a human, and appeared to be noble or royal. This concerned her as the upper class did not hang around the Slums so late at night unless looking for trouble.

Richard double blinked. Without his appearance, he realized he'd have to pay. Four coins weren't anything to an elf merely dust pay. Though he didn't ever carry coins, for his face alone had always paid his tab.

"Miss, I'm sorry I seem to have left my wallet in my home. Is there any way I can pay you in the morning?" Richard asked while he covered his panicky thoughts with a cool demeanor.

She considered his request. "Sir, to be honest, I've never heard of an elf not having a coin on him. Are you sure this isn't a stolen mare?" he jumped back at her prosperous institution.

He furrowed his brows and puffed out his chest. "Miss, I've never stolen in my life! This is my very own mare, and I could have your head for such an accusation!" he bellowed out red-faced.

She snickered at his clear offense. "She's"—the young lady said while she reached behind him and pet the horse—"beautiful, you can leave her for the night. A thief would have run off by now if I was onto him," she said. Her dismissal of his threat only made him angrier.

In the background, Richard heard some clunky guardsmen walking around. "Where is Richard? The king's furious!" distant voices barked back and forth.

The guards appeared to be on a manhunt for him. With his glowing skin, he knew he'd stick out like a pig at a party.

With the knights drawing forward, he viewed distant lanterns lighting up the pathway in agony.

Without so much as a thought, Richard threw himself inside the stable cottage. He fell on the young halfling, and with a palm to her lips, he muffled a squeal.

"Shhh!" he demanded while his heart raced like a cheetah. Richard huffed since now he truly looked like a thief or worse throwing himself on a lady at night.

To settle her down, the man removed his mask. When she viewed him, she let out a dramatic gasp to his unveiling. The halfling ceased her struggles as he lifted himself off her.

The girl had an instant change in attitude. She immediately bowed down and begged for his forgiveness. He shushed her again and motioned his hands forcing a smile to calm her stuttering.

Knights knocked door to door in their broad search for the young, missing prince. His father must have been very upset with him.

"When they knock, I need you to say I'm not here. You didn't see me, and you know nothing, got it?" Richard said to the starry-eyed girl. She nodded and fixed her gaze on the young prince with dreamy eyes.

He looked back at her from the corner of his eye. She was a breathtaking, young lass with eyes like blue like a knight's embers and peach, freckled cheeks. The lad appeared to be the beholder for the most beautiful woman in all of Heaven's Castle.

When a knock sounded on the door, the young girl flinched. She got up and paced to the door while Richard positioned himself under her cot.

"Young lady, have you seen the prince out tonight?" a male guard asked in an impatient tone.

Before she could answer yes or no another knight called out from outside, "Hey, this is the prince's horse, Chelsea!"

The guard at the door didn't bother to ask any more questions instead he barged in and chucked the lady into the wall with his knee. Richard cringed at the sudden attack. The knight stomped on through her small, studio cottage and opened some doors and cabinets.

Why would I be inside there? Richard asked himself.

The knight wasn't looking for Richard, for he was doing what he and every other elven knight had accustomed themselves to.

The castle guard filled up a satchel on his waist with fresh fruit and towels. He approached her nightstand, and with a jiggle to the old piece of furniture, he jammed it open.

"Nothing but an old mirror!" the knight grumbled to himself.

The young halfling got up and held the scavenging knight's wrist. "Please, sir, this belonged to my late mother, it's all I have left of her," she knelt and pleaded on her knees with her hands together in the air.

The knight slapped up her shaking hands and pressed her small body against the dresser. "It's mine now. Unless—you got something else to offer me?" the knight sneered with wandering eyes.

Richard groaned beneath gritted teeth while he drew a fist and attempted to restrain himself from under the bed. Were these savages the men whom his father trusted to protect the kingdom?

The lady shook her head left and right. "No . . . " she whispered as she pulled back with a bowed head.

"Then shut your trap, and I'll take what I darn well please!" the knight grabbed the mirror. He slammed the delicate item into his handbag and walked out the door.

When sounds of footsteps and a galloping horse disappeared, Richard emerged from under the bed. He ran to the woman's side.

"Are you okay, miss? That man will not get

away with what he did to you!" Richard reassured her with a grabbing hand.

The lady hid her head down. She tried to hide her sobs. Richard couldn't refrain from embracing the teary-eyed lady.

"What is your name?" he asked.

Through some soft hiccups, the woman whispered, "Stella . . . my name's Stella."

The next morning, Richard told his father what happened. To his surprise, his father didn't seem to possess any reaction whatsoever.

It appeared the king knew of these abominable crimes all along. This day marked the moment that Richard lost all his respect for his father.

He spent the evening finding the man who pilfered Stella's home and getting back everything he stole. Being an Ember Knight trainee and the prince of Heaven's Castle gave him just the connections he needed to track the sorry bastard down. To say, Richard went hard on the man, would be an understatement.

When the prince stumbled back to the stables

the next night, he pulled out the stolen mirror and handed it to a rejoicing Stella.

Though this wasn't the only time Richard visited Stella, regular nightly visits to her cottage became his new hobby.

Instead of training to be an Ember Knight till odd hours of the night, the young prince found himself being a vigilante of self-justice in the streets of The Slums. The name he joked about before with his father seemed less like a tease and more like a title now. If Howard wasn't going to keep the peace in The Slums, Richard would carry that burden.

It was after these regular visits that Prince Richard felt a flame in his heart spark. This young frail woman who worked in the Slum's stables captured his heart with her humble charm.

Shortly after their fate-felt encounter, they became lovers. The blossom of their relationship would carry on for many years after long after he'd married Clance and even after Earrie's birth.

He kept seeing her no matter how much his heart hurt about what he was doing to Clance and

Earrie.

A selfish flame only extinguished by Fae's birth. The love child exposed their long-concealed secret.

A few years down the line, Fae began resembling the king and his dwarven lineage, and Clance threatened Stella's life. This caused the king to cease his affair.

It wasn't long after that sickness took Stella.

Chapter 6 A City of Technology

Inside the royal throne room, Zenith sat on a stolen throne. He spent his hours building up his army of minions. The murderer felt satisfaction with each new mini beast hypnotized by his power.

His work halted when Acadash brought him something he hadn't suspected, Queen Clance.

She wasn't kicking and screaming instead she just waltzed in freely with a sinister smile on her lips.

The rightful queen stepped up to him and took a knee. "I have seen your power Zenith. You destroyed my husband and took his crown. You've done me a favor," she said in a humbling demeanor.

"Favor?" Zenith purred. She'd successfully captured the man's attention.

Clance looked up from her stance and drew in eye contact. "For years I've wanted this man dead. I've spent my better years loathing this man. He dishonored me day and night with his repulsing affair."

Zenith could taste the bitterness in her words. He knew that hatred firsthand, for he was hatred in human embodiment.

"Join me and become my queen," Zenith offered. He was entranced by this unplanned addition to his plans.

"Of course, my king," she walked up to him and took a seat in her familiar throne with a glowing smile.

"Royal queen, lower this barrier, and I will send my newfound army on all of Ephoreia to spread my power to every end and depth of its rotten land."

At his call, Clance spoke, "Barrier mode: off."

Just the command Zenith needed to start his game.

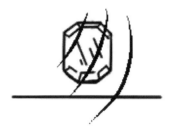

A sudden shake carried Earrie out of her slumber. She felt hands abruptly pulled her up like a bear catching fish from a river.

Before she had a chance to complain, the female knight heard a loud, cutting wind above.

The princess eyed a concerned Fae to her right. Elvador had sent her to wake Earrie. Due to his sharp senses, he heard many flapping wings in the distance; An army of dragons was quickly approaching them.

Elvador knew this attack was straight from Zenith. The hoarding beasts must have been a test of his power or perhaps an experiment with his minions.

Earrie ran out of her tent and met up with the others. Elvador faced her now that they were together.

"We need to mask our scent or trackers will reach us in no time," he whispered.

"Mask our scent?" Earrie questioned in a hushed tone.

"If we don't cover our smell, we'll be overrun by those beasts," Elvador remarked.

Earrie looked above her head to a sky covered in a meteor shower of dragons. She gulped. If she couldn't handle the few from before, how on Ephoreia would she survive this hoarding army?

Elvador was correct; They needed to run. To hide. Get far away from this army before they were to be eaten alive.

Fae appeared spooked, for she had no idea how to access her supposed Inventor powers. If they were spotted, Fae knew she wouldn't be any use in a battle.

"How do we hide our scent?" She questioned. Fae tried to mask the fear that coincided inside of her voice by appearing calm.

Elvador replied, "There's a river just below from us. We must take its mud and cover ourselves along with some leaves, so it will drown out our scents."

At his words, Benard grew agitated. "Isn't anyone going to question this man? He's an amnesiac who supposedly has no memories, and we're just going to blindly follow his orders. He could be an enemy spy for all we know?" he yelled in frustration with flying hands.

Earrie turned around to face Benard. "Look, we don't exactly have any other options, and certainly don't have time to stand here bickering about it," she said with folded arms.

Benard growled and stomped his feet down like a child who didn't get his candy. He paced his distance behind the group as he continued sulking.

The dragons dispersed from the clouds into all of Ephoreia. Each one possessed the same mission; They would show the power of their god Zenith and reinforce his kingdom.

With crunching dried leaves, the group ran through the outskirts of the forest. Their clock of safety was ticking. Sounds of flowing water marked their arrival to the river stream.

Elvador walked ahead of the group. He knelt and scoped out piles of slimy mud and covered himself thoroughly with it. Fae followed suit.

Benard threw the liquid earth on himself while he mumbled complaints about trusting this man under his breath.

Earrie was the last to drench herself. During this time, the elder princess never let her hand stray too far from her sword.

After they successfully veiled their scent, the groups continued on their march to The Mercernip Kingdom.

Elvador knew their map was outdated. Mercernip kingdom had a new name, Tuner Town. After all, he hadn't been isolated in the clouds with them for a thousand years, for the dragon was on the ground fighting a never-ending war with Zenith and his calamity.

The forest soon transformed into a desert after they passed some territories of bushes. The climate migrated with each step. Heat pulsated off their backs, and they regretted their disregard to bring canisters of water with them.

Elvador was the only one not succumbing to the dry heat, for he was a dragon; His endurance far outweighed the average individual like so with his lifespan. Elvador hardly aged a day since the day he became a beast.

Walking in the dry lands, Elvador thought back to his time training and the many days he'd spent walking through these very same dunes.

Through a cloud of hazed heat in the distance, the group viewed the tip of Tuner Town. An industrial town ran by tuned machinery left from the Inventors of Ancient's past.

A large church called the Church of Light held the ton together. The citizens of Tuner Town held tight to a solid theology involving protecting inventions and weapons of knowledge.

The kingdom's walls stood tall made with a mixture of mud and clay. They appeared tan in color and blended with the sands of the desert.

Inside the walls, a bustling city laid awake. Metal, tinkering machines rolled back and forth inside the town. They scurried in and out of small automatic openings.

Clunking about, the tiny machines carried dinner trays on their heads along with empty glasses. Some worked on vehicles that looked similar to the pods of Heaven's Castle.

The town was populated with a majority of human-sized, green brutes. They were the offspring of years of sharing a kingdom between dwarven people ogres.

Long ago, the territorial treaty between the two races became a new kingdom called Tuner Town. This new kingdom was filled with preserved Inventor technologies from a time past. Tuner Town was strong due to its many weapons of war upholding its foundations.

The brutes of Tuner Town spent their lives studying the machinery and performing hunts out in the desert whereas the dwarven people spent most of their time in keeping up their robots.

Many ogres protected the town as they were

trained guardsmen in a historic tradition to their kind's ways. War and battle had always been the source of an ogre's pride and glory. While many hated the war, they lived for a chance to get their blood pumping and bring honor to their name.

The group reached the town's tall gates. A large, muscular ogre viewed them and grunted, "Just who are you supposed to be?"

Earrie spoke up, "My sister and I are princesses from Heaven's Castle. Our kingdom was raided by a great dragon, and we are seeking aid from your kingdom."

The guard laughed, "So, that's what that racket in the sky was about. I thought you guys were having some sort of festival." His lighthearted comment did not amuse Earrie.

Fae spoke up from behind her sister, "The dragon that attacked us, he had on his wrist two separate technologies, and we were hoping you could inform us about them."

The ogre rolled his eyes, "Why should our kingdom help you out in any way. We haven't heard from you guys in a millennium. Word has it you stole our Inventor and ran off with her!"

Fae looked hopeful at the mention of an Inventor. "I'm an Inventor. I'm sure I could help you out in return for your aid."

Her words caused the guard's eyes to bulge. "If this is true, I'll bring you to our king right away! We haven't seen an Inventor ever in our town. All we have to remember the Inventors are our repaired ruins of the lost kingdom of Mercernip and the church.

"We have records and books but to see one in person . . . " the guard lost his train of thought. He stepped back and opened the gate with an echoing creak.

Fae wagged her head around to speak to Elvador, but his presence was absent. Just where had he run off too?

Benard gawked at the scene before him. He walked over to one of the moving technologies, and with a poke, he asked, "What do you call these?"

The ogre smiled a toothy grin, "Robots. Are you saying your kingdom is so behind in times you've never seen a robot before?" Benard nodded his head.

"To think we feared you elves up in your mighty kingdom. This whole time you lived in the dark ages up there. Frozen in time. A capsule of the era you disappeared," the guard said as they walked. He spoke more to himself than to them.

Benard spoke, "We had factories and pods, we just didn't need robots doing everything little thing for us."

"No, we had halflings do it," Earrie muttered under her breath with a sip of bitterness.

When they arrived at the castle's gates, the guard let Earrie and Fae in. He held out a long, strong arm to Benard that blocked his entrance.

"Not you!" the guard ordered in an authoritative voice.

Benard looked around in confusion, "Why not? I'm with the princesses."

"We never let outsiders in let alone from a foreign kingdom. An Inventor, now that's an exception. The other woman is only allowed to come . . . to discuss our deal,"

Benard huffed at the guard's response.

Earrie made eye contact with Benard. "Go enjoy yourself. You know you're geeking out anyway. We'll be back in no time," she commanded with a fake smile.

Her sense of casualness was odd. He agreed and headed off into the town.

Inside the castle, many people dressed in prosperous robes sat in an arrangement of chairs. They whispered muffled words into each other's ears with covered hands as if that masked their secrecy.

Fae felt like she was back at the Honor Ball with all the wandering eyes watching her. She guessed that all royals offered the same judgment.

Earrie put on her princess mask and smiled as if nothing was wrong in the world.

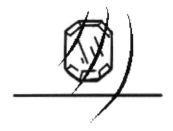

In town, Benard spotted a library. He went inside and collected various books. He found many copies that were updated novels of his favorites.

Stacking a castle of books in his arms, Benard stepped over to a large desk where an old, brute woman checked him out. Though he had no plans to return them, he pretended to be a man of integrity.

After the student exited the place of books, he took a seat on a bench outside the castle and read while he awaited the princesses.

A young dwarf approached him and asked, "Are you really an elf?"

"Why, yes, yes I am," Benard said amused. He flipped a page and broke contacted with his book.

"You know what the church says about elves don't you?" the dwarf asked.

Benard's brows raised. "No, I don't. What do they say?"

"They say that an elf will save Ephoreia and bring an end to the period of hostility," the young girl said. She looked hopeful.

"Is there a church nearby?" Benard asked intrigued.

The girl pointed. "This way," she said.

Entering an oval building, Benard looked around bewildered. Gold surrounded the walls and window seals, and pieces of inventions were plastered on the walls.

"What's this?," he asked, pointing to a plaque.

"Why that's the written code," the girl smiled. She looked down to her toes and dwindled her thumbs. "Though—I can't read it for you."

"Who can?" Benard said as he stared at the foreign text. Something about it was familiar to him, but he couldn't place it.

"Some priests can read a few letters, but the code isn't supposed to be read by anyone but an Inventor."

Benard's eyes lit up. Maybe Fae could read the text.

"Bring me my esteemed guest!" the king yelled above the whispering voices.

Silence followed his call. Brute guards escorted them to the throne.

All the brutes looked similar as they were tall, moss-green people with tan-colored robes. They didn't spot much defense for soldiers.

Earrie wondered why the guards looked so lightly dressed. Wasn't Zenith harming everyone? And what happened to the army of dragons from before?

They made it to the throne, and upon its seat, a short, dwarven king sat. Smaller in size than Fae at only four-feet tall. Although the new race of brutes dominated the kingdom, the dwarven people kept their royal bloodline in power.

It wasn't just Heaven's Castle whose royalty was filled with dwarven blood. They had a history of ruling a great number of cities as their people often built strong, lasting towns that withhold time.

The king wore a long, black beard with sprinkles of gray in it. His hair was placed in a low ponytail behind his back.

He was clothed in a velvet robe with multiple layers of different high-end fabrics of shades of purple and blue along with dust brown. The robe inched past his toes covering his black, pointed dress shoes.

"What do we have here? Have elven princesses come for help to a kingdom your people abandoned?" the girls gulped at his tone.

They knew nothing of the past that he mentioned.

Earrie walked closer to his throne and knelt on one knee, "Your Highness, my father along with many other Ember Knights need your help. Our kingdom was attacked several days ago by a towering, black and red dragon. I hereby humbly request your aid to defeat this mighty foe."

"Humorous at best. Were your people so isolated from Ephoreia you don't know who Zenith is? He's attacked every nation down here for a thousand years. Meanwhile, you elves slept peacefully in your stone castle among the clouds, contrary to our many sufferings.

"You even took your great Ember Knights with the power to slay dragons along with you while you elves continued to hermit up yonder. To add sears to our burns, your ancestors sealed our Inventor gene. The only hope of weaponry to defeat Zenith," the king said with anger and stowed sadness.

It was clear that he was blaming Heaven's Castle for all their problems.

Before the sisters could retaliate the king continued his speech, "I know most of this means nothing to you. A time before your generation. For what your kingdom did to Ephoreia, there is no mercy.

"Unfortunately, I fail to see any reason to aid you. It's a blessing your kingdom was attacked by Zenith after everything your nation caused. The

121

deaths. The suffering.

"All of us lay in the mercy of Elvador; The only dragon to ever hold his own against Zenith. Possibly the only dragon left that isn't in agreement with Zenith's ways. He is the only reason any kingdom still stands, and that any of us live. I have a proposition for"—he lifted his finger to Fae—"you. The young copper-haired girl." A smile filled his face. "Become my bride, and I will make an alliance with your people and come to their aid when they beckon my call," he offered in a sly tongue.

Earrie stood up to grab her sister. She wasn't about to let her sister throw her life away like some bargaining chip. Their father already did that. She'd seen the repercussions of marrying a soul you didn't love all too close in her lifetime.

Fae, on the other hand, was not about to marry this man she didn't know. She was far too young for him, and he gave off an eerie feeling with gawking eyes and wet lips.

The young princess moved to her sister, but silver spears that glowed blocked her way.

"What are you doing?!" Earrie asked the king regarding Fae in shock of his actions.

"I'm not about to let an Inventor out of my grasp. I offered you a peaceful option, but if you're denying it, we'll have to do things the hard way," he threatened and tapped his side in a signaling way.

Earrie grabbed her embers. "Blue Embers!" she called out.

Normally she would have been transformed by now, but her body remained the same. Could they be nullifying her powers somehow?

She eyed around in horror. The only thing that stood out was the glowing spears the guards held.

The ginger princess looked out of it. Earrie gave a concerned glance to her sister.

She noticed Fae's persist, trembling shivers on the throne room floor. Somehow this suppressor was hurting her sister.

The king stood up and pranced over to Fae. "By my beard, she is an Inventor!" he yelled, kneeling beside her.

King Pik cupped Fae's chin in his hand. She

groaned in pain. Inside her body, thousands of electric shocks went off. It was during this time that a familiar force awoke inside her.

A white-eyed Fae grabbed a hold of the closest spear. The blade's color went from silver to red letting out a force wave that infected all nearby blades with the same cherry color.

Earrie immediately tried her embers, and much to her relief she successfully transformed.

White text fogged around Fae aiding her every move. This wasn't like beforehand as Fae seemed to be coherent and directing her abilities.

Earrie surrounded herself with strong, gusty winds that knocked back the guards who cornered her. A small, dwarven knight walked up to challenge her. In his hands, he held an ax. She found it odd that the little soldier would come against her after witnessing all the brutes that fell due to a stream of her wind.

She called more wind, but the dwarf didn't budge. His legs held firm. He continued his approach. The dwarf's endurance reminded her of the robots she had seen earlier. Earrie drew her blade and prepared for a battle of blades.

The dwarven king stepped backward in fear of Fae's power. In his trace, he fell over the hem of his flowing robe.

Fae held up the red spear in her hand. With a sudden magnetic pull, all of the other red spears flew inside it.

She took the condensed technology and surrounded her body with it. The Inventor created a defense of armored technology. She walked over with her covering on and grabbed a hold of Earrie.

Fae shot her fist towards the sky, and a cannon type gunnery came out of her hand. A rocket smashed a large hole in the ceiling while dust and debris caved in on them.

The king gazed up at the concave. "If you walk out now don't ever come back! You've made an enemy of us." The king grunted on the floor while he banged his fist like a child.

Fae ignored him and transformed her legs into jet boots. She flew up into the air with Earrie in hand. When they reached outside the palace, she let go of her sister.

Targeting lock-on missiles fired at them. Together they danced in the sky as they dodged the incoming attacks.

Fae thought up a plan that she felt would be plausible. Given any normal elf, it wouldn't have been, but not for Fae. With the power of imagination on her side, she could do anything within technology's limitations.

She closed her eyes and hacked inside the mainframes of the machinery. With her touch, the attacks ceased.

Earrie and Fae gazed into the open sky, and they viewed a medium-sized, copper airship above their heads. Before they flew in another direction, the sisters noticed a brunette man on the edge of the ship waving his hand.

"Pup?" Fae questioned as she flew up to meet him on the deck.

Earrie looked at Fae, "I've got to grab Benard. We can't just leave him here."

Fae nodded, "Need my help?"

Her sister looked down at the city as if to weigh

her chances of success. "No, I'll be alright. As long as you have their firepower inline, they can't touch me," she said. Earrie quickly darted below.

She flew inches above ground level as she kept her eye out for Benard. It didn't take any time at all to spot the tall, red elf.

Benard was hunched over and fixated on whatever passage he was reading. He failed to notice the commotion in the air.

The wind knight swooped past the reader and grabbed him by the collar; The same collar she held up when they first met. He yelped and focused on holding his book.

"I'm guessing things didn't go as planned," he shouted against the sound of flight.

"Way to state the obvious," Earrie stated.

The princess transported Benard and flung him onto the airship with a clunk. "Ouch!" Benard squealed like a pig when his body hit the metal surface.

Earrie huffed and walked away towards the

hanger.

Fae felt like they were a safe enough distance from the town to release her hold on the town's firepower. She didn't want to leave them defenseless against Zenith's massacring tendencies.

A shout from Earrie indicated she made a naive mistake. "They're firing at us again! What happened Fae? Did we fly out of your range?"

Fae's range had nothing to do with it once she'd hacked the missiles she had them programmed for her hold. The young princess even had to rewrite them just to release them back to Tuner Town.

On sight of another missile, Fae jumped outside the ship and grabbed hold of the weapon and disarmed it. Earrie screamed when she viewed the risky jump.

The Inventor managed to change its direction into a reversal back to Tuner Town. The bomb's discharge was no longer a dangerous one, just a simple momentary EMP to disarm their electrical gunnery until they were out of reach.

Echoing yells of terror filled the air when the

incoming missile leaned into the town. Earrie and the rest of the group found the armed weapon to be an atrocious act. That was until they viewed the silver static come off it and a halt of Tuner Town's attacks.

"What did you do to the missile?" Earrie asked in confusion.

"Well, I got the idea from what they did to us back in the king's throne room. I nullified all their incoming attacks. Let's move through. It won't last forever," Fae said while her glance moved from Earrie to Elvador.

Elvador wore a tan robe that fell to his ankles. It had a small v-cut under his collar bones. Underneath the robe, brown sandals peeked upwards. The clothing covered his forearms. His covering drizzled down to his elbows as he held onto the ship's steering wheel.

"So, how did you get this airship, and where did you find the clothes?" Benard asked to soothe everyone's curiosities.

The dragon smiled, "I stole it from them. I just

had a feeling they wouldn't be of any help." His response caused them all to gasp. "For some reason, I just knew how to fly this thing, and I thought it might be of some use to us," he said while he kept up his act of possessing no memories.

"Are we still trusting this guy?" Benard said in an annoyed tone with rolled eyes.

"Hasn't failed us yet," Fae joked with an elbow to Benard.

"Unlike someone I know," Earrie threw in as she joined the teasing. Benard put his head down into his book while he tried to hide his obvious pout.

Earrie, Benard, and Fae discussed what they learned in the back of the ship while Elvador remained upfront piloting. Thanks to his dragon ears, he could hear everything that they said.

The truth was that Elvador hadn't stolen the vessel. It belonged to him. The ship was purchased with the many coins he'd earned from saving Tuner Town from Zenith throughout the years, adding that to a thousand years of saving their people, and he was quite a wealthy dragon.

The real reason he split up with them originally was to avoid being recognized. The whole town loved Elvador, for he was their savior, the good dragon, and Elvador had another reason for his separation. He took the time to go around back and have a private talk with the king Pik.

He and Pik quickly formulated a plan to test his new group of companions. He wanted to know just how powerful they were if put to the test.

The king meant a lot of the words he said, but in the state of Ephoreia, any foe of Zenith was their ally. Pik had fun teasing the girls until Fae blew a whole through his rooftop.

"His name is Zenith. Some dragon who's been attacking Ephoreia for a thousand years," Earrie said as she crossed her resting arms on a wooden table.

"There was a dwarven girl who told me of a type of prophecy from their church. It said an elf will save Ephoreia and bring an end to the period of hostility."

"She also took me to their church, and I saw text that looked to be the same code that comes out of Fae when she invents things. She said only an Inventor could interpret its text," Benard said.

"Maybe fate is on our side," Fae mumbled.

"Fate, or power," Earrie added.

"In this book of old Inventor's creations, I found something that talks about technology like the one on Zenith's arm. Get this, it says Melah made it long ago under the control of her father. It apparently can transport dragon's souls. I'm not entirely sure what its purpose was intended for, but I'll keep reading," Benard informed them. He licked his index finger and flipped a page in his stolen book.

Fae looked up at the group. "I'm not sure what happened when they shocked me. Something in those bolts gave me complete control over my abilities. I felt as though I knew everything, yet I knew nothing. I just thought of creations, and my ability filled in the blanks," she said with a curious tone and confused eyes.

Earrie and Benard listened while she spoke. "Well, I'd say that's a good thing," Earrie noted as she shook her head agreeably with closed eyes.

Benard chimed in, "So this Elvador guy they talked about, could he hold his own against Zenith?" Earrie and Fae nodded in unison. "We need to find that man, but first we have somewhere else to go," Benard chatted as he held up his all too familiar map. His finger aligned to a circled, red spot.

"The Inventor Trials," he noted out loud as he opened his book. "You see here," he pointed to a page inside of a book with many hands drawn pictures. "This is where they used to send Inventors long ago. It says you'll obtain tools to assist your abilities if you participate in this trial," he said. Benard mumbled a passage of reference under her breath.

Fae spoke up, "All right. I'll do what it takes to save our kingdom and take down Zenith."

With her strong words, they agreed. Elvador smiled in the front of his ship. Maybe together with this new gang, his thousand-year-old battle with

Zenith would finally have an ending.

Chapter 7 Darkness

Elvador cocked the sails to his massive airship. He spun it in the direction of Benard's map. The dragon believed he heard of the location before possibly even been there once or twice. He couldn't remember it's pinpoint location without the map though, but he felt a certain familiarity to its direction.

Fae walked around the deck and canvassed Ephoreia. She breathed in its vibrant colors with a deep inhale and smiled.

Down below, an uncountable number of sand grains filled the harsh desert. The sun toasted its hills like loads of bread. Fresh brown crisp peaks hunched over into dips only to peak back up.

With a stir in the engine, the ship turned. They arrived.

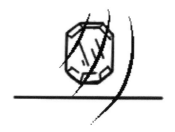

Above the boarding crew, Zenith kept a calm composure. On the armrest of his new throne, he flung his finger in an inward angle. Acadash walked over to his call.

"Lord Zenith, what do you wish of me?"

"While my dragons are toying with their prey, I want you to do . . . a separate task."

Acadash looked up with hunger in her eyes for bloodshed, "What's your command?"

"Siege Aspen Bay. It's time to add my old hometown to my board," he sneered.

With a nod and a turn, Acadash exited the building. When she faced the opposite of Zenith, a monstrous gleam covered her face. It was time to show off her power.

The throne room's tall, golden gates hung open. Before she exited Zenith said, "Take Clance with"—he reached in his pocket and grabbed a Blue Embers—"you. I want her to use this. I can visualize her utilizing her husband's embers to slay her no-good daughters. Just marvelous!"

"Before you go, bring her to me. I have a . . . gift for the lady," he flicked his fingertips, revealing a spark. He held in his palms a touch-activation bomb. She grinned and clapped her hands in approval.

"You never fail to impress me, Lord Zenith."

He then tossed the blue, glowing chain her way. With a snatch, she grabbed it and went to fetch Clance. The two of them were about to have a playdate.

The queen changed out of her purple, satin gown into a much lighter piece. She observed the new dress in her body-length mirror.

Clance adored her new short, silk slip as it was something Zenith picked out. Clance's blood hair matched it perfectly while her peach, glowing skin decorated its outskirts.

A knock on the door caused Clance to leap. She wasn't planning on getting her hands dirty this soon.

Acadash flipped open the room and peered over to queen's getup. "You're a red rose. Stop hiding your thorns Clance. This is the hour to show yourself," she said with a smirk.

Clance turned around with a worried look. As a queen, she had never trained for battle. A few times in the queen's past, she rode on a horse or shot a glance over to her daughter's training, but she was not in any means prepared for a battle.

A familiar shine caught her eye when Acadash dangled a jewel in her face. "You will prove your worth," she spat.

Clance walked up to her with a changed expression. With a clamp of her fingers, she possessed the embers.

"Gladly," she whistled.

Before leaving Acadash brought Clance to Zenith's feet. "As you commanded Lord," Acadash said with humbleness.

Zenith got up and slid his feet toward the queen. He cupped her chin up in his hands.

"The dress looks lovely on you, my dear," Zenith snickered.

He kissed her and tapped her shoulder with his lit hand. Clance was oblivious to his true intentions. She smiled and wished him goodbye.

Acadash only grinned. She knew first hand Zenith's backstabbing ways.

The two willing servants flew down from Heaven's Castle to the home of the humans.

Aspen Bay was an old trading town on the coast of Ephoreia's split continent. The town was filled with hustle and bustle. Humans excelled in special crafts. They clothed their town with beige, wooden pieces. Made from the many aspen trees that outlined their town.

On these elegant crafts, skilled artisans used black, blotchy inks to create unique designs. They told stories and mocked breathtaking landscapes. All the pieces followed the town's wood-painting tradition. Small towns from all over Ephoreia paid a plethora of coins for their furniture.

These creative trades kept the town alive. Hundreds of routes with trade wagons came in and out daily.

Aspen Bay used to be called The Kinster Kingdom. Like Tuner Town, this Kingdom was renamed sometime in the past thousand years.

A kingdom that once belonged solely to the humans and their dragon soldiers now belonged to Ephoreia.

Races of every kind filled its streets. Brutes, elves, humans, dwarves, ogres, and halflings were all equal in these walls.

Elected governors under a united rule of neighboring nations ran the town. Instead of royal rulers, Aspen Bay was led by its citizens.

Behind Acadash and Clance's descent, a couple dozen of Zenith's minions followed.

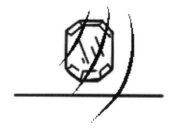

Harbor Bay had no time to prepare for their attack. Zenith's terrorism was familiar with the people of Ephoreia, but not his new army.

Folk skidded into basement sanctuaries designed for war. Doors slammed tight with strong, metal latches. Town guards ran through the streets with swords awake in their hands.

The knights of Harbor Bay rushed to their defensive positions. Armies of blended Ephoreians were ready to defend their city.

Before breaking ground Acadash licked her lips and sprayed a shower of paralysis venom over the town.

The acid rain caught many fighting men off guard. They froze in their places only to be at the mercy of their attackers.

Clance summoned stone boulders that crushed

many innocent bystanders. She shielded incoming arrow attacks with a created wall.

The attackers placed their feet on the ground.

The few fighters left found little hope with Acadash's cheetah speed. She jumped from victim to victim leaving a cold trail of bodies behind her steps.

Mini beasts cleared the air and dived into the military barracks. They chopped up archers like ravaging wolves.

Citizens of the once quaint, trading town shivered in utter fear when transformed dragons flung open their bolted doors.

They brought traumatized civilians to the town square where Clance had fashioned herself a stone stage. On her stage, the red-haired queen stood up with a proud look.

Acadash inside of Maxwell's possessed body stood by her side. Together they sported sinister, crooked smiles. The audience quivered at their terror.

"Quiet down onlookers!" Acadash silenced the

crying crowd for the queen's speech.

"Hello, my beloved Ephoreians. As you can see, you've been usurped into Zenith's loving hands," Clance said with a voice of authority.

"As Zenith's queen, I am now your queen. Your town was a . . . project of sorts. A starting block for our new nation under Zenith to form," she looked around with a dropped smile.

"You will serve Zenith. You will serve me. You will obey our rules without objection. No freedom of speech exists anymore. A tongue that speaks against our Lord Zenith will be slain. Anyone who attempts to rebel against us will be obliterated.

"Now, let's wean out those of you who are strong-willed. Shout out praises to our God Zenith and me!" Clance's speech came naturally to her. After all, she was a queen.

The crowd looked with blank faces too scared to show any emotion that didn't please Clance. She viewed a small boy in the crowd who wasn't clapping or singing.

Clance walked past the crowd and stood in front of him. "Yours?" she asked the young woman holding his left arm.

The woman replied, "Y-Yes, my queen, he is."

Clance glared at the boy while he glared back. Tipie, a young lad always was as stubborn as a horse. At his disobedience, the queen stomped her foot and threw her arms together.

"You know, I'm a mother of two. One is mine, and one is an abomination to my eyes," Clance said. Her voice sounded vicious.

Before the woman could respond the queen grabbed hold of his neck. He didn't scream at her tight squeeze instead he bit her and kicked her in the leg. This resistance triggered Clance's rage.

She dragged the squirming young boy in her arms to the stage. She was about to make a statement. Clance viewed Acadash, "How about a dragon's clamp?"

"Love it!" Acadash said with enthusiasm.

Clance held the specimen up for the whole crowd to see. "Watch what happens when you resist Zenith!" she yelled out as she flung the boy in the air.

A dragon swooped down and gobbled the boy

whole crunching his bones like twigs. The audience winced at the display of power.

"Now, do any of you want to join the boy. My dragons sure are hungry," she threatened.

The boy's mother stood pale-faced in a trance gaze into space. Acadash flew behind her.

"Will you be joining your boy tonight?" she purred into the woman's ear as she slid her fingers across the woman's neck in tease.

A long pause fell over the crowd. When it seemed as though the woman would give up her life, she said, "All hail the queen!"

At her words, Clance smiled. Exactly what she wanted; A town of enslaved followers bound by fear. Folk were too scared to fight back and frightened enough to turn on their kind if it meant saving themselves.

Acadash clapped and giggled up a storm. "What a delightful day today has been!" She glistened with psychopathic joy.

When darkness befell the city, all signs of hope left as their light vanished.

The town sat covered in a layer of the beasts that hovered over the sky. This barrier of dragons left them with dark, monstrous shadows that flew house to house and a clouded sky.

Chapter 8 The Trials

The group exited the copper ship into sinking sands that covered their ankles. Sounds of crunching sand under their steps caused Elvador to wince.

Fae looked back to the copper ship. It's brass reflection blinded her, causing her to glare.

"Won't this just be obvious?" She questioned in worry of being spotted.

Earrie set her hands on her hips as she thought about it. "You're right. The ship will give away our position."

With an idea inside her mind, Fae walked over and touched the ship. A glow inside of her eyes signified the release of familiar white text. She package condescended the ship into small, square earrings.

Elvador's stomach turned at the deconstructing of his airship, and he sighed in annoyance. If the beast was going to keep up the part as an amnesiac, he needed to remain calm. With a few pleasant thoughts, he reassured himself that she could invent a better model sometime.

Fae placed the copper hanging squares into her ears. She turned around in adorable mannerisms and asked, "Do you guys like my new jewelry?"

Elvador looked at her and touched the earrings, "Your work is unlike any other. I've never seen such boxed pieces before. It looks beautiful on you."

She twitched backward. The young princess looked up into his endearing eyes with a blush and said, "Thank you, I'm not entirely sure how I did it though."

Benard turned around with his quick-witted spirit, "So—you say you have never seen something like her earrings before—what exactly do you remember?"

"Not enough to tell a story of it. Bits and pieces of different places and technologies around Ephoreia are scattered around in my mind," Elvador replied.

Benard huffed with aggravation as it was not the response he wanted. He wasn't pleased with Elvador's vagueness.

The red-haired boy wanted him to come clean and say his true identity, for he was sure this man would betray them at any moment.

Benard rolled his eyes and stuck his nose inside his torn map. He directed them behind slow steps with points of his finger and irritable mumbling under his breath.

"Are you sure you know where we're going?"

Earrie asked doubtfully.

"Well it's not exactly like I've been here before," Benard said in defense. He threw his map to his side in frustration.

The dry, dessert conditions were taking a toll on the parties' minds.

The boy sighed and reached for his dropped map. With a glare, he gazed toward Earrie. Before the two could continue bickering in the desert heat, Benard tripped over something astray in the desert.

Earrie turned around with her hand clasped over her mouth as her body started convulsing. Fae let out a small giggle. Meanwhile, Elvador masked a grin.

Benard got up and dusted off his gray trousers. He walked over and tapped her shuttering shoulder, "What's wrong? Are you choking?" he asked.

Earrie turned around with light tears in her eyes. She smiled heavenly and said, "Well, it's just like who else"—she brought her hand to her cheek and wiped a single tear—"but Ben. You're such a clumsy fool."

Benard stood mesmerized by her beauty. Earrie's bright, pink skin flashed against the tan terrain behind her. The princess's eyes glistened behind warm tears.

He'd never seen her so relaxed. Her emotions were like an unwrapped gift; They brought him a sudden surprise.

He smiled back and scratched the back of his head. Benard stood just a couple inches away from her face and subconsciously spoke out loud, "Beautiful."

Earrie blushed and held her hand over her crooked elbow. "J-Just, who are you talking to?" she mumbled embarrassed.

Benard's cheeks burned a deeper red than his usual glow. He gazed behind her and spared himself embarrassment by saying, "The desert lands. They're beautiful—just breathtaking."

At his comment, Fae and Earrie gazed at the endless desert. They gasped at its enchanting, vast lands. The sun danced off the grains of sand causing sparks of light to clap in an appraisal.

"It's quite lovely, isn't it?" Elvador added.

Benard looked back to study what caused his fall. A bright shine to the corner of his eye struck him. Bending over, he noticed a metal surface beneath the sand. To his amazement, the spectacle appeared to be a hidden entrance.

"Guys, look here!" he shouted with a pointing finger.

"What is it now?" Earrie asked, agitated.

"The trials! This has to be the entrance." Benard said with excitement. He jumped up and down like a high-school girl.

At his words, the group ran back to his side and helped him shovel off the sand that had blown over the underground latch hiding its entry.

Earrie noticed how much time it would cost to uncover this whole doorway, so she decided to transform and use her wind to speed up the process.

It was during the time of concentrated digging that Elvador perked up his keen ears to the sounds of screaming in the distance. The dragon knew the location of the chaos very well, Aspen Bay; The town was the remaining remnants of the city he grew up in. He stepped back from the group and nonchalantly ran to their aid.

Fae heard a dash behind her. She snapped her head around to eye its source.

With notice of Elvador's disappearance, she asked the others, "Hey guys, where is Pup?"

Benard turned his head, "I don't know maybe a sinkhole got him."

At his insensitive remark, Earrie smacked his head. "What a jerk! Someone goes missing and that's what you say about it," she yelled.

Benard wasn't sure if Earrie was this concerned for Elvador or if she just chose to take the opportunity to jump on him for any little thing he did.

It was a game of bait and switch with Earrie. Benard was always wrong in her eyes; Her quick snaps were a natural element to their relationship.

"Well, there's nothing we can do about it. He probably just chased a bird. I don't know," Benard said in a pathetic attempt to offer up some sympathy.

Fae crossed her arms and shook her head. "You're right. We can't do anything about him right now. After all, I need to get this trial over with," she said as she approached the latched panel.

Fae wiggled the lock, and to her fortune, it shattered to white dust at her touch. With Earrie and Benard's assistance, she flung open the old, metallic door. It fell with a muffled clank as the sand softened its blow.

Inside the hatch, they viewed stone walls that spiraled downwards in what appeared to be a never-ending pathway. A yellow, transparent laser covered the doorway.

Fae took the first step as she slowly poked her finger to test if it was safe. With no reaction, she stepped inward.

Behind her, Benard and Earrie took turns attempting to cross the barrier. It rejected them with a buzz and a slight burn each time they pressed.

Benard reached into his leg pocket and grabbed out his book about the Inventors of Ancient. He fumbled through the passages with his right thumb. With furrowed eyebrows, he tried to make sense of what happened.

With a gulp to clear his throat, he read out loud in a loud, narrating voice, "It says, 'only Inventors may participate in these trials.'"

"Fae, come back you're not doing this alone," Earrie ordered with a shaking head after she fully comprehended the aforementioned text.

Fae bounced her head like a disobedient child. "No . . . I've got to do this Earrie. Just wait for me outside," she said with resolve.

Earrie stomped her foot, "Stop kidding! You can't be serious!"

Benard grabbed hold of Earrie's hand, "She needs to learn about her powers. She's Ephoreia's only hope right now. You can't take this way from her," he sounded lost in thought.

Memories of his mother drilling his father to let him attend Penate College filled his head. He knew what it was like to have someone close to you not support your dreams.

Earrie slapped his hand and yelled to Fae, "You could die, sister! Don't be stupid! Just come out, and we'll find some other way to help you!" her words were more and more desperate as she viewed her sister turn away and pace off.

"Don't come crawling back when you get hurt! Think you're so strong Fae, but you're just a kid!" Earrie shouted. Her words haunted Fae as they echoed down the swirling staircase.

Fae waved from behind but refused to look back. This wasn't goodbye, for it was simply a see you later.

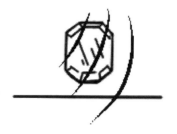

Back in Aspen Bay, Elvador surveyed the town. He eyed the extensive amount of beasts above in the sky. With the activation of his tracker powers, he noticed orange strings that led to that of a royal-blooded elf.

Who on Ephoreia could that be? Elvador thought.

He had a strong feeling that something was off. Zenith had possession over this town. Normally, he never bothered to enslave people. He was always more into massacring and tormenting them. Zenith had never been the type to involve himself with political powers, for it was always a waste of his playtime.

Elvador threw on his robe's thin, layered hat. He needed to remain aloof if he planned to continue his investigation of the town.

He walked to the streets, and at first, they appeared to be normal. This was until he viewed the faces of the local Ephoreians instead of their normal, polite smiles and waves hello, they remained unresponsive. It was as though life itself was sucked out of them.

He stopped by a restaurant to grab some food and remain inconspicuous. Ordering his dish, he noticed that everyone gave him blank faces in response to his questions.

While Elvador sipped his brewed tea, he eyed a

family of four at the wooden table across the room. The children showed signs of emotions inside them.

Two siblings peaked their heads up to inhale warm stews with big, beaming grins. When the beast watched their delightful anticipation for their dinner, he noticed the father kick their toes from under the table.

For some reason, the people of this town were choosing to act this way. He observed that they could control it, yet they played this role of hidden, facial expressions with dull neutrality.

An evening bell sounded that startled Elvador. His tea split over on his lap causing him to groan. People around him glared at his vocalization as if he might get them in trouble.

At the sound of a chimed bell, everyone stood up and started clapping and shouting praises to their beloved Lord Zenith and his queen. Elvador not wanting to be spotted copied them with some claps and mumbling under his breath.

Just the name Zenith caused Elvador's stomach

to twirl. He despised that man. To even think back to the times that they use to be comrades sickened him. He resented himself for ever having trusted Zenith.

Outside of the restaurant, Elvador heard trumpets and loud banging drums with sounds of marching. They grew louder and louder as he visualized instruments coming into the window's view.

The mother of the family said, "A celebration for our God!"

Elvador flinched. He couldn't believe anyone would be this happy to serve Zenith.

Maybe he was wrong about them choosing this as they seemed to be under some means of control.

The family he studied earlier walked out with forced smiling faces, and the entire restaurant followed in an orderly fashion behind. Elvador joined them in the curiosity of their destination.

In the streets, a parade took place. He noticed the orange, royal-blooded string was inside of an approaching cart.

On a red-carpeted float, an elf dressed in red stood. Her face and body shape appeared similar to Earrie's, except for the fact, she was several feet taller than Earrie.

Her hair matched her dress while her skin glowed a sandy hue. Elvador played the role of a local while he observed intently.

Everyone seemed to be worshiping this woman in red. They shouted in her direction and flew flowers along with strings of glitter in the air.

He thought she must be in alliance with Zenith. He hid a glare when her float approached.

Suddenly, the source of this madness dawned on him. The people were bound by the most powerful method of control; Fear.

The people clapped and shouted because they knew what would happen if they didn't. They worshiped the red queen as slaves.

When the cart passed by, the noise soon dissipated. People went back to their daily lives along with their absent expressions.

He continued to walk around the town to scope out its defenses. This seemed to be a stronghold of

Zenith. Whatever evil he was concocting, Elvador would put an early end to it.

Meanwhile, back in the desert Earrie pouted inside the edge of the trial's doorway as it offered her shade from the desert's harsh, beating sun. She crossed her arms and legs as she awaited her sister's impending return.

Benard sat to her side and read his novels silently. He'd given up any attempts at small talk. That was until he noticed a passage that would be of interest to the pink-haired princess.

He tapped her on her bare shoulder and pointed to the text, "'Trials are held on the participants' eighteenth birthday. They consist of three trials. One trial of wisdom, a second of knowledge, and lastly one of endurance. All winners are condemned as royalty inside The Mercernip Kingdom and given a place in the palace, whereas all losers are to be put to death.'"

"Death?" Earrie screamed.

To which Benard continued reading, "'Hanged and executed by The Mercernip Kingdom for the crime of dishonor.'"

Earrie relaxed somewhat at his words. "This must have been a big deal to Inventors," she said in wonderment.

Benard shook his head and continued reading. The two fell back into their silence.

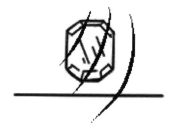

Below them, Fae reached another laser doorway. This door was colored a different color; Green.

With a deep breath, she walked through the door. She looked down and jumped when her clothes disintegrated into mist particles. They vanished just like the lock from beforehand.

Her outfit was replaced by an elastic black suit. This suit's seams glowed a multitude of colors.

Small glowing text crawled up her side legs and reached across her arms. The new suit covered all but her face.

She noticed the only thing that remained from her possessions were her cubed earrings. She was comforted to know that at least she still had her technology with her.

The room Fae walked into was unlit. The only light in the room came from her suit's edges and the flooring tiles that glowed flashing, Inventor text along with her natural shine.

Overhead, Fae heard a robotic voice from an unknown device. "Commencing trial in three-two-one," it said.

When the voice ceased, Fae felt the ground shake. The floor in front of her was a dark blue with bright, green text inside its tiles.

With a sudden shake, the flooring separated to reveal large cubes. They floated in the air in different, trained patterns. Some of these cubes went up and down while others paced left and right. However, none of them provided a clear pathway to the next door.

Fae reached for her earrings. She transformed them into a jet pack and placed it on her back.

She smiled and thought to herself about how this test would be a piece of cake.

Fae flew up over levitating pieces. She made it halfway through the trial room when air vents opened up in the sidewalls and blew fierce, pressing winds against her.

With the force of the winds ushering her backward, the ginger-haired princess fell back to the beginning of the trial. She tilted her head up and noticed a sign.

The sign listed the trial's rules: no flying, no super jumps, and no hacking the trial.

She got up and sighed. Her previous thoughts vanished and were replaced with nervous worries.

Fae approached the first floating platform. The tile arrived close to the edge of the walkway then flew in the direction of the next door. She decided to hop onto the glowing cube.

The floor piece brought her to another block. This one was above Fae's head, but it was too high for her to jump to.

The young princess used her technology to create a ladder to it before the plate underneath her feet left her.

She scanned the next platform, and it appeared underneath her but still in a closer range to the door. With a leap of faith, she jumped onto the platform. Her legs felt wobbly as she stood.

Fae viewed the rest of the floating tiles. Inside her mind, she started to imagine all of the missing pieces. She could see the completed puzzle now.

This trial required her to use her imagination to fill in those flooring gaps. The test was very much in opposition to that of her Inventor powers. Normally, Fae's power filled in the gaps for her while she just pictured ideas.

With some more leaps, ladders, and created tiles the Inventor found herself at the exit. The next-door appeared to have a blue, laser barrier guarding it.

Fae continued with the trial. The room she

walked into was pitch black, and she couldn't see anything. Despite her glow, it appeared to be utter darkness.

Like the previous trial, she heard a voice beam overhead, "Commencing trial in three-two-one."

When the voice finished talking, a bright light flicked on. It's brightness caused Fae to stumble back. The once darkroom now appeared bright white almost as though she was inside of the white room she traveled to the first time her powers were released.

It was a much smaller room than the previous one. Fae viewed two statues in front of her. When she walked over to them, the speaker shot on again.

One statue was that of a dragon with flames coming out of its mouth, and the other was a statue of a dwarf holding up an ancient, clock-like machine.

"Approach the statue that answers this question. Who came first the dragons or the Inventors?"

Fae halted in her steps. She honestly never thought about it before. The princess knew some information about the War of the Ancients.

A thousand years ago, all the kingdoms were at war with each other. Each kingdom had its weapon as humans had their dragons, dwarves had Inventors, and elves possessed Blue Embers.

She knew that dragon souls powered the Blue Embers, but she had no idea if those meant dragons were created. She considered how all the dragons that she'd ever read about had a human form. Maybe this meant that humans created them?

Fae shook her head in a mental struggle. If that were true, why couldn't they create dragons to destroy Zenith?

She contemplated back to all of the inventions she heard were made by past Inventors. Was this power of creation more powerful than she ever thought?

Fae knew that long ago there was a time when Ephoreia had a united nation called Utopia Kingdom; One where all kingdoms lived happily together under a joint period of peace.

The girl believed dragons were unheard of back then. Perhaps Inventors came first regardless if the dragons were created or not based on their recorded history.

With a step of her foot and a stir in her stomach, she walked towards the Inventor statue. Fae closed her eyes and held hope in her heart she had chosen the right one.

The overhead speaker shot on again, "Correct. Proceed to the next trial."

The princess sighed relieved to know she was correct, but with the truth about the possible creation of dragons, she felt extremely confused yet simultaneously intrigued.

Fae proceeded to the next door. The entry was barred off with red lasers, unlike the others. With a deep breath, she entered the new room.

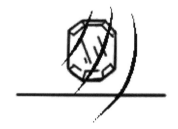

Above Fae, Earrie tapped her toes impatiently and shifted her legs in nerves. Being alone with Benard caused her to be uncomfortable. It was clear he had a fondness for her, yet the wind knight already had a love who meant everything to her.

Benard paced on the sandy outskirts of the ruins while he read a chapter. Something in the text caused his eyes to bulge in awareness.

"Earrie! It says the trials end underground Aspen Bay. It's just north of here, but we better start in that direction so we can be there for Fae," Benard said worriedly.

Before Earrie got her chance to bring Benard down for not knowing ahead of time, she saw a dark, falling star above her eye. She placed her hand above her eyebrows as she gazed at the figurine.

When the shadow descended above her, Earrie instantaneously recognized it, Maxwell. She thought he must have somehow gotten away from Zenith, or the battle was already over.

"Maxwell! He's alive!" Earrie shouted rejoicing.

She dashed through thick, sand sheets that slowed her down as she skidded to approach Maxwell.

On the ground, she threw her arms up and down and yelled, "Down here, Max!"

Behind her, Benard lifted an arm at her passing body as if to stop her. She brushed him off to continue her loving sprint to Maxwell.

"Princess wait! This could be a trap!" he screamed in warning.

Her ears tuned him out. Benard was not about to take this moment of joy from her. When Maxwell descended to her side, she reached out to embrace him. He wore a smile that soon turned sinister when he held her tightly in his arms.

Benard viewed his evil smirk and a glimmer of ill intent in his eyes.

Without backing down, Benard shouted again. "Princess! Stop! There's something wrong with him!"

In naive love, Earrie shook her head and refused. Right as she pulled out of the hug, Acadash inside of Maxwell's body grabbed her and shoved her fangs into Earrie's neck.

"Max"—Earrie mumbled confused as she attempted to pull away from him—"Max . . . please

. . . stop."

Acadash stood and gleamed at her work in self-admiration. She barely lifted a finger and already had the princess under her pinkie like a puppet.

"His embers, Ben, I can't move. It's his venom paralysis," Earrie said as her body started to fall victim to the poison.

Benard stood in his own paralysis; One of fear. He was never one to battle. After all, he was just a civilian-medical student at Penate State College. On the other hand, Earrie was the knight who trained for this kind of battle her entire life.

Before Earrie's lips froze she managed to say, "Run! Run, Benard, save yourself! You're no match for Maxwell! Get out of here while you still can!"

Benard couldn't run. His stubborn legs would not budge. They were frozen like a statue.

"Stop calling me that. Maxwell is gone. It's Acadash now," Acadash grunted.

Earrie noticed Maxwell's Blue Embers were aloof, yet he was transformed. She knew with certainty what events must have occurred.

When the paralysis reached her mouth, her speech failed her. Though she was speechless, a single tear filled with heartache dripped from her left eyelid.

Benard felt ashamed of himself. The girl he cared for was being attacked before his very eyes, and he was incapable of doing anything to protect her.

After some self-pity, he thought back to the medical ointments he created on the beach. He remembered that he did indeed have a poison remedy. Though he wasn't sure if it would nullify the effects of the bite, he knew he had to give it a shot.

If he could reach Earrie, then he could have a chance to save her. He had a sudden idea. Benard knew the princess would kill him for it later, but it was worth a shot. Due to his inability to fight, it was the only shot he had.

With his hand rested at his side, the boy secretly fumbled in his satchel for the correct antidote. He had a vague memory of putting it inside a thin, tall vial, unlike the other ointments he concocted.

With his touch, he attempted placement. Benard knew he couldn't just open his bag and search for the antidote in front of the enemy, so he had to remain aloof.

With a grab, he slid what seemed to be the correct one into the cuff of his long-sleeve shirt without ever being able to glance at it. He had to rely on his touch memory for this miracle.

Benard paced up toward Acadash. As Earrie heard impending footsteps she inwardly sighed.

Acadash grinned at his approach, "A willing surrender? Are you a coward? What, you're not going to fight me, or can you even hold up a sword at all?" she purred in continuing teases.

Benard maintained his approach, "You're right. What can I say? I am a coward. I know I can't possibly harm you. I'm nothing but a fly to you," he said with his hands held upward in a motion of surrender.

"Please, before you finish me to allow me to kiss the woman I love. Let me bid her farewell," Benard said half-truthfully.

Acadash glowed with pride. She felt no concern about this boy's antics. What could a fly do to a snake anyway?

"All right, entertain me, HAHAHA!" she blurted out in hysterics while clapping.

Benard turned to face the princess. Her face was frozen, eyes wide open, and mouth agate. He was about to put on a show for Acadash in an attempt to save Earrie's life.

With a couple of forced coughs, he nonchalantly placed his hand in a fist by his mouth. Inside his grip, the hidden vial remained cloaked. He gulped it while pretending to have a coughing fit.

"Get on with it already before I get bored," Acadash growled, as she patted Maxwell's back bow for emphasis.

With the warm liquid in his mouth, he moved his face to Earrie's. His frail hands shook on opposite sides of her cheeks, and he leaned in. He felt a slight hesitation at first but shook it off.

Benard was several feet taller than Earrie so the liquid had no trouble after falling into her throat like a waterfall. While he kissed the woman of his dreams, he could only consider her ailment.

Earrie felt the substance flowing into her mouth. Her soul relaxed at the realization of his true intention.

"Enough! You're making me sick," Acadash said visually repulsed.

Benard turned to face Acadash and wiped the medicine off of his lips. She eyed him with a smile without a single worry in the world.

"Since I so graciously allowed you to say your goodbyes, you're going to run for me. I want a"— she licked her lips—"chase! Run for me little boy haha . . . It's just so boring when my prey gives up," she whistled into his ear.

With a tight reassuring squeeze to Earrie's hand, Benard bolted off.

"Ah . . . haha, purrfect, run little boy! Run as fast as your legs can muster!" she giggled.

The princess's feet felt tingling sensations. Her nerve control was returning to her; A new warmth coated her body. Each limb was cured of numbness bringing her reassurance that she would live.

Earrie knew now that she would risk her life to save Benard. Just like he'd done for her. She would be a willing sacrifice for her friend.

Benard's heart pulsated as he ran through thick, desert sands. Endurance had never come easily to the medic boy. His legs shook and buckled inwards.

Droplets of sweat fell quickly from his face while his body cried for him. Benard put everything into saving Earrie, and he still wasn't certain if the medicine would cure her.

After giving him a running start, Acadash shot arrows dipped in poison. She flew in the air and laughed at each touchdown of her arrow.

"Whoops! Almost! Keep running little mousy!" she taunted.

Benard's run managed to keep Acadash distracted as Earrie wiggled her toes and her fingertips.

"Faster, mousy, faster!" Acadash cooed above.

Right as her arrow closed in on Benard, Earrie jumped in the way and deflected the arrow with her blade. The wind knight was transformed and ready to fight.

To fight your love knowing he had no control over his body, it was truly a cruel fate for the young princess.

"For a mouse brain, Benard, sure is intelligent," Earrie with a sly grin to taunt Acadash.

With a growl, Acadash lunged forward. Benard watched as they dashed through the sky. He viewed them as an angel and a demon. Before him, dancing knights marked the sight of opposing wings, as one, was from the side of darkness and one of light.

Acadash leaned in on Earrie, but the speed of her wind kept her out of reach. The princess dashed and darted to invade the array of incoming arrows.

Between her escape, she siphoned wind in her blade. With a strike of her weapon, cutting air zoomed in the direction of Acadash. The breeze knocked her enemy over, but soon the archer regained her composure.

Earrie took the opportunity to dart behind Acadash. She placed her sword to her lover's throat.

"Didn't anyone ever tell you not to turn your back to the enemy?" she said in a cold, emotionless tone.

Acadash kicked her fiercely to break free, and Earrie fell to the floor. In a moment of defense, she blew sand up to create a covering storm of dust.

Acadash found the storm to be a well-suited target. It was obvious to Acadash that Earrie was inside the storm. She flung her arrow back and loaded it with ammo. With a release of her fingertips, her bow set forth a barrage of arrows that fell into the flowing storm.

The storm's strong winds cut fallen arrows in half. At the sight of her failed attack, Acadash backed up. She started to doubt her ability. Could her powers be any match to Earrie's wind?

While Acadash hovered in the storm, Earrie, with haste, channeled her storm into a burst of condensed air. She brought the storm into her blade, and a tornado of dust danced on her weapon.

The wind knight swooped underneath Acadash and with the full power of her abilities, she hit her with everything she had.

"Arghhh—" Acadash grunted with a hold to her gut.

Earrie drove her to the ground. She shot all of her wind inside her body, but because she viewed Maxwell's face in pain, she held back.

The strong attack caused Acadash's back to slit open in a long cut. Blood splattered beneath her decking Earrie and a distant Benard.

"No, you fool! NO!" Acadash screamed out. She fell on her knees and slammed her hands to her face as she tried to suppress Maxwell.

His limp body stumbled toward Earrie. With blood dripping from his stomach, he fell into her arms. She looked stunned.

Maxwell raised his head and gazed at Earrie, "My little fairy."

"Max!" she screeched.

Benard grabbed Earrie's shoulder from behind, "It's another ruse Earrie!"

With a shake of her head between falling tears, she mumbled, "No, it's Max."

She fell limp to his side, and the young couple

embraced. Earrie's usual, hidden emotions were now visibly apparent. There was no hiding how she felt about Maxwell.

"Max!" She shrieked as his soft, gray skin dimmed underneath her fingers.

The smell of salty tears lingered inside the air as Earrie wept in his arms. Would Maxwell pass so soon after the lovers reunited?

Chapter 9 Sir Maxwell Penate

Two years ago inside the royal gates of Heaven's Castle, an eighteen-year-old Earrie stood outside the palace in the courtyard. Behind some trees, she practiced her abilities.

Above her, sounds of birds whistled in the treetops. Flowers of every kind sat decked inside white, molded beds. Sky-blue, marble benches surrounded the canvassing viewpoints. The arch walkway was covered with trees and vines full of blossoming flowers. The garden smelt pleasant, contrary to the odor of the Slums that resided on the edge of the kingdom.

With a swing of her blade, the princess summoned sharp winds to cut down the tree before her. Earrie swiped her wind into thin, combusting attacks. With a deep breath, she brought forth as much wind as she could muster into one final attack.

A loud thump was heard through the courtyard. The tree fell at Earrie's feet. A symbolism that she was accustomed to, for she was a princess next in line for the throne.

When Earrie ran to the stump to cut it in half, she was blown back by the force of her wind. Before she could plummet to the green grass, strong familiar arms broke her fall.

She gazed up to meet silver eyes. Maxwell.

"What would a princess be training in her formal clothes for?" Maxwell asked suspiciously.

Earrie sighed and transformed back to her normal self. She got up and dusted off her ankle-length, flowing skirt. The pink-haired princess grabbed her frilly, button-up sweater and threw it on so no one would notice the holes ripped out of her maple, silk blouse.

The boy looked away while she composed herself, "Another hand-fashioned shirt ruined," he shook his head with a masked grin.

The wind knight scuffed her nose and clamped her arms together tightly, "I've got hundreds more than I could ever need. No one will notice it," she said with a slight attitude.

"My guess is you've been out here blowing off some princess meeting to train again, and you think a few more minutes of training is all you need to get strong enough to beat me in a duel."

"Stop analyzing me, Max! You know I hate that, and you're wrong I was just on my lunch break. I thought that I would tune my wind strikes," she said back in defense.

"It's not even nine o'clock. You've got to be the worst liar I've ever met," he said.

"We both know if I tried hard enough, I could easily triumph you in a duel!" Earrie exasperated with puffed cheeks.

"Look, princess, we've dueled almost every day for years now, and you've never once beaten me," Maxwell said bluntly with his hands out by his shoulders in a shrug.

Guards ran back and forth above them inside the castle walls. They called out Earrie's name. Maxwell looked at her as she hid her head in self-admission.

Maxwell walked up to her with an overly confident tone and reached for her wrist, "Guards! Worry not! I've found the princess!"

His acting caused Earrie to roll her eyes. She grabbed his wrist with her spare hand and dug her nails in while he forced a smile.

"Tomorrow, let's duel. I'm serious. If I win, you will take me out at night time past curfew."

Her words caused Maxwell's heart to pound. Just what on Ephoreia was the princess implying?

"Look, princess, I-I can't be caught with you after hours. My family could lose their college, and I would certainly forfeit my rank in the Ember knights"—he turned and viewed her directly in her eyes—"I would lose you."

With castle guardsmen approaching, Earrie mumbled under her breath, "You will do this for me," she used her princess tone. Maxwell could tell this night was very important to her.

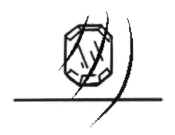

At dawn, Blue Embers arrived at their training camp. It was Tuesday, the day for dueling. Different Ember Knights were pinned up against each other in a ring to test their abilities and prepare for a real battle.

Earrie along with the other knights stood in line patiently as their instructor called them by name. The instructor Arron spent his previous night arranging duels best suited for each person's abilities.

Knights had a choice in choosing their partners, but the majority stuck with their assigned duelist. Earrie, on the other hand, walked up with confidence to Maxwell.

"I challenge you, Sir Maxwell Penate."

Many young men sighed. They wished she would be as infatuated with them as she appeared to be with Maxwell.

Her offer was nothing unusual. Earrie always picked Maxwell. Arron attempted to change her mind, but she was as stubborn as a mule.

Everyone sat down with their partners in the stadium watching the matches. The crowd gawked each battle hunched over with their fingers clinging to the stone bleachers in anticipation.

All the Ember Knights took Tuesday duels very seriously, for the competition was their life, their pride, and their honor. Some members only joined for the glory achieved in winning these battles.

The king, along with many royals and nobles, would often come to the stadium every week to view the matches. There was never an empty seat among the benches.

When the time came for Earrie and Maxwell's duel, they both sat up and walked upstage. Maxwell's mind was off in space. He kept dwelling on what the princess said yesterday. Just where did she want to go?

Together in unison, the two shouted, "Blue Embers!"

While the crowd roared, Earrie and Maxwell fully transformed. His scales were green and dark blue.

Maxwell led the battle to a start with a reach behind his back. He grabbed three arrows to fill his bow for his standard, arrow attack. The princess had dodged his plays thousands of times before and this was nothing new.

His attack was a simple one after another spray. With each released arrow, Earrie flung in routine flips and kicks. The wind knight knew his style all too well. She even could predict his next attacks.

Rather than focusing on herself, Maxwell always figured she spent too much time trying to memorize his tactics. This lack of self-awareness always gave Maxwell the upper hand. With just a little bit of spontaneity, she would always attack right where he wanted; A wrongful, predicted assault.

Earrie smiled as she believed she had finally

envisioned an opening. She darted to Maxwell while his hands were preoccupied filling his bow.

Maxwell grinned, "Not this time, little fairy."

Earrie's eyes widened when she heard an overhead arrow. He must have used a break-off decoy hidden in one of his arrow's shadows.

"Always so predictable princess. You seem to have fallen for my trap," he narrated with cockiness.

She fell to the ground with the arrow pinned between her two wings, but she wasn't about to give up. The princess summoned her wind to lift the arrow out of the ground in an attempt to release her constraints.

A sudden numbness overtook her as his shot was coated in venom. Her body trembled, and while she was about to collapse to the ground, a worried Maxwell broke her fall.

He yelled for medics as he held her with concerned eyes. The venom knight never meant to hit her with his paralysis shot. He just wanted to scare her out of his range.

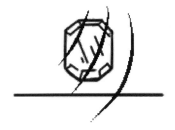

A few hours later, an unconscious Earrie awoke. She looked around only to realize she was in the infirmary.

"Just great! Now I'm never going to get out of here! That man . . . why can't I just beat him one time?" she said out loud to herself.

"Lighten up, fairy," an elusive Maxwell spoke.

His voice caused her to jump, "By my crown! Why are you always sneaking up on me?" she shouted red-faced.

"Why is your guard always down?" Maxwell shot back.

Before Earrie could continue her bickering, Maxwell leaned over her and held her up bridal style.

"W-What are you doing?" Earrie held her hand in her lap to keep her hospital gown from flapping up.

Maxwell looked at her, "Well, I'm taking you out of course."

"But . . . I lost," she mumbled with her face hidden under her pink strands.

"I never cared about the duel, Earrie, it was you I cared for. If you would have been more patient, I would have let you win anyways."

Earrie's cheeks burned bright red as Maxwell walked over to the window and unlatched its hinges.

"The w-window?" Earrie whispered in a nervous stutter.

"How else are we going to remain undetected?" Maxwell smirked.

With a quiet transformation, Maxwell flew out the three-story high infirmary. When he reached the ground, he noticed Earrie's blushing cheeks.

"Just where is my princess off to anyway?" he teased.

"The horse stables in the Slums. Well, wait . . . let's head to the general market first."

Maxwell's face cringed at her desired

destination. He took her request without resistance, and the two proceeded to sneak out of the castle.

They ducked between houses and hid in high grass. Neither one of them had long before Earrie's hourly nursemaid would tune in on her disappearance.

Maxwell handed Earrie his evening coat to conceal her face. She walked in the rundown market with a lowered head while Maxwell waited outside against the store's walls.

When Earrie walked back outside, it started sprinkling. Light showers coated the two sneak outs. She rushed over to Maxwell and ran through the dark streets.

In Earrie's right arm, she held onto a light-brown basket with a blue covering. Inside the container, she placed several warm loaves of fresh bread along with bottled jams. Alongside the food, she placed long ribbons for a woman's hair. Some were pink and others were plaid, multicolored pieces.

Maxwell eyed her purchases, "Grabbing

snacks?"

"It's not for me."

He watched in curiosity as Earrie slipped in her leftover coin and then some. His eyes shot up at the amount. Just how generous was the spoiled princess?

He wondered who this person was that Earrie was going to meet in the stables. When they closed in on the Slums, Earrie became more and more clumsy. Her pace slowed down as well.

Maxwell wondered why Earrie was so worked up about this meeting. He chose not to ask and instead opted to just stay by her side.

Earrie paced up to the shack, and with a soft tap, she knocked on the stable door. The door creaked open to reveal a small, redhead halfling. The young lady looked distraught.

Her eyes were puffy, and her cheeks appeared damp. She seemed reluctant to open the door to her surprise visitors.

"A-Are you okay? I brought this for your birthday. It's some bread and gifts. Fae, is your mother around?" Earrie said. She held up the basket with an offering smile.

Fae shook her head, "No, Stella passed last week."

At the devastating news, Earrie's face drained of color. Here she was smiling and offering up gifts when this little girl was in mourning.

"Do you have any family? Someone, to take you in?" Maxwell asked behind Earrie.

"Look around, sir. Kids younger than me are all on their own with mouths of their own"—she said as she held back cracks in her voice—"own to feed. These factories take the lives of our loved ones every day."

"The factories?" Earrie asked.

"You know, where weapons, clothes, and armories for the kingdom are crafted.

"Yes, but what about the factories?" Maxwell asked for Earrie.

"People die from the smoke that comes from them as it pollutes the air. The upper class don't live close enough to the factories to experience their smoke or frequent gas leaks.

"Our water here runs brown from toxic exposure. People here fall ill, and they die young. They live their short lives with breathing problems. Their bodies grow weak from working long hours daily. We don't even have the coin to afford medical treatment," the halfling said in a hopeless voice.

"I'm so sorry . . . " Earrie uttered, but it was of no use. Words alone couldn't fix this.

"It's not your fault," Fae said. "Born in rags and die in them," she muttered.

Maxwell and Earrie listened intently. Why had they never heard of these horrid conditions? They both had proper schooling, yet they'd never been taught anything like this about the castle's ghetto.

"We weren't meant to live in the clouds. We're boxed in with minimal resources. There is simply not enough to go around," Fae finished. Her eyes drifted past the two acquaintances at her door and to the familiar smoke trails of the factory's rooftops.

Earrie was amazed by how educated and mature her half-sister was. She had an idea. With a turn to her shoulders and without saying anything else, she ran towards the upper sector.

Maxwell tried to stop her as he followed close behind and shadowed. Earrie's feet clashed into puddles while she pounced off to the castle like a cat on the move. The puddles splashed back onto Maxwell causing him to be drenched in muddy rainwater.

He called out to her, but his efforts were in vain since she ignored him. When they reached the courtyard, he viewed her as she slipped into the palace.

He walked over to the garden's bridge and sat underneath. Earrie tended to come here when she was upset.

Maxwell enjoyed studying Earrie. She never failed to surprise him. The princess was stubborn, irritable, and snobbish. Yet, she was such a kind hearted individual. When Maxwell managed to get a smile from her, he felt the greatest satisfaction.

Earrie wore many masks. She owned a princess mask of polite remarks and political speeches. She also possessed one of a knight; It was strong in nature and strikingly composed. Relentless. Confident. Among her many masks, he found out that in rare pastimes she sometimes took them off.

The bare mask. Her true self. He spent many years attempting to place all her masks with their different occasions, but the hardest mask to place was when she wore nothing.

Maxwell enjoyed pushing her buttons. The princess never expected him to act proper mannered around her, and he loved that down-to-earth nature about her. He sat under the bridge for the next hour complementing all the new things he learned observing his favorite fairy that night.

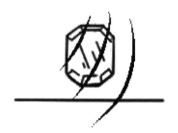

Back in the castle, Earrie panted while she held her hand to her chest to compose herself. The princess stood outside her father's throne room with patience. Once she caught her breath, Earrie walked up to the doors.

She told the king's guard that she desperately needed to speak with her father. The guard tried to restrain her and told her that the king was in a private meeting and she was not to disturb him.

With a loud kick, Earrie busted in the room causing guests inside to gasp. Maxwell's father was among the many royals present in the throne room. They'd been discussing plans to expand the Penate College and various business ordeals.

Earrie remained in her hospital gown when she ran up to her father's knees and knelt on his lap. "What"—Richard pet her quivering head lightly—"my child, are you hurt?" he questioned.

"Father, I bring you terrible news. Stella has passed. I've grown very fond of her threw my trips to the stables, and now that she's gone—"

The princess sobbed into her father's lap and took a deep breath before she blabbered off in tears as her mother clenched her fist in jealousy.

Richard spoke no utterances. He appeared as though the news hurt him worse than it hurt Earrie.

"Father the child . . . she's left alone with no one to raise her at the young age of sixteen," Earrie said with pain smeared into her words.

"Adoption. I will adopt this child," the king said.

"Adoption? Why, you can't be serious!" the queen yelled.

King Richard looked at her from the sides of his eyes and in front of his guest, guards, and daughter said, "Need I remind you who made you a queen?"

Her resistance let up and she turned her face in shame. She married into her queen status, while Richard was born a prince with the very same dwarven bloodline of Melah.

In Richard's eyes, Clance was just another royal-born elf. She wasn't his queen and never would be. A forced marriage for the tradition.

Earrie flinched at her father's harsh words. She looked up to give comforting eyes to her mother, but Clance's face was drawn away.

The king took his hands and clapped; A signal for some guards to line up.

"Bring me the girl. Bring me my child, Fae."

Outside in the courtyard, Maxwell heard clanking boots above him that rushed across the bridge. Their vibrations made him wonder as to where they were rushing off to. He knew all their nighttime routines, and this was not a normal activity.

With curiosity, he perked up and stalked close behind the guards. He followed them past the merchant roads, through the middle-class homes, and into the Slums. His interest heightened when he noticed them tap on Fae's door.

Without a quick enough response, the guards kicked the door down to disrepair. Something that a halfling like Fae would never be able to afford to fix. The guards went inside with lit torches in hand.

He didn't see what happened, but he noticed the girl being dragged out of the shack kicking and screaming. She was dressed in a light-blue, striped nightgown. It was old but taken care of well. A stylish piece she inherited from her mother. Stella received the gift long ago from none other than the king himself.

"Shut up, wench! You're going to wake all the kingdom!" a guard yelled.

"Shouldn't you speak a little nicer when talking to a lady?" an eavesdropping Maxwell hopped in.

Seeing his silver-plated armor with a dragon molded onto its chest plate, the guards knew he was of the Ember Knights. They gulped in fear of their witnessed actions.

"You men reek of ale. Why would good working men be down at the brewery?" Maxwell observed as he took out his blade and leaned on it nonchalantly.

"It's not like that! All of us went before our shifts to the inn and just got one glass is all!" one sputtered out embarrassed.

"So, do you usually come to work drunk?" Maxwell continued to poke them. "I'm sorry, but it's my duty to report his kind of behavior to the king."

"No! Please!" they all said together in various pleadings.

"Well, how about you guys retire from your shift early, and retreat to your homes? Just take it easy tonight. What do you say? I'll escort the girl," he said smoothly with his organic charisma.

"She needs to go to the throne room. King Richard called for her summons," the last remaining guard said while the others ran off.

Maxwell nodded and escorted Fae towards the palace. She looked up with blatant fear in her eyes.

"Sir, why are you bringing me to the king. What crime have I committed?"

Maxwell was uncertain about how to answer her question because he truly didn't know why she was summoned.

When he reached the palace they walked calmly into the throne room. Fae canvassed red, narrow carpets with gold borders. She looked to her side to view white, laced walls with silver molding panels all around their borders.

Fae stopped and peeked outside the many windows inside the exquisite palace. Clear skies filled her vision, unlike the windows back in her home.

Fae's heartbeat paced when large, throne-room

doors creaked open. She surveyed the inside to witness sparkling, white floors with golden walls. Jewelry of every kind hung from the walls like draped curtains. She stood still in front of the throne.

A small, petite staircase with six steps led to the king. She looked up to witness the same girl who'd befriended her many years ago, Earrie.

The princess sat in a medium-size golden throne to the left of the king. To his right, Clance the fiery-haired queen resided.

All of them possessed intense faces that only made her more nervous. She looked over to Maxwell, and his gaze seemed to be studying Earrie's.

"Fae, on this day, I've decided to make you my daughter. Earrie's cries have opened my heart to your sufferings. You will be my child from this day forth," Richard said. He avoided mentioning the fact that Fae was his real daughter.

The king knew of Fae for her entire life, but Clance's persistent pestering continued to hold him back from taking any action. On this day, he put his foot down and decided to make the best choice for his youngest daughter despite the queen's dissatisfaction.

Fae couldn't believe what she was hearing. How could a halfling like herself could be adopted by the king? It didn't register in her brain. She was still trying to process that Earrie was the princess of Heaven's Castle as she had never seen the princess's face.

At night, Fae packed her bags and said goodbye to the Slums. She moved into her rightful place in her father's house with her sister Earrie.

In a short time, the two princesses would form an inseparable bond of protection and sisterly love.

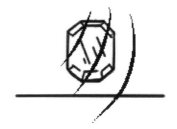

After the hectic events of the night, Earrie met up with Maxwell in her favorite spot. He skipped pebbles while she spoke.

"She's my sister, you know."

"Yeah, I know . . . he adopted her," Maxwell said with a hinge of sarcasm as though it was the most obvious thing in the world to him.

"Max, she's my blood. Richard is her true father," she said in a non-joking attitude.

Maxwell stared at her to study what mask she may have been wearing. He could tell instantly that she was being truthful to him. He knew her too well to continue any disbelief.

They talked for the rest of the night, but something felt closer between the two Ember Knights. This day of sneak outs and throne-room meetings brought them new planted closeness.

Chapter 10 Reunions

Fae passed through the next door. This time she felt a new confidence. Inside the new room, she viewed a gray, blank pathway that led her to the other door.

Like the previous times, an overhead speaker chimed in, "Commencing trial in three-two-one."

Fae's head rang in a confusion about this trial; Nothing seemed out of the ordinary until the normal floor shrunk into the wall. Underneath thin tiles was hot, boiling magma.

When the flooring vanished, Fae quickly invented hovering boots to save herself. She gasped and looked around to find a refuge away from the vines of steam.

With no gushing wind pushing against her, Fae assumed that she was allowed flight. After all, they did take away the tiles. She looked behind her, and without seeing a plague of rules, she continued to fly.

The Inventor realized she would need a mask to breathe. With a thought and a touch to her mouth, a mechanical covering hid her lips. Without any fresh air, the machine didn't offer her much support.

She flew against the buzzing magma as high up as she could muster causing her body to brush against the burning ceiling of the room. Fae viewed a shadow in between the smoke. With bulging eyes, she witnessed her late mother.

"Stella?" she questioned surprised.

"Why do you waste your breath on me?"

"Mother?" Fae asked again with a stir in her

voice.

"Murder! Murder!" the familiar shadow yelled in her direction.

Fae continued her flight to the shadow. The once small room appeared to have grown a whole acres length. What first appeared to be just a small flight only seemed longer with each passing second.

Fae shook her head. That wasn't her mother in front of her. Stella died in her arms many years ago. It was nothing to her, just the trial's cheap imitation of her mom.

The pressure wore down on her. She felt herself drawing weary. Fae lost control of her powers and fell inches in front of the magma. She held herself up with a thought-out bridge.

The metal bridge scalded her thin, padded feet as she ran across. Behind her, shadows appeared to torment her. They were all familiar faces.

Kily, her childhood friend, was a simpleton lassie that worked at the bakery. Pau, on the other hand, was a father figure to her growing up. His profession was the local blacksmith. A woman she'd seen a few times on holiday was there, Reaki, her mom's sister. She was The Slums' seamstress. All of the steam clones were fellow halflings that died an early death. She knew each one personally.

Their roaring familiar voices pounded in her ear.

"Princess, why did you do nothing for us?"

"You've clothed yourself in your father's fine silks while we rotted in dirty rags!"

"You're nothing but a snobby elf! You're not one of us! You never were!"

Fae held it together while she crossed over the bridge. Her soles in her shoes seared off completely. With a wince to the pain, she collapsed. The fall only caused her to scream a higher pitch when the metal stung her fingers and legs.

The halfling looked up, and the door appeared to not be as far. She needed to hold it together for a few more seconds. Fae dragged her body across the newfound bridge in the direction of the door. Her suit tore down the sides around her hips and bottoms of her legs.

The breathing filter she created earlier fell off

when she lost full control over her powers. Between coughs and heavy breathing, she skidded to the door. An instinct to survive, to keep going, took over her flesh.

Fae's face filled with charcoal, smut, and ashes. Her normal yellow and orange colors were covered with a layer of gray soot.

"Look at the high and mighty princess. She's come down from her throne to grace us with her presence. Rags and smoke, maybe you are one of us," Stella's imitation growled with a sinister giggle that sent shivers down Fae's spine.

The beginning pieces of Fae's bridge fell into the magma only to dissipate in the heat while she crawled on her belly to the door. With oozing burns all over her flesh, the princess placed her hand inside the green, blue, and red laser door. With one final pull, she gathered up the strength to somersault herself into the next room.

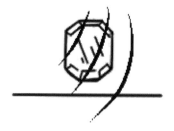

Above Fae's desperation, another existed. Earrie cried out for Maxwell as she shook his limp body back and forth.

When Benard realized that the person in control was Maxwell, not Acadash, he pulled out his medical supplies and started working.

With a streamed pour, burning ointment spilled onto Maxwell's back to prevent infection. Maxwell let out a persistence groan.

The practicing medical student placed taped wraps of bandages on his disinfected wounds. Lastly, he bandaged his entire chest up to ensure that the wound was sealed.

Earrie watched as Benard's delicate hands went into action. She marveled at his skill. For the first time since she met Benard, she deemed him useful. All of the times beforehand, the lady Ember Knight only thought of him as baggage.

It appeared she wasn't as skilled at judging someone's worth as she thought.

She eyed Maxwell, and he coughed while opening his yes faintly.

"Thank you," he said to Benard.

Earrie offered an arm and shoulder to Maxwell as he stood up.

"We have to get to Aspen Bay, Fae is going to be there all alone, and we don't know if it's a safe town," Earrie informed Maxwell.

"I can make it. Just don't get mad if I lean on you a bit."

"You can lean on me anytime, Max," Earrie said.

Benard growled silently and rolled his eyes. He was so used to being alone with the princess that he had forgotten about the knight who loved her.

The princess was ecstatic to be reunited with Maxwell. She asked him about Zenith and the deadly battle above their heads, but the only information he could offer her was that the last thing he retained before his blackout under

Acadash's control. He told her about the scene that was engraved into his skull. Where the last squad of remaining ember knights along the king were battling to the death against the massive dragon.

The group walked onwards towards Aspen Bay. As they spotted the tip of the town in the distance, they noticed Aspen Bay was layered in swarming dragons. It was clear, Zenith had possession of the coastal city.

Not wanting to take the fight directly to Zenith yet, they opted for a stealth option. They sat down behind a rock covering and discussed how they would meet up with Fae and avoid forced entry.

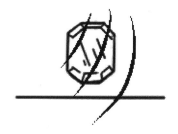

Inside Aspen Bay, a curious Elvador canvassed his multitude of orange, tracker bands. The investigating dragon watched Clance's string merge with nearby others as he noticed a strange movement. It appeared as though their strings were traveling underneath the city. He viewed the cords pull downwards like stomped on blades of grass. Elvador decided he would follow them.

The pursuing beast paced over to a hidden entrance behind an old cemetery stone. He pushed it open, and with a loud creak, the tombstone revealed a receding staircase. Elvador stood amazed at the depths of this cave.

He was thankful for his night vision when he reached its depths as the cave possessed no natural lighting. Elvador continued to follow the people through its windy tunnels. Airy screams clung to his sharp ears. The foundations of the underground pathway appeared to be that of hard rock as it was a natural formation of some kind.

Deep inside the ruins, Fae progressed to the next door. The young halfling felt something was off when she patted herself down and noticed that her clothes remained intact. She pinched her skin up like a tent to check and see if she was dreaming. In doing so, she realized that none of her flesh had burns, and all of the pain that she'd felt before had vanished.

For a second, Fae thought she may have died due to the reversal of her ailments. She looked around her new surroundings and canvassed a space, unlike the other rooms.

This room was well lit, and to the right edge of the room many boxes laid with flashing fuzzy pictures like living portraits on them. They displayed scenes of each trial she'd partaken in. The wide boxes even looped displays of herself.

"Amazing," Fae said flabbergasted.

"I know, isn't technology fascinating?" a startling voice rang behind her.

Fae jumped back. "Who are you?" she stammered out in a cracked voice.

The close sound appeared to have emerged from the speaker she heard beforehand.

"Relax, Fae. I'm a friend."

The young princess viewed a small glass ball

float from behind a chair that was facing toward the displays. The clear globe was about half the size of Fae's face. When the object spoke, different colors of light inside the sphere danced inside its dimensions. The orb appeared to be filled with the same code that birthed from Fae when she invented.

"I'm Delka."

"Wait . . . you can talk?!" Fae said in a sudden realization that the globe possessed speech.

"Yes, I'm the consciousness of a past Inventor. My task is to forever persevere the"—Delka floated closer to Fae's entrapped eyes—"legacy of the Inventors. As of today, I hereby proclaim you an official Inventor."

Fae smiled, "I-I passed?" she stammered out.

"Well, you made it past each trial, didn't you?" Delka questioned in a sarcastic tone.

Fae nodded as she watched closely. Delka hovered over to a podium that stood in the center of the room. The stand was rectangular shaped and stood waist tall.

"Come over here, and place your hand on the pad," Delka said while she spurred out instructions.

"What for?" Fae questioned with her left eyebrow up.

"For the database records. We preserve your hand print along with a small sample of your blood. This happens to every registered Inventor."

The color drained out of Fae's face, "Blood sample? I-I don't know if"—a small needle poked the top of Fae's hand while she slid it in the scanner—"Ouch!"

"You managed just fine," Delka said in a blatant tease.

Fae removed her hand, and the podium retracted into the ground. The stand disappeared under the ground's blue tiles as though it was never there in the first place.

"About that last trial, what was that?" Fae questioned in evident confusion.

"The trial, it dives into your mind. Your thoughts. Your heart. Picks together the best memories and fears to test for your metal endurance. It's designed like all the others to see if you have what it takes to be a registered Inventor."

Fae felt a sense of intrusion. Her thoughts? To have gone so far back in her life that the trial could have gathered all those imitation shadows, the test must have seen every memory she had.

"All of the trials, not just the last one were created personally for you."

"It just seems . . . impossible that this knowledge exists inside our world today. Most people don't even use machinery yet," Fae said in bewilderment.

Delka tuned in, "Well, it's because it doesn't. This entire trial was created by the Inventors themselves. Their past knowledge is lost to all the Ephoreians today."

"Lost knowledge?"

"You've seen it yourself. With constant wars and the destruction that flows them, knowledge gets lost. Organized kingdoms opt to deceive their kind with false information to keep the peace. Knowledge gets lost when people fail to preserve intelligence in its context and in its correct form. This knowledge exists in the world, but without the ability to harness it and protect, it gets lost over time."

Delka stood up and walked over to a glass tank that stood close to the exit of the room. A pair of goggles ascended inside it. They were black with orange lenses.

Delka continued, "Kingdoms rise just to cause others to stumble down in their shadows. Inventors preserve technology in its purest form. If that means having to take down certain kingdoms that have harnessed knowledge to harm others, then that's what we have to do.

"Before the dwarves discovered the Inventor gene and implanted it only into their kind, we were always a secret organization. Our kind didn't ever come out of the shadows. We stayed back like a guardian angel, and kept the Ephoreia in a peaceful state."

"You speak as though Inventors have been around forever," Fae said.

"Well, that's because they have," Della stated abruptly.

"That's not what—"

"What you were *taught*?" Delka emphasized the last word.

"So, I'm confused. Dwarves didn't create the Inventors?"

"No, the Inventors are from a much higher power," Delka replied.

"Higher power?" Fae asked with uncertainty in her voice.

"Now, that's something you have to figure out yourself and through your journey. Here take these goggles. They are your reward along with the clothes you have on for passing the trial.

"Your new suit will allow you to control your abilities easier as a beginner, and these goggles have blueprints for inventions. They have plans inside them that you couldn't begin to conceive yourself."

"Thank you! Hey, I have an idea. Why don't you come with me?" Fae asked with her usual childlike enthusiasm. She placed the goggles on her head like a hairband as she pushed up her top strands into a bubble and listened for Delka's response.

"I have a duty here to guard the trials. I can't just leave."

Fae shook her head. "I'm not sure you understand . . . a lot is going on up there. An evil man named Zenith is going around taking over kingdoms and destroying all harnessed knowledge as we know it. I'm the only Inventor that exists right now, and if I fail Ephoreia will lose it's only hope," Fae said in a serious demeanor as if she knew her purpose now.

"How could you be the only Inventor?" Delka asked, taken back by her words.

"I'm not too sure myself. But if I can't get the help, I fear I will not be able to stop this man. He's a great dragon who's able to grow half the size of an entire kingdom and use multiple powers all by himself."

"If this is true, then he must have stolen"— Delka floated back and forth—" Inventor technology. I'll come with you. I have to train you in the ways of the old, or this man will surely destroy all of Ephoreia if left unchecked."

Fae smiled in relief. She ran up and pulled

Delka's glass ball in for a tight squeeze to which her new friend irked.

The past consciousness looked up to Fae, "I have to warn you. I don't have my Inventor powers anymore. I won't be any help in battle, but I can give you wisdom."

"That's okay! I'm just so happy to know you're going to help me!" the young princess said delightfully. She retained her blinding smile and twirled around in a playful demeanor.

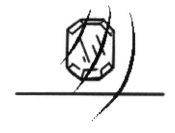

Together the two walked outside of the trial. Fae viewed a tunnel formation of rocks. Silver, icicle-like rocks hung down from above and shot up from beneath. The ginger-haired princess's glow lit up the cave while they walked out. Fang shadows followed her path as she walked by odd figurines.

"What direction are we going?" Fae asked.

"A mile or so, we will emerge in the city of Aspen Bay. It's not too far," Delka said back in response.

The newly registered Inventor shook her head and continued onward until she noticed a familiar statue approaching her.

Out of the shadowy cave's depths, the queen emerged seemingly alone. Fae beamed her bright smile and ran to greet her adoptive mother.

Chapter 11 Breaking Entry

Earrie eyed Benard ready to plan an alternative path, "What do we do? We can't just waltz in there?"

Benard placed his hand to his chin in thought, "We dig."

Maxwell smiled and eyed Benard, "Not to prod, but I'm not sure you have the endurance needed to dig under the city. To be honest, I couldn't in my condition either." He held his back in reference to his words.

Benard rolled his eyes, "Not that. I just meant Earrie could use her wind to cut us to the tunnels, and when we get closer, we could melt it."

"Melt it? Now you've lost your mind," Maxwell said in sarcasm.

"If I combined my medicine with your venom, I think it'll be just what we need to gain entry," Benard said with certainty. He twisted around and walked a couple of feet in concentration until he spotted a point. He stared intently and lifted his finger.

"Here, we dig here."

The princess nodded her head in compliance, "I'll do it. Blue Embers!" she shouted.

On the other hand, the male Ember Knight didn't need to transform now. When he molded himself with his embers, it resulted in him never being able to obtain his normal form again. His very body showed how much control that he'd given over that day in desperation.

Earrie flew into the sky siphoning all the surrounding air all into her spin. With a typhoon of wind, she clashed into sandy grounds tunneling away its covering. The determined, female knight kept going and going like a worm until she struck a hard surface.

Benard fumbled in his satchel as he reached for the different remedies that he concocted. "Eureka!" he shouted.

Maxwell grabbed Benard and brought the bookworm down through the dig in. Together with a spill of his medical mixtures added to Maxwell's venom, the two successfully managed to break entry with a bubbling goo.

Earrie descended along with the others until touchdown. They viewed puzzling tunnels before them that darted every way.

"We need to make markings while we walk so we won't get lost," Maxwell said, and Earrie nodded in agreement.

They walked in the direction of Benard's compass unsure if it would lead them to Fae.

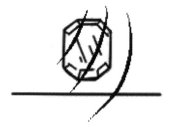

Deep in the tunnels, Fae held her adoptive mother in an intimate embrace. "Mother, how are you here?"

"Fae, I must tell you. You're father . . . he's passed," Clance said with disheartening sympathy.

Fae's body drew limp at the words. She fell to the ground, and in her arms clinched to Clance's red dress.

Richard was Fae's real father. The man she never got to know.

The king always hid his true self in front of the queen and the civilians of Heaven's Castle. His antics fell in similarity to that of his eldest daughter.

The young princess felt a numbness in her heart knowing what could have been. She yearned for a time when Zenith was gone and she, Earrie, and their mother could live happily ever after.

"He gave his life protecting his people. The king died ensuring that everyone who could make it out would escape without harm.

"Richard passed in Zenith's arms while Maxwell tore his throat out," a sinister smile quivered on the queen's lips as she attempted to keep up her act.

"By the crown! How did you make it out alive?" Fae asked, startled as she stood on her shaking legs.

"Well, you see, I didn't make it out necessarily . . . I'm part of it now," Clance chuckled and reached behind Fae.

Sharp, metal cuffs pierced Fae's wrist, and she stumbled back in horror.

"Mother, what are you doing?" Fae questioned with shaking lips.

The ginger-haired princess would've never thought that the queen would betray her people let alone her. She believed this to be a ruse, or maybe Clance was forced into compliance for survival.

"Something I should have done a long time ago," Clance said with a chuckle.

The dark queen moved her hand in a signaling fashion. Dozens of dragons surrounded the mother and daughter.

"You see, child . . . I'm *with* Zenith now."

Her words felt like repeated stabs to her chest. Delka stood back behind her but never uttered a word.

The young Inventor's eyes lit up to protect herself, but the shackles around her wrist neutralized her abilities just like in Tuner Town. The white lettering that came out of Fae seeped back into her like a wilted flower.

Fae attempted to hold her tears. She didn't want to give Clance the pleasure of seeing her cry.

This pain felt worse than the third trial, for this pain was real. Raw and non-manufactured betrayal.

Clance snickered while she eyed her dragons, "Rip her apart boys. Just make sure to leave the chains on to keep her powers at bay."

Fae scooted back and tried to hide in a ball terrified of what would happen.

In an abrupt change of events, a strong arm

grabbed the princess up by her stomach. She coughed at the force of the hold.

With a gaze, she looked up to see warm, brown eyes that met her stare with sympathy.

"Pup?" Fae asked.

"Hold on tight!" Elvador commanded.

He wasn't about to flee. The newfound savior heard everything Clance said.

The dragon couldn't believe that Fae's mother would do this to her, but he knew the evil that Zenith was capable of bringing out in a person. A drip of power reveals much about a person's true intentions.

Elvador wasn't aware of Fae's adoption though as he believed the queen to be her birth mother.

He jumped on the first dragon he viewed and swung him by his neck into a wall. His ear's tickled as he heard the man's neck crack.

These mini beasts were no match for Elvador, for he was a true dragon of ancient times. Faster. Stronger. Better reflexes. Larger. More durability. Built for war.

After he'd thrown another dragon, he jumped onto its body like a frog and reached with his free hand for the guard's sword.

Elvador viewed the next mini dragons as they rushed him. He swiped one down after another like fallen trees. Each one went down with a thud.

Clance backed up as she watched in horror.

Screams of the dragons echoed through the tunnels. Their shrieks reached Earrie and the others.

The gang picked up their pace in a clenching pursuit of the noise.

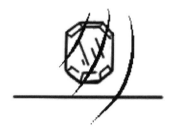

Between high leaps and sounds of blades clashing, Fae held on tightly. She pressed her head into his chest as if to avoid witnessing the graphic slaughter.

Her hands shook in fear. She didn't know where her companion was pulling his strength from. This was her first time witnessing his powers, for Elvador had revealed his true strength until then.

The dragon was strong and quick in with his blows. Blood dripped into overflowing piles under his victims. Their bodies built upon each other like bricks to a wall.

He lunged at his final opponent only to stop short at Fae's screams, "No! Don't!" she pleaded with a stray arm out trying to reach for his stepmother.

Elvador froze at the princess's pleas. He looked at frightened, green eyes and backed up in horror of what he almost did. The beast had been so carried away with saving the girl that he forgot she was in his arms.

The dragon panted, and peered around at the blood-stained cave. He wasn't going to be able to hide his identity any longer.

At Elvador's hesitation, the queen reached into her chest and pulled out the long, flowing necklace, "Blue Embers!" she yelled.

The embers darkened into a violet blue as they transformed with her Clance's heart. Scales rippled through the queen's red dress and dragoon wings shot out of her back.

Admits the confusion of, a sudden, foreign blade pieced inside Elvador's back. Earrie stood behind the pair as the culprit. She pulled her sword back, and her face shot pale in the realization of her actions.

With Fae's screams and blood covering Elvador's face, he'd appeared unrecognizable in the dark cave. This led the elder princess to jump on him in a mother-like instinct to save her younger sister.

She attacked without taking in the scene and sentenced him to a quick death.

The dragon fumbled coughing out blood and set Fae down before falling into a limp stagger on top of the fallen minions.

Clance gazed at the scene and snicked a devilish laugh.

With a dash, Earrie jumped in front of her mother. She eyed her mother's body covered in silver and white scales.

Earrie stammered her words trying to make

sense of everything, but her sister's crying only caused her to feel a sense of foreign fright.

She grabbed her heart and stepped back while her stomach turned.

"What is going on here?" she muttered through a dry voice.

Delka flew beside the elder sister. "The queen sided with Zenith, and she attempted to kill Fae."

The ancient robot knew Earrie from diving into Fae's mind during the trial. She too felt a sense of betrayal from Clance. It was as if she lived part of the girl's lives with them and knew them more than anyone else did in those tunnels.

The princess eyed Delka and covered her face scared she would be attacked. Her legs shook, and she felt it impossible to hold her sword in its unusual, striking stance.

"Ma?" Earrie whispered.

She stepped a few feet back placing a space of distancing comfort between them.

Fae stumbled back to a wall with her heart

pounding. The younger princess fidgeted inside of her shackles, but her efforts remained relentless.

Benard stood aside from her and attempted to comfort her with a reassuring touch on the shoulder. His kind words offered nothing to put an end to her hysterics.

On the other hand, Maxwell backed up and placed his hands on his face. The ember-melded man started to shutter his shoulders back and forth, and underneath his hands, muffled sounds of joy presented themselves.

His convulsions caused Benard to dart his glance. "Maxwell?" he asked in a confused tone.

"It's time mommy dealt with her children," Clance said as she licked her a blade of stone creation.

It seemed the queen did have a few tricks up her sleeves. She had been forced to watch Richard duel when the two were engaged as part of their arranged courting. His skills seemed to have rubbed off on her.

Madness blanketed Clance and Maxwell.

Earrie held up her sword and shook her head. She had no plans to fight her mother, for she fully believed Clance must have been possessed. Earrie knew she would have to defend herself though.

The traitorous queen made the first attack when she shot out stone boulders Earrie's way. With a kick upwards, the female knight dodged the rocks and sent progressing, ranged attacks towards her mother avoiding to make any contact in fear she may hurt her.

Clance continued to giggle like a sociopath, "HIS FACE! I SEE THAT BASTARD'S FACE IN BOTH OF YOU!!! I'LL WIPE THAT MAN'S LEGACY OFF THE FACE OF EPHOREIA!"

Earrie noticed these were her mother's words. They weren't a separate person like Maxwell. She felt like something broke the woman she once knew to create this monster before her.

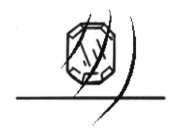

In the background, Maxwell spoke out, "hahaHAHA! To think, you fools believed Maxwell could restrain forever! His soul is weak and emotional compared to mine!"

Earrie heard Acadash's awakening behind her back and felt her gut stirring. Her heart dropped at his sudden change of character, but she tried not to let it interfere with her battle.

"Don't listen to her! Maxwell will always be stronger due to his compassion!" Earrie said with determination while she kept up her relentless attacks.

Acadash slowly pulled out Maxwell's bow and aimed it at Benard. She wore a wicked smile that sent goosebumps down his arms.

"I'm sure you remember this game, mousy. RUN!" Acadash slurred. She motioned up the arrow a few times to emphasize her intent.

Benard felt a returned fear. He turned around and without hesitation bolted off into the depths of the cave.

Following the passing marks they left earlier, he darted forth in the hope of escaping Acadash's chase.

Behind them, Elvador twitched his fingers. Between two blurry eyes, he managed to take his razor-sharp teeth and pierce them into a body underneath his. He sucked up the warm liquid and with a loud gulp swallowed it.

When the blood entered his body, his wound healed shut. Elvador felt alive again. With a cock of his neck, the dragon eyed Fae. He knew she needed protection.

Elvador dashed in front of Acadash's trail and shoved her into the wall. "You're going to play with me," he said intimidatingly.

"Long time no see, Elvy . . . I missed tormenting you!" Acadash said with a hiss as she licked her lips.

She pushed him off and regained ground. Acadash attempted to string an arrow, but his speed outweighed her.

There wasn't enough time for her to utilize her bow instead she was the one on the run now.

Benard continued his sprint to their point of entry, but he didn't stop there. He kept moving his frail legs until they felt like they would break off. When he tripped over a stray rock, the young medical student moved his hands and covered his head.

He felt like a loser. Fae was in no condition to fight, and he saw the shackles she was locked in. He had run from both of the princess's sides only to care for his own life.

In a depressed state, he crawled to the wall and leaned against its cold surface. Shoving his head into his knees, Benard dwelt on the overwhelming enemy that the group he had aligned himself with faced.

Zenith was an unstoppable dragon allied with hundreds of beasts that obeyed his every call, and Benard believed Maxwell to be too far gone to help and Elvador to be deceased. He sat there shaking while he waited for what he believed to be his end.

Back at the battle, Earrie clashed against Clance as Elvador trailed Acadash. He eyed around her orange line and noticed she had somehow swept behind him.

With a twitch to his ear, he heard Fae squeal out.

Dashing back to the girls, Elvador felt blood pumping to his heart.

Acadash loved to play games with people's lives. He knew the snake girl very well, for he once dated her long ago.

When he arrived, he spotted Acadash with her hands on Fae. He instantaneously dashed toward her.

"Uh-uh-uh. One step closer, and the little brat gets it!" Acadash said with a tip of her arrow pressed against Fae's throat.

Fae squirmed and held up her chin as she tried to slip out from under Acadash's pinned arms.

Elvador stood unsure of what he could do to save Fae. Right when it felt like the situation was under Acadash's control, the young princess managed to turn the tide of battle.

Fae remembered the trial's rules, and a risky idea plotted into her mind. With quick action, she hacked into the cuffs and turned them into shackles for Acadash. Her protector dashed to her aid, but she did not need it; Acadash was already subdued.

Elvador, seeing that Fae was okay darted to help the elder princess. Fae followed his direction.

He held down Clance while Earrie snatched the embers out from under her.

The younger princess used her powers to manipulate the technologies that she brought from the trial. With her imagination, she created a wheeled prison to place the two captives in.

Elvador threw Clance and Acadash inside and slammed the door shut tight. They both insisted on making useless noises and comments, so he muzzled them with torn clothes he scavenged from the fallen dragons.

A distant Delka flew over to Fae's side now that the battle was over. She hovered still for a moment as if to regain her thoughts.

"I'm sorry Fae, but I couldn't risk getting hurt

and the Inventors losing me," she said apologetically. Delka spoke slowly as if to show the sincerity in her robotic tongue.

"It's all right. I don't know how I would continue if I lost my only hope at figuring out my powers," Fae smiled.

"Who's this?" Elvador asked regarding the glass globe that stalked her.

"Delka, she's the stored consciousness of an Inventor of Ancient. She's also the protector of the trials. I convinced her to leave them, so she could help me on my journey. She plans to aid me in the bring down of Zenith to ensure the safety of Ephoreia's knowledge," Fae said proudly.

Fae proceeded to enthusiastically tell anything and everything she'd learned about the Inventors during her time apart from the group.

"That sounds . . . different," Elvador kidded with a toothy grin and a scratch to his head.

Fae looked at Elvador, "How on Ephoreia are you even alive, and how did you do . . . what you did?" the halfling asked in a frightened whisper.

Elvador looked at the horror in Fae's eyes and felt a stab to his heart. He never wanted to scare her. He just wanted to save her life.

Looking away into the caves, Elvador said, "My name is . . . Elvador. I'm the dragon that protects what's left of Ephoreia."

"Y-You're a dragon?" Fae asked in amazement darting her head beneath his. She thought back to how fondly the king of Tuner Town spoke of him and smiled brightly.

"Yes," Elvador said. He sighed in relief at how quickly Fae's demeanor softened.

Beyond them, Earrie held her father's glowing embers close to her heart. Fae sensed her sadness and walked to her sister's side. She offered a hand to Earrie's side and hugged her for a moment.

"He's gone, Earrie. He's passed."

Earrie felt a pit in her mind. She should have

known when she witnessed the embers. No way would her father have given them up alive. He would have died cold and stiff with them still on his neck.

The elder princess looked over to Elvador, "If you're a dragon, that still doesn't explain how you lived." She had been listening to him and Fae.

"Rejuvenation. I heal off of my kind's blood." Elvador said bluntly.

Fae and Earrie both cringed. "Isn't that a little . . . cannibalistic?" Fae asked in repulsion as Earrie's face sickened.

"More like realistic. I'm a super soldier built for war. Healing off fallen soldiers makes an army of dragons have unimaginable amounts of endurance."

Elvador pulled the prisoners while the group followed the markings back to the other side of the tunnel. Along the way, they ran into Benard. He was in a corner feeling sorry for himself.

"What's wrong with you, you fool?" Earrie asked as she kicked him. With no response, she squatted down in front of him and waved her hand in front of his open view.

Benard looked up from his crossed arms and shook his head, "I'm a loser. I don't deserve to be alive."

"Ben, you're acting like we don't already know this," Elvador teased. He threw in a reassuring tap to the man's shoulder.

Fae knelt next to his side with Earrie. Her empathetic heart led her to say, "Benard, if it wasn't for your vast amount of knowledge we wouldn't have even found this place."

"You saved me, and you saved Maxwell with that wound clean up," Earrie added in to aid Fae's encouragement.

The elder princess clenched onto her father's embers in her hand for comfort. She noticed their flame appeared violet in color. It's dragon heart needed a strong soul to contain it.

She looked up to Benard and an idea struck her mind. The determined pink-haired princess stood up and crossed her hands together and sighed.

"Stop your sulking, and get up and do something about it! If you don't want to be a coward then don't be one! Make a decision now when you stand on your legs to walk forward and strive for a future where you aren't a crybaby!" her sudden change of demeanor caused everyone to jerk backward. She stomped her foot down between Benard's legs, and he jumped in fear.

"H-How can I achieve a future like that?" Benard asked with hope in his golden eyes.

Earrie reached for his hand, and his cheeks flushed a deep red at her touch. She forced his clammy hands open and placed the violet embers inside.

"Use them. Embers give us the power we need to change the future and the world. Fight by my side, and help save Ephoreia," Earrie said with cold eyes.

Fae looked at the scene with endearment. She knew how much the embers meant to her sister and how much they mean to all of Heaven's Castle. Elvador, on the contrary, didn't feel like Benard was the right type of candidate for an ember, but he chose not to speak of it.

Benard closed his fingers around the embers

and with a tight squeeze, he said, "I will! I'll do anything to protect you, princess, from now on my life is yours! I will serve you and the kingdom of Heaven's Castle for the rest of my years!"

"Prove it," Earrie said.

He shook his head with sincerity. Elvador tried to embrace the moment with a positive outlook, but he believed that Benard fighting front line with the stone embers would be his death sentence.

Fae smiled, and Earrie laughed like nothing was wrong in their lives. Their playful demeanor was as though they were just too normal sisters joking around.

The elder sister changed the joyous tone when she brought up Aspen Bay. "Now that we have them contained, we need to retake Aspen Bay. Zenith cannot have his hands on them!"

The others nodded their heads in agreement. "How do you want to go about it?" Elvador asked with curiosity.

"We walk straight in the center of the town from the exit, and attack them from the inside," she responded.

"I like that idea. I can use this impending battle to train Fae for what is to come," Delka said in thought-out preparation.

The female knight clenched her fist, and placed on her battle mask, "We're going to take initiative—make the first move. Zenith will know what it's like to come against us."

With a nod of his head, Benard agreed with Earrie's strong words. He wasn't sure how he'd do in battle, but he trusted in Earrie's power. The elf knew he would do what it takes to protect her even if that meant he would have to give his very life. The princess owned his life now, and he was going to prove he wasn't a useless coward.

With a halt of the cart, Elvador looked over to Earrie, "What do you plan to do with Maxwell?"

She turned over and looked at him, "Simple. I'll save him."

"Earrie you can't save him . . . I've seen this dozens of times. He is gone forever. If you keep him alive, he'll just be a puppet for Zenith's game," Elvador said with an earnest tone.

Delka flew between the two, "Well, I'm sorry to

burst your bubble, but she can"—she hovered in front of Earrie—"save him. To the northwest of Aspen Bay, there is a fresh spring. The pond is filled with what's known as the Water of Life; Its water can heal any injury or any ailment."

Elvador looked down, "That's nothing but a legend . . . " he spoke as though he'd attempted those waters before.

Delka lit up bright pink when she spoke, "I'm a legend, Elvador, and so are you. Anything that exists long enough and has something to offer people becomes a legend."

He tilted his head down while he appeared to be lost in thought. It was as though, his mind was trapped inside memories from long ago.

The group continued to the exit. With a hatch in view, Earrie eyed the group. "Everyone get ready! Transform Benard! Call your Blue Embers!" her fire reassured them.

He placed his hand to the stone embers and looked up determined, "Blue Embers, hear my call!"

Benard's body started a transformation at his words. His legs filled with silver, white scales that tore his trousers, followed by arms that sprouted scales up to his shoulders. Out of his back, dragon-like wings emerged that caused his shirt to fall off completely. The cloth piece hung on his left-wing and flapped like a war flag.

Elvador couldn't help but grin as Benard's appearance struck a similarity to his old comrade, Elliot. His old, dear friend was also an ember knight. Together, many years ago, they battled against Zenith's uprising.

The group stood a few seconds from the latch, "Every victory won is one step closer to taking Zenith down!" Earrie shouted while she held her hand up in passion.

Delka hovered over to Fae, "You will provide them with the most support possible. Create firepower, armor, and weapons for us and the civilians who wish to fight. You can do this, Fae, I believe in you."

Fae nodded her head. The halfling was unsure of her capabilities. but thanks to Delka's encouragement, she felt coerced into confidence.

Chapter 12 The Battle of Aspen Bay

Elvador was the first to exit. With a loud plop, he flung open the hatch and squinted his eyes. The outdoor light blinded his brown eyes. The dragon walked over to an open space, and with a roar, he began his dragon transformation.

The super soldier's body mutated into his fighting form. Out of his back, a long, narrow-pointed tail came forth. His palms morphed into claws, and his face shaped into an image of a beast while his nostrils sneered out musky fumes.

The group watched in amazement while they wondered what his full potential was. He looked back and threw his head into the sky.

Elvador let out a ground-piercing shriek. Fae stumbled at the vibrations of his beastly sounds.

Earrie and Benard nodded their heads to Fae as they were about to put an end to this stronghold of Zeniths. Together, they darted into the air in the direction of the hoarding beasts.

Fae stayed behind on the ground. She needed to remain close enough to the prisoners to keep them subdued.

Delka viewed her, "Fae, I'm going to fly up and view the battlefield. I will tell you what to do from there."

"How will I hear from you?" Fae asked bewildered. She peeked left and right with worried eyes in her shaking fear of being left alone.

"Use your goggles to show you blueprints for

radio communication," Delka commanded.

Fae fumbled with her goggles, "All right, this should work." She spotted a mapped out invention that she was sure would do the trick.

With a reach, Fae touched Delka. She managed to create a radio receiver and broadcaster. The young princess then created one as an addition to her goggles.

The Inventor stood ready on the ground and shot out sheets of numeric, white text. Transparent codes floated in the direction of nearby technology. She then shaped them into blasters for air-born targets.

Earrie used the natural wind flow of the dragons' flight to throw them down. A minion propelled out of the sky by her fierce breeze and launched into a building's decorative, sharp pole. The beast's body flinched like a crushed bug until it fell limp.

Squawks of the mini beasts integrated with people's shrieks filled the air.

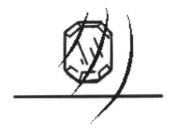

In the sky, Elvador remained surprised by how well Benard performed with the Blue Embers. The beast felt that maybe he was wrong about Benard's ability after all.

Elvador was ashamed to admit it since he was a fully trained weapon of war, but he found himself being sheltered by this new Ember Knight's walls several times.

The elder princess felt a sense of peace when fighting by Benard's side. It was as though she was back at home with persisting flashes of her and the other knights battling against the usual mechanical, dragon dummies.

Earrie smiles as memories of her and Maxwell dueling fueled her blade. She dwelt on her decision to save him and just what it might cost as the battle went on.

Meanwhile, Delka shouted at Fae, "Aim behind

Elvador! They're prioritizing him!" Fade nodded and obeyed with targeting lock-on missiles. In her mind, she envisioned hitting multiple beasts behind her friend as her powers followed through those images while they became reality.

The once thick barrier of minions started to dwindle. Openings tore, and the sun glimmered through. The new peaking light marked fresh dawn for the people of Aspen Bay.

Crowds watched the knights battle for their sake. They cheered and clapped their hands while tears befell their eyes.

All was going well until a mini beast snuck up on Fae and flicked her off guard. Her vulnerability was just the second the enemy needed to gain the upper hand.

The knock back caused Fae to lose control over the makeshift prison, and as a result, Acadash kicked open the door joining the battle with a hold on Clance.

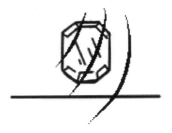

Zenith stood elevated in a stolen throne above them. His minions fell bewitched to his mental connection. With his bond, he could see, hear, and even feel the very events of the battle. Instead of growing angry, he tapped his fingers against his throne and snickered.

"I'll have my way here," he sneered mischievously. He placed his stray hand on his chin, "I always do."

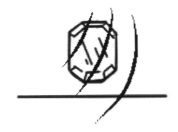

Earrie viewed a flying Acadash. She turned her back towards the battle, and in a change of pace, the female Ember Knight dashed in the sky to her sister's side.

Fae surrounded herself with a multitude of fighting robots to aid her. They stood knee high and held a copper appearance in the likeness of Elvador's deconstructed airship. In their hands, they held electric chainsaws and fire-bullet guns.

The machines danced around Fae in a ring of protection. When she moved, they followed like bodyguards. Delka continued to shout orders down at her.

The young Inventor dropped beads of sweat from her head, and she panted while placing her focus on her creations.

Earrie yelled at Acadash, "Hold on, Max. I'll save you!"

"How many times do I have to tell you that I'm not MAX!" Acadash screamed while she pulled out a clump of her hair in hysteria. She strung repeating arrows at Earrie.

Benard viewed Earrie dodging arrows. He knew first-hand whose bow was cocked at her. With a swoosh, he dashed in to aid the princess.

Earrie gazed into the clouds. She dodged but failed to make any reprocessing attacks.

Her mind seemed to be off inside those clouds. The knight moved solely by her natural-battle affinity, yet she continued to make close calls in light-heated ducks.

Benard sensed that her absentminded attacks were not suited for battle. With his heartbeat raised, he summoned a wall of defense.

The medical boy breathed deep breaths to contain his composure. He felt that it was his time to act on his words of servitude beforehand.

With a fling of his fingers, Benard conjured up a large golem out of his wall. His spontaneous idea flowed to him earlier when he saw Fae's creations supporting her.

The rock humanoid of gigantic boulders of stone sewed together moved slowly, and pieces of stone sanded off the monster along with clouds of dust and rock chips. The particles fell downwards causing watchers to cough and scatter.

His Goliath swung its bulging fist into a clasp on Acadash and Clance. The newly made Ember

Knight held onto them tightly while he struggled with his concentration.

Acadash managed to kick open the stone, hard grip and fly upwards with Clance in her arms. The venom knight looked down with a peek at her surroundings and understood that Elvador was on his way.

The fused, dragon soul knew she couldn't take on this many at once let alone the strongest dragon alive next to Zenith.

She thought back to the touch bomb placed on the traitor queen by Zenith. With that desperate back-up plan in mind, she dropped Clance from high above into the direction of the mighty, three-story golem.

The queen screamed out manically, "SAVE ME YOU IMBECILE!" Acadash only glared back saying nothing.

Sounds of impending bomb ticks mixed with a repetition of shouts from Clance's daughters. No one besides Acadash and Zenith knew of the bomb that would soon detonate.

Acadash used the distraction of Clance's

dramatics to attempt to demolish Earrie. With a rogue sneak, she flew behind an off guard princess. Right as she went for the final blow, Benard swooped in as a chevalier saving his heroine.

He used a makeshift, rock defense to protect her. Upon the sight of his aiding barrier, Acadash grunted and soared off towards Zenith along with the fleeing mini beasts.

As Benard used his golem to grab Clance, something horrible happened. The bomb inside the queen's head hit its last beep. Zenith watched the entire battle awaiting his chance to cause the greatest amount of damage.

The bomb disrupted Benard's golem, and it's particles shattered all over Aspen Bay. A fragment unfolded into view and flew towards Earrie. The medical boy directed all of his efforts into stopping the blade.

His actions led to many civilians in the underskirts of golem perishing from sudden deaths, for he did not protect them.

Earrie whimpered out when Benard smacked into her. The force of the incoming shard collided into his wall and sent him flying. They flew back into a hard fall on the ground.

Underneath them, Fae perceived a paralyzed Elvador. The young halfling darted to his ailing side. She paid no mind to the collapsing golem overhead instead the princess held tightly to his neck.

She gazed at his side and spotted a stray arrow; Acadash must have targeted him during the confusion.

She closed her eyes and squeezed unyielding as she tried to free him from the venomous arrow.

"It's no use, I can't save you!" she shouted while buildings collapsed above.

Fae looked around and tried to find any technology to help her, but she was too weak to call on her aid.

"Help me, Inventor codes, why aren't you helping me?" she shouted in despair.

Elvador saved her life back in the cave, and she wasn't about to let him die here. Fae held on his neck and closed her eyes hoping for a miracle to save them as the buddings collapsed above them.

The dragon managed to summon all his strength into covering Fae with his wing taking most of the stone onto himself.

Several loud, pulsating screams along with Ephoreians' cries bellowed through the town. Earrie stood up on shaking legs as she stumbled over to a headless corpse. The corpse was clothed in red. It belonged to her mother, Clance.

Her daughter hugged her limp body and crying hysterically. She flung her head to the sky and screamed. Earrie's shoulders bumped up and down in rhythm with her tears.

Loud screaming caused Benard to tense. He scooted up close to her and attempted to provide comfort, but her shouts only grew more booming.

The boy looked around and viewed spattered droplets of blood all around him. Distant screams tickled the boy's ears.

As a studying medic, he knew every second mattered after injury. Each. Second. Mattered. Anytime the boy wasted in mourning or shock was another moment for the wounded to bleed out.

Benard paced over and saw Elvador laying ground-level underneath dozens of fallen boulders on top of him.

He didn't notice the young princess at first as all he saw was orange dragon scales and limbs peeking beneath stone.

Benard, still transformed, lifted the boulders off the dragon only to spot a pair of bloodied legs detached from a body.

The scene caused shivers to fall down Benard's spine. Fae laid pale-faced leaned against Elvador breathing heavily with both of her knees detached from her legs and covered in dripping blood.

The boy dashed to the princess's side and held up her hand. "A-Are you alive?" he asked.

Fae's eyes blinked open, and she mumbled, "My powers—they didn't save me." Tears fell down her cheeks, and she attempted to lift her head to view her injury.

With a glance down, the crippled princess viewed her lower torso. She turned to her side and vomited blood.

Benard grabbed his medical bag like a safety net and reached for wrappings with determined hands.

Without finding the proper supplies, he told Fae, "Don't move! Stay still! I'll be right back!" He held out his hands as if to motion her body from sliding any further down the dragon's limb.

With a dart of his foot, Benard went into autopilot mode in an instinctive effort to save the devastated town before him.

Benard darted through streets and ran past fallen buildings. The boy approached the first door he could find. When he jiggled the door, it gave no entry. The medic kicked it open with a crushing bang.

With a bustle, he thumbed through rows of shirts and grabbed some plain whites. Without looking back and ignoring others who were in pain, he paced back through the town until he reached Fae's side.

He whispered calmly to her, "It will be okay. I'm here to help. I'm going to place some pressure to stop the bleeding."

With a gentle touch, he poured stingy liquid to prevent infection. The ointment cleaned out bacteria in her wound, and she grunted in pain while her head twisted back and forth.

"It'll be alright, Fae," a comforting Delka said.

Elvador spoke no words, but he heard everything. He cursed himself for having not been able to save the girl.

"Pinch into my shoulders to help you endure the pain," Benard offered while he created tight wrappings around her legs. He knitted strong knots of torn cloth to sever the bleeding.

"Arghhh!" she winced. The young princess dug her nails into his shoulders to fight the pain in acceptance of his offering. He pulled intensely on the wraps to seal off the open wound.

Fae glanced over to Elvador. With thoughtful eyes, she scanned him intently. The princess spaced out in lost in thoughts while Benard finished her medical aid.

"Get him some dragon blood . . . it'll cure him," Fae mumbled and then fell back into unconscious slumber.

Benard caught her by her right arm just before she hit the cement. With a light touch, Benard placed her head on Elvador's leg to elevate her body.

In a remote white noise, he listened to Earrie's sniffles. He informed Delka that he was going to be back and headed off once again. His steps led him back to Earrie.

"Your sister is hurt badly! You need to help her," Benard said as he advanced to Earrie.

She hadn't moved at all from her place of desolation. He positioned himself behind her and eyed the crying princess. With a lean downwards,

Benard placed his arms around her from behind.

For a few moments, the two stood there in silence until Earrie turned around and in a split second and embraced him. All her tears fell out like hard drops of ice. She cried until her soul found the strength to wobble upwards.

Benard stood by her and pushed over a piece of her hair that stuck to her tear-stained cheeks. "You need to be strong, Earrie. Fae is hurt, and she needs you. This city needs you. Be the city's refugee. They need your strength . . . I'm going to help as many as I can."

Earrie looked up to him with red-veined eyes, "Okay . . ."

She got up and stepped slowly next to Benard. Her side shoulder leaned against his while she tried to keep on going for Ephoreia.

With her sister in view, the elder princess picked up her pace. With jogging arms, she reached Fae's side.

"I'm here, Fae, I'm here," Earrie said faintly between sobs.

She knelt next to her broken sister laying on the ground next to Elvador, and held Fae's body on her lap while looking with a blank stare at Fae's missing legs.

The female knight thought that if she only could have been more powerful then she would have been able to prevent this, contrary to, a weak fairy pretending to be as strong as her father.

Holding her mask in line was an impossible task. Earrie slammed her right arm to the ground and lifted her head in the air to continue her sobs.

The princess was now without parents, and her sister laid broken on her lap.

Earrie gulped and wiped her tears. She panted and cried out, "I will never hesitate again!"

In this very hour, she would be a new person. A person who didn't let naive thinking block her judgment calls in battle. If Maxwell endangered her sister's life again, she would finish him.

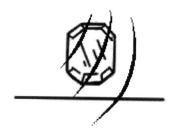

Benard stepped away from the two sisters and ran through town over to what appeared to be a run-down, medical building. He went inside its caved-in, rustic doorway and opened up a multitude of cabinets as he searched relentlessly.

With a peer, he opened his eyes to dozens of fresh unopened ointments. Before his bulging eyes, the medical boy viewed an assortment of reserved stashed medicines.

Benard decided he would use this space along with a branch out to another close-by building for the injured.

Outside, he found countless stragglers. They wandered around aimlessly as though they lacked any direction. Lost souls with broken homes.

With some loud shouts, he decided to bark at them much needed orders. He told them to gather up the wounded and bring them back to the old infirmary.

When word spread among town that a doctor was present to heal the sick, many rushed the seriously injured over.

He assigned an arrangement of volunteers, to assist him with bandaging and cleaning out the injured wounds. Benard was lucky enough to find some medically trained professionals along with trainees in the great crowd of disembodied spirits.

Even though Benard might have been just a student, he was at the top of his studies. He spent his entire life learning about different ailments and remedies. With mixed concoctions of fuzzy fumes, he never knew what impending discovery awaited him.

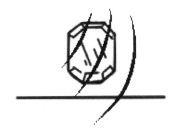

Earrie eyed a wooden wheelbarrow full of debris from the fallen golem. With a gentle slide of her hand, she pressed Fae's head to the ground.

The elder princess approached the wheeled cart. The cart's lower half was buried in the ground.

She pulled the cart out of the wreckage with a forceful tug that caused her to stumble backward. As she raised her palm, the barrow tipped over. Silver rocks bustled out like a chunky mudslide. The stream of rocks licked the surface beneath it in a gathering pile.

With a couple of resisted pushes, she tested the wheels to ensure that they were in a working condition. Pulsating, old wheels brushed against Aspen Bay's dirt road as Earrie pressed the wheelbarrow to her struggling sister's side.

The elder princess tossed her arms in the air. With a whistle and using her knight-like commanding tone, the Ember Knight ushered in some volunteers to help her efforts.

They aided her by lifting Fae's body and placing her in the wheelbarrow. With fluttering eyes, the young princess drifted in and out of awareness. The halfling mumbled out words about Elvador that caused her to worry about his condition.

Earrie whirled her sister with haste over to the makeshift infirmary. Volunteers inside the old hospice elevated Fae to one of the few, unoccupied beds.

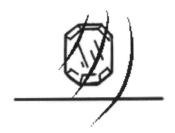

After a few hours of medical attention, Earrie was allowed to visit her sister.

The elder princess held on to her sister's hand, "I'm going to the Water of Life." Her words were barely heard over the roaring background noise.

"Earrie, you're too drained I need you. We all need you," an exhausted Fae whispered as her face cringed desperately.

"I know that. That is why I'm going. I will bring you and everyone else water from there," Earrie muttered. She spoke her words with fire, but her eyes looked distant.

The Inventor looked over to her sister, "What

about Maxwell? Is our mother alive?"

Earrie shook her head side to side, "Clance perished . . . She should have never joined Zenith. Maybe it's better this"—Earrie placed her dominant hand softly onto Fae's—"way. Max is fine. Acadash got away, but I'll get her back and save Maxwell." A lump in her throat hid the pain she felt inside her words.

"Zenith is just toying with us," Fae said in a moment of brokenness.

Earrie stood abruptly knocking over medical trays full of sterilized equipment, "Yeah, and we don't know the kind of game he's playing!"

Fae winced at the clanking tools. The sisters silenced as though the racket was a punishing parent.

Earrie bent over and picked up the equipment. She squeaked out loud as one the stray pieces pierced her.

"'Every victory won is one step closer to taking Zenith down!'" the older sister shouted out loud as she mocked herself in frustration.

Earrie grunted and stood still eyeing her sister.

"Who was I kidding?"

"You weren't kidding anyone and certainly not me," an eavesdropping voice said beyond a cracked doorway.

Benard walked through the doorway. He stood suited in a medical robe.

The long white clothing had a type of clear apron attached to it, and the see-through accessory was full of liquid, pain relievers, colorful pills, and medicated ointments.

"Sorry for eavesdropping, Earrie, but you're wrong. We made a footprint in history today with this battle. Lives were lost, but life was gained.

"These people had everything stolen from them before we showed up. They weren't even allowed to show their emotions. Don't sit here and beat yourself up. These people need leadership and a willing hand," he said. It was clear this town made an impression on Benard.

"You're just a student here playing doctor. Do you have any idea how serious things are?" Earrie asked in a cold tone as she confronted Benard with her hands on her hips.

"Call it what you want, but I'm trying something while you're just sitting here feeling sorry for yourself like—" Benard stopped himself before saying something he might regret.

With an unfolding of her hand, Earrie reached for a smack only to drop her hand and turn around.

The princess walked silently out of the room before eyeing Fae and Benard with one last look.

"Thank you for saving Fae's life," Earrie said.

Benard nodded, and Fae fell into a medicated slumber.

She decided she would go and retrieve the miracle water with or without Fae's blessing.

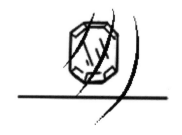

In the center of the town, she canvassed Elvador. The female knight touched him to see if he was still breathing.

Benard forgot to give him dragon blood because of all the patients he was taking care of and the people he was directing. Earrie remembered him speaking earlier about dragon rejuvenation, so she ran outside to some distant corpses.

With a lift of her sword, she drove its end into a cocked, limp body. Out of the body, a waterfall of blood oozed.

She held a vase under the outpouring of blood and gagged. Earrie placed a hand to her nose to muffle the corpse's reek. When the vase was filled to the top, she skidded over to help Elvador.

The wind knight pulled out the arrow that Fae hadn't and placed her hands on his jaw while Elvador's mouth remained paralyzed but slightly agape.

She held his jaw up on her knee and patiently poured the blood inside of his mouth.

In a few seconds, Elvador flinched awake. When he regained full control of his body, he transformed into his human form. His nakedness caused Earrie to scream and cover her eyelids.

The dragon covered himself with his hands and ran to a building's stall. She eyed around to find him some clothes. After she found a decent pair, she threw it to him over.

The covering was a white, male blouse with brown pants that matched his hair. The dragon punched his legs into the new outfit and arrived out of the room composed.

"Where's Fae? Is she still alive?" He demanded, concerned.

"The infirmary . . . but you're not going there," Earrie said in a serious tone.

"I have to see her!" Elvador said with pleading eyes.

"You can't! There isn't any time! We have to go to the Water of Life," she said with her arms out in a demanding gesture.

"I'm telling you that that won't work!" Elvador shouted in annoyance while he turned and looked for Fae's tether. His eyes relaxed as he spotted the princess' string.

"She's okay," Elvador whispered to himself.

"You can tell?" Earrie asked.

"I can see her tether. It's moving a lot as if her soul is fighting to stay alive . . ."

"That's why we have to go, can you see now?" Earrie said.

"Okay—let's hurry!" Elvador said.

The dragon and Earrie set off into the sky before eyeing the town in one-last, reminiscent stare.

Elvador thought back to his memories of the Water of Life, and he felt a tug at his heart. Earrie's tone and mannerisms reminded him of his last journey there with his long, passed-friend, Elliot and their desperate attempt to save a friend.

Together they flew off in the sky with the direction of the mysterious water of legend marked into their hearts with an 'X'.

Chapter 13 Soft Water Village

In town, Benard felt the pressure of his work. Many died under his care that day while few pulled through.

He felt first hand the many difficulties that came with spur-of-the-moment decision making. He knew he would have to practice this pressure daily when he finished his schooling.

The medic wiped his sweaty brow and sighed. "I guess, it's kind of like a battle in that regard," he mumbled to himself at an operating table. Others around him looked to him for wisdom and nodded agreeing.

Everyone faced a battle that day in Aspen Bay. Citizens and knights alike.

The medic student handed orders out to townsfolk during his off time. People gladly brought extra blankets and remedies. He soon discovered that no one else was standing to take charge of the town, so he decided to do it himself.

Men worked together to bring hurt and lost children to shelters with makeshift stretchers of bouncy fabrics and logs of aspen. When Benard observed the town supporting each other without racism, contrary to Heaven's Castle, he witnessed what could have been for the elves.

In only a few hours, all of the injured were collected and brought into the town's medical buildings. Ogres, humans, and various kinds all arrived together for a joint issue.

Soon the whole town had split-up tasks. The harbor city wasn't defeated by Zenith, if anything, they were brought together by his attack. Aspen Bay held itself together by a strand of survival.

Many men and women stepped up to the plate. All of the emotions that they tried so hard to hide under Chance's control bundled out at once. Their feelings for justice aided them as a striving force to continue. What once had been suppressed by the enemy was now their driving strength.

Benard knew he was partially to blame for the chaos that fell onto the town, but he was taking responsibility for his actions.

The boy was now a man on a quest for redemption. He would try to save as many as he could and give it everything he had to reorganize the shattered town.

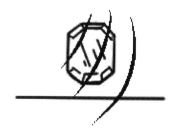

Benard told Fae that Earrie had left town, and Elvador was nowhere to be spotted. In her heart, she'd known where they ran off to. She sighed and leaned back into a familiar rest.

Her condition seemed to be worsening by the hour. Fae's natural glow faded little by little, and the young princess's state concerned Benard.

He sent volunteers to check on Fae every thirty minutes and provided her with fresh water and towels. When he viewed her lethargic activity, the medic man feared the worst.

Benard felt Fae's head with the back of his palm. Beads of sweat trickled down onto his hand like morning dew off a bent leaf. Fae was burnt up with a flashing fever. Her lips appeared chapped and her eyes looked clammy.

"Infection!" he yelled in a serious tone.

With a clumsy dart, he jolted out of the room in search of antibiotics. All of the cabinets appeared to be empty of the care they needed. He dug through them and thumbed relentlessly.

Finding nothing that could be of use, he offered Fae natural foods with organic antibiotics, but he continued to feel worrisome. The sunset was falling, and he was running out of time.

Benard laid down on a cot in a spare cleaning room to collect his thoughts for a few seconds.

He worked harder than he ever had in his entire life today. His hands pressed against his cheeks, and he laid on his side feeling clammy while trembles of anxiety befell him.

With his eyes pulling down on him like claws, he found himself drifting away in shuteye.

Benard drenched his sheets in sweat as he tossed and turned all night long. For some odd reason, no one woke him. He visualized nightmares of those lost by his golem and Fae breathing her last breath while begging for him to heal her.

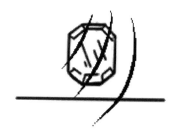

In the sky, Elvador viewed the jungle that surrounded the Water of Life. He dove down like a penguin until sharp arrows flew by his side.

Villagers of a local town were ready and armed

with bows.

Earrie wasn't transformed instead she had fallen asleep on Elvador's back during the trip.

When a sudden arrow pierced his left wing, Elvador crashed down. Both the dragon and the princess fell unconscious after the traumatic landing.

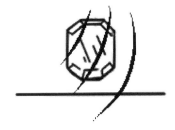

Rumors passed back in Aspen Bay through the night. Their whispers passed word around of Clance's death, a failed battle, a runaway princess, and of a certain lively bunch who freed them from Zenith's clinching grasp.

Some people in the town felt a blossoming faith in this group while others mocked their efforts. Townsfolk talked of destroying this newfound group to gain Zenith's trust as the fear of Zenith's power hung heavily over this coastal town.

An evening crowd formed around the town's center. Unsure of what would come next, they pleaded for answers and a leader.

Their bellowing cries heard no answers as Benard laid fast snoring in the hospice instead Delka brought word from Fae's bedside.

"'Trust in my sister, Earrie, she will save us all,'" Delka spoke in regards to the younger princess.

Booing rushed over the crowd while others clapped loud bangs of trust. The crowd soon dispersed and went back into their homes for the night. A few randomly selected watchmen guarded the town while it slept like a newborn baby.

Somehow in the last few hours, the town elevated Benard to a near king. They placed his efforts above that of Earrie's and the others who placed a rule in freeing them.

Benard was unanimously elected by the hearts of those rescued as the town's hero and their mighty shield.

They remained unaware of his choice to let go of the golem that cost them so many including that his reasoning for stepping up was purely damage control.

The town viewed Fae as just another one of Zenith's victims. She was a sign of what he does. Destruction. Fae was a crippled princess with an impending death on her shoulders. They mourned her before she'd even met her end.

"What a tragic ending to a beautiful girl," some uttered.

"Zenith's a bastard!" others shouted with raised hands.

They welcomed Fae with open arms but doubted she would be of any use now that she was injured. She marked a lost card for the elves of Heaven's Castle.

Some of the escapees from Heaven's Castle spoke well of the princess when they learned of her Inventor powers. Others wanted their beloved Earrie to return to them.

For most of the residents of Aspen Bay, not refugees, believed Earrie to be a coward, for she played the same stereotype that all elves possessed; An elf always runs away. They believed that maybe she'd gone to hide in the clouds like her ancestors and labeled her as the Runaway Princess.

Aspen Bay's people possessed a love-hate relationship with Elvador. In the end, he'd always come through, but his usual disappearances meant they had no real security with him. Most felt like he held back on Zenith many times where he could have easily ended this millennial-long war, and they hated him for it. A tossed-around nickname of his was, the Beast of Unfounded Grace.

Empathetic townsmen brought many gifts for Fae. Some wrote her notes of sympathy, meanwhile, others thanked her for her sacrificial efforts. They wrote in their cards about the things Clance did to the town when she was in control. These words of tyranny caused Fae to shutter.

Fae held a lit hope in her heart as the afternoon came. A hope that her sister would soon return with a miracle.

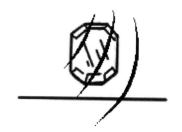

Elvador woke up in a deep, dusty dried-up well. He looked around him and tried to spot Earrie in this place of captivity. He turned on his tracker senses but to no avail. All he could tell was that she was above him, for the string climbed up the tunnel like a growing vine.

Earrie's eyelids slowly flapped open. She viewed a beaded pillow under her hot-pink locks. Above her body, a heavy, wool blanket laid; The covering presented a variation of brightly, dyed colors.

She sat up and the blanket fell revealing a thin, animal-skin dress that hugged her body. Someone had undressed her.

Earrie grabbed on tight to the colorful blanket before her and backed up into the bedpost. She clenched the fabric around herself in shame.

With burnt cheeks brighter than that of her hair, she eyed around the room. The open space seemed to be similar in appearance to Aspen Bay's decoration.

Possibly, the town may of one time been connected to Aspen Bay or maybe it split off. The village, after all, was not too far from the trading town.

A young woman entered the room through a wooden door. Her skin was olive and her hair was as black as a raven. She walked quiet steps and turned toward Earrie.

On her body, was a mirroring dress. She wore open-toed sandals while her raven hair was tied into a looping braid.

"The Head Chief is ruling against you."

Her words rang back and forth in Earrie's ears. "Ruling against me? Who are you people?" she asked, offended.

"We are the people who spared your lives. You attempted to fly into our village!" the young girl said in defense.

The village girl broke eye contact and viewed her toes. She twitched her toes in a nervous front. "You're being sentenced to death."

"To death?" Earrie asked dumbfounded. The princess didn't have time to die, for she had to save her sister.

"After we brought you in, my father, the chief

head, put you to trial. The clansmen deemed you guilty of intrusion. They've decided to use your life as a sacrifice to the Goddess of the Waters."

Earrie grabbed around her neck wanting to transform but felt a barren collar bone. "My embers?!" she shrieked.

The woman was unsure of what she meant instead she bowed and turned around. Earrie looked across the room. She eyed a thin, decorative sword placed on top of a black box. She pulled out of the bed covers and lunged to the blade.

The decoration's top was boarded off by a slick sheet of glass. With an act of desperation, she punched through the barrier cutting her hand on chips of glass.

The knight grabbed the blade and flipped behind the woman. She placed it against her chest and cupped her spare hand over her mouth to muffle out her screams.

"Chief's daughter? You'll make a useful hostage," Earrie said as she peeked outside the holding.

The princess looked down to notice their

elevation. This village was built throughout the towering treetops of Ephoreia's western jungle.

She heard foreign, bird noises and trees bristling full of nature. With an inhale, she smelled a distant campfire. Perhaps, they started their sacrificial ritual on Elvador.

Earrie wouldn't allow that. Elvador was their strongest ally, and she wasn't about to lose him. She pulled the squirming girl out of the studio, and a local tribal man eyed her as she exited.

He had berries drawn down his cheeks in a line to his neck. With an authoritative voice, he spoke out in a jumbled up tongue. Bits and pieces sounded familiar, but the rest made no sense to her.

Earrie eyed him and shouted, "Give me my embers, now!"

The guardsmen grabbed behind for his bow. "Stop! Move another inch and the girl dies!" Earrie yelled.

In the distance, Elvador listened to her desperate shouts from inside the well. He decided it was time to make his move.

The dragon used his inhuman strength to

maneuver himself out of the well. He gripped onto stray roots, and with a pull, he jumped to new levels. When Elvador emerged, he peeked his eyes up and spotted a guard.

He lunged at him like he did all his prey. With a swoop of his hand, the beast stole the man's sword and knocked him unconscious. Elvador opted for a stealth mission since he already knew the diplomatic approach was not going to work.

The escapee darted to Earrie's orange band. He was a tracker dragon, after all, so locating the princess was a simple task for the man.

Earrie walked past many tribal men until she spotted what appeared to be their chief. He sat on a glistening, rock chair.

A feathered headdress sprang from his head, and he wore many colorful beads around his neck. He clothed himself in a furry, bear robe with a stuffed head that hung off his rear. His toes were bare and full of jewelry.

"My embers!" she shouted at him.

The man looked stern-faced, and he reached to his right hip. Out from under his satchel, he pulled out a small, animal-skin bag. With a toss in the air, she noticed that its layers had a glow glimmering through.

"Give it to me or the girl dies!" Earrie didn't want to play games with them. She made her intentions clear when she sliced a drop of blood from the squealing chief's daughter.

The chief replaced the bag at his side as if to test her. It appeared as though her threats were meaningless since the chief didn't hesitate to draw signals to his men.

Sounds of arched bows caused Earrie to doubt herself. The chief was placing equal pressure against her.

Before things got ugly, Elvador dashed behind the chief and tossed the embers to Earrie. He used all of his speed to then grab onto her and leap into a nearby tree branch.

Just as he removed her, dozens of arrows landed where she had been standing. The chief daughter was inside of her father's arms crying while Earrie grabbed her embers to transform.

The female knight was about to teach these fools a lesson that needed to be learned. Don't mess with a princess on a mission to save her sister.

"Blue Embers!" she yelled.

Her familiar green and white scales filled her salmon-pink body. Earrie dashed with a wave of wind and knocked over the crowd.

Something odd occurred when villagers knelt over and worshiped her. They shouted out praises and admiration.

"Our Goddess of the Water Life has graced us with her presence!" a tribal shouted.

"Bow down to our Goddess!" the chief yelled. His spooked daughter remained cradled in his arms.

Earrie was shocked when they all started to speak her tongue. It appeared as though everyone in the clan spoke two languages fluently.

Elvador thought to himself that this couldn't seriously be happening. He had seen humans worship just about anything in his lifespan, but this rang to a whole new level. The dragon had a strong feeling that he knew who just who their goddess was.

"Show me your waters!" Earrie commanded. The princess saw this as an opportunity for herself.

The villagers beneath her flight were more than ecstatic to bring her to the waters. They escorted her through the town to a pile of water.

Elvador frowned at the sight of his old-friend Alice. Earrie looked into the body of water. In the center, a statue of a woman stood frozen. She appeared to be an Ember Knight, such as herself, who was covered in a layer of stone.

"She was my friend. Zenith imprisoned her inside this stone with stolen, Inventor technology. I brought her here in hopes of a miracle along with her love Elliot . . . As you can see, the water did nothing for her," Elvador said while his thoughts wandered around lost in memories of long ago.

She stood an average elf height much taller than Earrie. Her body was petrified with her arms raised tall as if she was reaching for something. Her hair laid draped around her front in a long ponytail that fell like a curtain down to her knees.

"She's beautiful, isn't she?" Elvador said while gazing at her.

Earrie nodded at his words. She glimpsed over and eyed Elvador, "How do you know if she's even alive?"

"I'm a tracker dragon. I see soul tethers. They appear in orange, and once I know someone's scent, I can follow their trail. I can see hers. They always . . . disappear shortly after when people die."

"Maybe Fae can heal her?" Earrie inquired as she interrogated him.

A lost essence of longing for Alice's rescue returned to Elvador's eyes, "You're right."

Earrie walked over to the water and knelt to bottle water. With a reach, the princess grabbed out a brown-skinned rolled up rag. She opened the brown cloth to reach for tied, glass vials.

Elvador tapped his toes in frustration. The roaring shouts of the ignorant crowd behind him were wearing him down.

Earrie sensed his weariness as she too was mentally worn by their persistent shouts. They fogged her mind with repeated phrases. With hurried hands, she finished filling up the containers.

When Earrie finished, she eyed Elvador, "Let's go back!"

Her beast friend transformed. With a smile, she walked up to him. He willingly lowered his dragon neck so she could board effortlessly.

"Our Goddess summons dragons to her call!" clansmen bellowed with their puffed chests.

"I'm not your goddess!" Earrie screamed in fragmented frustration while Elvador grumbled out an escaped giggle.

They soared back conjointly to Aspen Bay.

Chapter 14 A New Mission

A door knock shot Benard out of his trance. He spied around unsure of his surroundings. With a view, the man noticed light peeking under a doorway across from him.

After a few seconds, he remembered yesterday's events. Memories came flooding like a broken dam, the battle, Maxwell, and Aspen Bay all exploded in his mind.

He groaned and tossed himself from bed.

Footsteps approached from the hallway.

"Benard, wake up! Earrie and Elvador have returned. They've asked to see Fae," a voice belonging to one of his volunteer underlings said in a frantic state.

He shoved one of his boots on and staggered to the door with a shoe still hanging in his mouth. The practicing doctor smacked the door open in a rush and eyed a young woman before him. Her face spoke volumes.

Fae condition worsened.

Benard placed his second boot on and dashed past the girl without speaking to her in the direction of Fae's room. He danced between medical staff and ducked under carts.

The elf couldn't let his friends know he'd fallen asleep when Fae was at her weakness as they'd trusted him with her.

With shaky hands, he wiggled open the lock to Fae's room. He looked over and spotted Fae. Her color was absent. He ran to her bedside and quickly checked her pulse. At the feeling of a faint beat, Benard sighed and wiped his drippy forehead.

Fae's yellow skin appeared to match some of the human's skin tones without its glow. Her eyes were shut tight, and her hair looked like a washed-out copper.

A door flung open to unveil Earrie and Elvador.

The elder princess pushed past Benard and reached for her vials. She quickly grabbed a container with trembling fingers fumbling with its lid. Once removed, she commanded Benard to hold Fae's mouth open as she gave her sister the water.

A familiar shine drifted into Fae. This brought joy to everyone in the room. Her friends stood around her with smiles on their faces as they eagerly waited for her recovery.

Fae's infection left the young princess bit by bit, and the wounds closed over without scar tissue, leaving her bottom-half legs nonexistent.

Earrie stood in a stool next to Fae and clung to her. She pressed her head into Fae's lap opposite to how she had held her sister not too long ago.

An irony felt past them. The girl who just

recovered from her deathbed was the one handing out comfort to those near her.

Later that night, Elvador came back to approach the princess alone.

"Fae," he said in a whisper as he stood in the doorway.

She peeked open her eyes and smiled brightly.

"I'm glad—you're alive," they both said in unison causing each to turn their blushing faces.

Elvador pulled up a chair and sat beside her. "W-Why didn't you get out before you were injured?"

Fae looked away at a medical tray across from her. "I wanted my powers to appear and save you. I wanted to save you the way you saved me just before in the cave. I didn't want you dying on me. . ."

"I have never met someone who would risk their life for merely a dragon. In my times, dragons were always viewed as expendable, and even now, I feel as if I'm just a tool sometimes . . . I know that we haven't even known each other for long, but you cared enough to try to protect me. I won't forget this," Elvador said staring into Fae's soft, lime-green eyes.

The two made eye contact for several minutes before Elvador turned and faced the door.

He wasn't sure if he could let Fae in. She was innocent, kind, and beautiful. Everything a guy could ask for in life, but he wasn't a normal human.

He didn't want his baggage and years of misery to become her burden. This never ending fight with his once-friend Zenith was his and his alone. He couldn't live with himself if he made it her problem.

It didn't matter that she was an Inventor. He wasn't going to give up his plight to end Zenith.

Elvador's reason for concealing his dragon form wasn't just a test. He was a secretive man who didn't know how to trust people anymore.

The dragon placed his hand over her and thanked her. "I'm so sorry that you got hurt. I don't want that to ever happen again," he said.

He brought some food in from town and ate

dinner with her before parting ways.

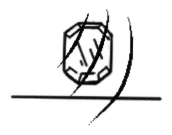

A few days later, a silence kissed the town's doubts about the princesses. Fae was alive and Earrie was back leading her people.

Since then, Benard had fully established a system of temporary relief and shelter for Zenith's victims. In such a short time, the town became known as the Resistance Force.

They were captured by Zenith, yet they resisted and broke free from his chains of hatred. Rumors spread across Ephoreia that Aspen Bay's resistance had slain the evil queen who allied herself with Zenith.

Many hidden people from all over Ephoreia came rushing into the trading town for asylum. Even though Zenith would make this town one of his targets now, Ephoreians materialized with a new hope that their efforts would bring down their suppressor.

Civilians liked what they heard, and since all of Ephoreia was wary of this man's oppression, it was time that Ephoreia allied itself against the rampaging tyrant.

Followers of the local church spread word of their ancient prophecy of a troll who would end hostility. Many believed Benard would be their savior.

This newly lit faith brought smiles to the people of Ephoreia.

Zenith's attacks on Heaven's Castle, his murdering sprees on every elf possible, and his multiple attempts to kill Earrie and Fae, all were in his hope of halting his impending defeat. His objectives were revealed. Kill every elf.

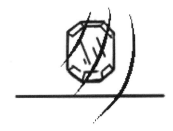

Back in the hospital, Fae asked for all of her

creations. Some locals gathered them up and brought it piece by piece to her room.

They carried them on carts as the parts weighed too much for them to carry barehanded. She scanned the technology while an idea floated in her mind.

Meanwhile, Benard expended the last drop of miracle water to an ill child. He stepped outside after washing his hands and decided to repair any broken down structures with supportive beams and secure the borders of the town.

He built homes from scratch for families that lost theirs and for fresh arrivals from all over Ephoreia.

Elvador spent his time boosting morale. His presence kept the town of resistors hopeful. He walked by the barracks and helped correct poor-stance soldiers, and the beast used his tracker senses to reunite lost loved ones to their families by following spare pillowcases or forgotten neckerchiefs.

When the dragon witnessed Benard reshaping the town, he offered to transform and carry large, stone walls to create a border of protection. Townsmen clapped and watched in awe as two worked together elegantly.

Benard and Elvador were making a statement. Aspen Bay was under their protection; A Resistance Force guarded by a dragon and an elf.

Earrie busied herself with aiding the growing army of volunteers. She found an old armory full of knight gear. Some were antics while others were old decorations.

All of the pieces were of fine quality. They were sturdy, reliable pieces.

The humans once owned exquisite blacksmith's shops for their royal guards, and their craftsmanship appeared to have been mastered.

The pink-haired princess distributed the wares between resistors.

Earrie took a thin rapier to replace the one she lost in the water village during her blackout and abduction.

She eyed a set that appeared similar to her own,

yet it was much lighter. The wind knight felt lik the sword's weight would allow her to utilize he abilities to their maximum effect as she was knight of speed.

The armor shined gray with polish, and it sheets reflected the morning sun. Unlike he standard Ember Knight armor, this piece appeare bland in comparison. Simple, yet the quality of th piece suited her more than that of her old armor.

She cut out a flap in the back for her wings. Th human armor hung high enough on her that sh didn't need to cut out its legs or arms. Her dwarver blood from her father caused her height to b stunted allowing her to utilize human clothes anc wares.

Earrie slashed a tree stub as she wore in her new blade until her arms fell weak. She decided it wa time to take a break and laid against the trunk while she ate a pre-packed sandwich.

In her heart, she held precious memories of he time with Maxwell. She looked to her side and visualized him sitting beside her teasing her and patting her head. These moments in her head kep her going.

A windy breeze swept her hair feeling her with a comforting peace.

Over the next few days, the elder princess spent Benard's free time training him. Together they swiped down trees and flew up to high distances. She gave him pop quizzes on Ember Knight basics while he put forth his entire being into their training.

Benard found himself falling behind Earrie in the sky. His failures weren't entirely his fault since the training was designed to push him to his limits to teach him endurance.

Earrie turned around and waved to Benard, "Stop falling behind, you moron!"

Her teases caused Benard to blush. He felt reminiscent of all his memories traveling with the princess of his dreams.

For a couple of hours a day, Benard pretended the weight of Ephoreia was lifted off his shoulders instead the man filled his thoughts with Earrie.

Benard envisioned himself swooping in and saving Earrie during a battle with Zenith. He imagined her dramatically falling in her arms and declaring her unyielding devotion for him until an image of Maxwell stuck his thoughts.

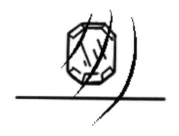

In the infirmary, Fae told Delka about her plan. The Inventor's consciousness had spent her time in and out of the infirmary. She checked on Fae daily, but she also used her time wisely to collect new data. Delka did what needed to be done with her days.

Fae summoned all over the machinery in front of her. She flipped through her orange goggles until she found the blueprint she was looking for, robotic, prosthetic legs.

Fae felt relieved at the sight of the prints since she knew in her heart that as long as she lived, she would be able to find a way to use her powers to walk again.

Through Delka's guidance, Fae created two sturdy-bottom additions to her legs. The young princess fastened the bottom tip into that of a boot successfully overriding the need for shoes. Both of the created legs were mirror matches in appearance.

Fae decided to link the boots to her black and lit up suit. The boots stretched out into the fabric of her elastic outfit. If she wanted to change her outfit, she could easily detach them.

The boots had side seams of text colors, and they shined a numeric code. She followed the same blueprint of her suit as its structure allowed the boots to further help to control her abilities. By giving her a tighter control over her power with a decreased range, Fae was able to contain her raw potential at an early stage.

The Inventor called in her physical therapist.

The young woman surveyed her new legs. Among her struggling attempts to utilize her new legs, she created a walker to aid her in her recovery. The female assistant helped Fae walk to different goal markings every day.

Her sister along with the others paid her visits and brought her encouraging words, and Benard arranged for her to have a visit outside. He brought her to a bench to watch her sister and Elvador train soldiers in the barracks.

Fae sat on a new bench outside of the barrier of her old home, yet she remained trapped. The halfling was restrained by her journey to recovery. She gazed at them and dreamed of a time when she would rejoin the fight again.

Delka documented the battle of Aspen Bay in her stored records. She went around the library and gathered new information to fill her databases.

She felt that Fae's recovery would grow the young princess as an Inventor and make her stronger. The new start would allow her to trust her powers and herself.

Delka allowed trained professionals to aid Fae

in recovery, but she often found herself pushing her mentor to do more and go further until she passed each goal mark. This wasn't the end of Fae's journey, but a new beginning.

In just a few, short days, Fae found herself able to walk small steps without the walker. With just a tug by a friend or therapist, Fae was able to walk again.

She thought back to Earrie's strong words about how each step was one closer to defeating Zenith and let an accomplish-marking tear.

Earrie brought Fae a basket of fresh bread. Bringing baked goods to her sister reminded Earrie of all those late-night visits she used to make to visit Fae back in the Slums.

Their sisterhood started with baskets of bread and stayed together with an everlasting bond of friendship and love. Smiles and laughs exchanged between the two were a rare wholesomeness mostly forgotten in a barren Ephoreia.

When Fae mentioned that she was to be released today, Earrie gasped. "Well it's only been a week . . . are you sure?" Earrie asked in disbelief.

"She's ready," Delka said as she peeked from behind Fae.

Earrie attempted to hold back tears of joy while she watched Fae walk freely out the doors of the old hospital. Elvador and Benard stood side by side with a fresh bundle of yellow dandelions in their hands that matched that of her glow.

Fae ran to them and flung into their arms. They both held her up and spun her around in circles. She wiped her joyous tears with a swipe of her left hand.

Benard handed her the roses to which she jokingly bowed while the others laughed.

With a sudden change of mood, Earrie looked at the three before her, "I've heard a word about a volcano a day or so from here that used to be Zenith's base."

"It's inaccessible . . . Zenith uses his volcano powers to mold magma around him to allow him and him alone entry," Elvador added as he drew eye contact with Earrie.

Earrie stood in front of him, "My sister will

guide us. I trust her ability. I'd say it's time you do so as well."

Elvador looked at Fae. For one of the first times, he viewed her wearing a serious face.

"I already sought out heat resistance blueprints. We can get to his base," she said in confidence.

That new feeling of hope reentered Elvador's heart. These people were for him. For the first time in hundreds of years, he felt like he wasn't alone anymore.

"Okay," Elvador said with his mind made up smiling.

Benard eyed the others, "I'm coming as well. I'll go give some orders to the medical staff on my leave."

Earrie turned around and pointed to the tip of the sky where Heaven's Castle laid. "We will destroy Zenith and bring a new life to Ephoreia!" she said in encouragement.

With three nods in agreement, they bolted off in separate directions. As soon as they reemerged, they would head off to their new mission.

Chapter 15 Zenith's Base

After the gang of resistors finished their preparations, they grouped up at the base of Fae's newly created warship. A silvery, gray-colored ship with a red, circled pattern. Along the ship's body, spiraled Inventor text that spun around to an unknown rhythm.

"Wow, it's grander than mine," Elvador said as he witnessed the creation.

"Than yours?" Fae questioned uncertainty.

"That ship from Tuner Town was mine. I didn't steal it. I just had to make up some lie to mask my cover."

"Why did you hide who you were, to begin with?" Earrie questioned as she tuned in to their conversation.

"Yea, I'm still curious about that," a nosy Benard intervened.

Elvador turned around and his brown locks floated in the sun, "I needed to know if I could trust you. My battle against Zenith is centuries old. I couldn't risk the wrong connections."

Fae and Earrie nodded their heads intently as though they could see where he was coming from, contrary to their agreement, Benard remained against Elvador.

"It was clear we were Zenith's enemy from the start," the stone knight said in a challenging tone.

Elvador fought back, "I'm over a millennia-old, Benard, I've seen people who are against someone join up with that very soul hundreds of times. All it takes is a little bit of desperation for power or weakness and you've got the ingredients lined up for betrayal."

"We can talk about this once we board the ship. We don't have the time to sit around and bicker," Earrie barked in a spirit of grumpiness.

They all followed through with her orders and filled the ship. Elvador decided to take command and give Fae rest before they reached the volcano.

Benard joined him in the co-pilot. "So, do you have any idea what you're doing?" the medic man asked Elvador aggressively.

He flipped on a multitude of switches unsure of what they did to show off to the dragon. He glared over to Elvador as he awaited an answer.

"Well, I mean I did own my airship before, and I've flown similar mechanisms in the human wars long ago . . . Um, do you have a clue what you're doing?" Elvador said nonchalantly with a glance to Benard.

He then eyed the buttons that Benard touched and reached over to flip some off. "Try not to . . . touch anything." Elvador said while he placed his hands back on the ship's wheel.

In a flustered state, Benard twirled his chair to his right and daydreamed out the window for the rest of the trip.

The man's embers appeared to be a darker purple. Benard glared at Earrie across from him and wondered why she never spoke up for him.

Ever since Benard bonded with his embers, a wicked spirit laid festering in his heart. A spirit of darkness created by Clance's hatred and jealousy.

No one in the group seemed to notice Benard's change in attitude, and they didn't notice his embers as they were all too focused on their own paths.

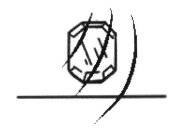

In the back of the ship, Fae memorized blueprints. She studied an abundance of battling techniques for Inventors while Delka went over

their past lessons. The young princess breathed deeply as she attempted to inhale all the material she learned like she had a final exam to take.

To her side, Earrie played with her rapier. She glanced at her reflection on her polished sword. Hot-pink hair glimmered back to her. The princess flipped up her left leg and positioned it under her right.

If they could gain any information about Zenith and his stolen technology, then just maybe, they could gain the upper hand.

The wind knight dazed into a blank spot inside her head for the rest of the trip ignoring Benard's stares.

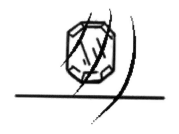

When they arrived at the peak of the volcano, the group felt a looming thickness that clouded the air. Fae deconstructed her ship with a touch and familiar white text that flowed from inside her body.

With white eyes, she morphed the material into her studied plans. The object's shape was sturdy, and its crevices ran smooth. The bobbing, heat-resistant submarine weighed a ton, yet it managed to float.

Her mind focused on the inner workings of her newly created transport. Many bolts tightened, and the gears spun into fashion. Her thoughts painted it piece by piece as the submarine materialized in front of her.

The side of the dense ball lifted into a doorway. Inside the ship's continents, four benched seats laid.

Before they spun in, Elvador spoke with a worried face, "There's a whole lot of dragons down there . . ."

Earrie turned towards him with fierceness in her green eyes, "Benard and I are Ember Knights. If we can't handle mini beasts we will never stand our guard against Zenith."

"I like your confidence, but we have to be careful. Zenith is always watching through the eyes of his beasts. If he traps us somehow, we will be in a deathbed!" Elvador said as his voice cracked in stress.

"Trust in me, Pup," Fae said in a soft smile. She held his hand in hers and eyed him in a silent plea.

"Okay," Elvador uttered softly, and his heart pounded.

The dragon breathed out a deep sigh. It was hard for him to trust anyone other than himself. He didn't want anyone getting hurt, and he didn't want anyone else to have to clean up his mess, Zenith.

There was something special about Fae. She had the ability to bring forth light in others. A sparkle in her eyes lit the dragon's heart with a fresh flame of hope.

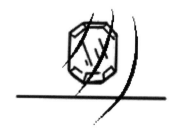

The group finished their discussion, and they ducked their heads to enter on Fae's built-in bridge. When they sat down, automatic, seat buckles drove them into benches.

Fae shouted, "All aboard!" Her usual glow appeared to sparkle along with her enthusiasm as she waved her hands.

Fae, contrary to her friends, stood with hands resting on the central, motherboard scanner. The technology was similar in that of her boots and outfit as this scanner assisted her control over the situation.

Elvador stood awestruck at Fae's power, somehow, this little elf had come into Ephoreia and created a new beginning for the lost.

New things were happening, and with it, a remodeling of everything they even knew was occurring. The dragon had seen nothing but destruction and attempts at preservation for the past millennia, but nowadays, things were changing.

Lifted hearts and spirits were normal around this Resistance Force, and with that elevation, a new standard of living was established. The hope the dragon lost many years ago was now with him again, and he wasn't going to let Zenith steal his fire anymore.

While Elvador thought on the new light in Ephoreia, Earrie couldn't wait to get back into the battle, for she hated Zenith; All the princess wanted more than anything was to see his demise and restore her kingdom.

Earrie's body shook in anticipation of gaining any new information on Zenith. She couldn't contain her fidgeting.

"Nervous?" Benard asked. His eyes remained fixated on the princess as they made way into the volcano's depths.

She clenched the cuff of her blade, "No, I'm excited to bring Zenith down."

Her serious demeanor caused Benard to gulp, but she was right. Zenith stole everything he could from her. He was the embodiment of evil and needed annihilation.

The stress of the impending war dangled over the passengers of the submarine. As the pressure and heat built up, a nerve-wracking intensity fell upon those who were unsure of themselves.

To break the ice of lingering fervent that

brought heat over the group, Fae said, "So, Pup, it seemed like Acadash knew—"

"That's because she used to be my girl . . . A thousand years ago before she allied herself with Zenith's human, she was a normal soldier like everyone else. She once had a heart that desired goodness and justice, but after she started dating Zenith, something changed in her eyes. She wasn't the girl I once loved," his words poured like a cup of bitterness.

The dragon folded his hands with a cross and placed them on his chest. It was clear this wasn't an easy topic for him.

"What was it like being a soldier back then? And how did the three of you meet?" Fae pressed.

Earrie and Benard both paid heed to his past. No one knew much of anything about Elvador, for he was always more reserved than them. The beast had a quiet nature about him.

"I used to be a young, seventeen-year-old boy just looking to get by. And one day, I heard about a new, government-funded project, dragons. The needed volunteers, so they offered a large amount of bills for participants," Elvador said as he shifted into a more relaxed stance.

"Human, super soldiers," Fae said while she remembered his words in the cave under Aspen Bay.

"All-out, indestructible, roach soldiers," Earrie mumbled in the background.

Fae watched Elvador as his face grew dark.

"I enlisted because of my desire to make a good income and do well for myself. I met Zenith at an elimination camp. Weaklings were rooted out quickly. Only the smartest, and most likely to succeed candidates passed.

"Zenith was a normal, average guy. Other than the fact that he passed his initial exams with flying colors, nothing ever stood out to me about the guy.

"We became friends during training as only a few of us ever reached the later-level stages. Zenith and I shared bunks during our rise to the top. After several months, a small group was selected to undergo dragon experimentation."

"Well-trained, lab rats," Benard speculated.

Elvador let out an annoyed sigh and continued,

"It wasn't long after the war with the dwarves and elves alliance that humans began to . . . abuse their dragons. Suddenly, dragons weren't seen as humans any longer.

"Out of fear, they stripped us of our rights. Oppressed by our creators for the very power they gave us. We ended up being nothing but weapons to them. They invented touch devices that stripped us of our powers to keep us in place with unmovable, shock collars.

"We weren't *permitted* to think for ourselves, and any form of the uprising resulted in more restrictions, even death. Our humanity was stolen from us . . . " his words dissolved into a faint whisper.

Fae's eyes built up with tears hearing his story. "That's horrible— Pup, I have no words . . ."

Earrie looked over and said, "Thank you—for sharing with us. I know this can't be easy to talk about, but the information you've given us is invaluable. I think—I understand our mutual a little bit better now."

Benard stayed quiet as he thought of the history

of dragons and the abuse they went through. He felt bad from his original stance to Elvador, but he knew he couldn't let his guard down for the princess's sake.

"We're approaching his base!" Fae yelled causing everyone to turn their attention.

Quaking metal echoed through the under-lava ship. Fae stood firm while the others gripped to their benches. With a loud clunk, they landed into his base.

"I-I can't hack it. I can't get entry," Fae said with devastation present in her tongue.

She forced her coding to Zenith's secret base, but they failed to give her access. The halfling shook her hands and glanced at the others with tears in her eyes.

Delka swam over to her side. "Fae, the systems, they're built like the Inventor ruins. I just checked, and I have full access."

At her words, color returned to Fae. "All right, I'll dock you at the ship bay!" the young princess said with determination in her lime-green eyes.

With some sparkling colors, Delka opened the base's gate and Fae boarded the ship. Opening the door, they all walked out and approached a pathway of halls.

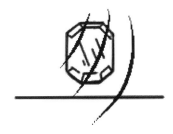

At Delka's command, a hallway door opened and Elvador looked over to Delka, "I want to go scout ahead. Can you continue to open doors for me?"

Delka lit up gold, "I have access to the whole system. The doors have senses that scan who is entering. I'll know it's you."

Without another word and just a wave, the dragon dashed away. He used his inhuman speed and tracker senses to trail above the group.

Along his sprinting, he canvassed maze pathways made up of square, gray platforms. They sparkled reflections of tin. Large bolts with colorless skewers were drilled inside its edges. Elvador's feet buckled against the slick flooring as he picked up his pace.

Earrie silenced the group, "If there are really as many dragons down here as Elvador said, then we must be quiet. Whisper and use hand signals. Be sneaky."

Her sister and Benard nodded their heads, while Delka remained focused on providing Elvador a distant opening. The group tiptoed through the building room by room, and they surveyed everything they could access.

Some rooms displayed chairs with restraining straps hinged on their sides. Other rooms were full of cut-up samples of dragon flesh tilted underneath telescopes.

The inspected rooms were packed tight with square, flashing screens. On their lenses, pictures of dragons DNA were flashed. Next to the charts, written words in Inventor language that no one could decipher showed themselves.

Delka being only a remnant of her old self still didn't know how to read them. The codes were foreign and jumbled up. They seemed to be constantly creating a new way of speech as the lettering went on making it impossible to understand.

"Just what on Ephoreia was he researching?" an intrigued Benard asked. He placed his fingers gently across the screens.

"My coin is on minion control. We also have to take into account his growing powers and the sheer multitude of his abilities," Earrie mumbled in a moody tone. Everything about this man Zenith made her sick.

"Well, we know he's got stolen technology for transporting dragon souls, and dragon creation. So, through the process of elimination, I would say his growth must be linked to the power he has over his minions. Possibly, he found a way to alter the dragon creation machine to make mini beasts that obey him," Delka said.

"Wow, Delka, you are a lot more intelligent than I ever gave you credit for," Benard complimented.

They left the room and continued onward until they reached two diverging doorways. To ensure that they both had dragon slayers with them, the sisters stayed together while Delka and Benard went on a separate pathway.

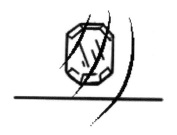

Elvador managed to make it to the center of the facility. He viewed a large, circular room that had many doors all leading to its base.

In the center, there was a large globe. The sphere appeared identical to Delka, but it towered in size.

He approached the glass structure and tapped it with a thud. To the dragon's surprise, the machine lit up with rainbow text. They danced in zigzags and stripes when the technology spoke.

"Hello, old friend," its vibrations rung familiar to Elvador, Zenith.

"Just what the hell are you?" the dragon shouted. He flinched his fingers backward in noticeable disgust.

"Don't pretend you don't know me," the see-through computer said.

"What do you want, Zen?" Elvador said with folded arms as he rolled his eyebrows.

"There. You see, that's not so hard now is it?" Zenith purred through his ball.

Light flashed bright and the tyrant continued, "I don't want anything. I have everything. Every dragon who's ever crossed paths with me has been . . . let's call it, erased. Nothing has ever stopped me nor will it ever!

"Your little group of savages won't even scratch under a single scale of mine. I'm the new king of the world that I re-birthed! I've carved out my empire with my very own claws that my enemies gave me," Zenith finished his prideful speech.

"Sure are confident, aren't you? You seem to

forget that I'm still standing," Elvador muttered as he paced around the globe in a huffed stance.

"Are you? And for how long will it last? You know you won't live with your group. They're young. Juveniles. I have something better to offer you though."

"Oh yeah, wagging-up deals? You must be desperate. That's not the forceful Zen I know," Elvador teased with a devilish grin.

"Name a kingdom and it's yours. You want ale, woman, or coin? I can give you all and more. I will share this world of mine with you. Think about it. You and me; Just like old times," Zenith said, dealing his cards.

The dragon decided to entertain Zenith for a moment, "So, what's the catch?"

"I want the heads of each one of your companions."

At his offer, Elvador couldn't help but bellow out in laughter, "Hahaha, I'm"—he raised a hand to catch a falling tear—"sorry, but I could never side with a villain like yourself."

"And when did you become the hero? Your

hands are stained with the same amount of blood that covers mine!" an offended Zenith barked.

"I protect people, save them, and risk my life for them. Yes, my hands are stained, but I am doing everything I can to redeem their taint while you're only added to your sins. You're nothing. Just a murdering suppressor. A faint shadow of the man I once called my friend! Ironic how you've become the very thing WE stood against one time!"

"Don't you dare try and act like you're better than me! What's the matter Elvy, still hurt your little whore Acadash clang to me? Why don't you get behind Richard's rotting corpse?" Zenith's paired consciousness yelled with flashing colors.

Before Zenith could go on, a door folded open revealing Delka and Benard. They rushed over to Elvador's side in investigation.

"Ahh—Delka, the Protector of the Inventor Trials. What a pleasure it is for you to make an appearance. NOW GET OUT OF MY SYSTEM NOSY LASS!" at Zenith's shout, electric sparks flung towards Delka.

With a connection to her sphere, all of her colors dissipated as if they were never there. Her glass body fell in slow motion to the ground.

A thunderous shatter flicked everyone's ears as her globe made landing. Elvador shut his eyes and positioned his chin off to his side.

Another was lost by Zenith's bloody hands.

Benard fell on his knees into sharp grains of glass. He attempted to shove the pieces together as if that would bring her back. His shaky hands placed them together like a puzzle, but his thumb nicked the formation crashing it down all over again.

"She's gone, Ben," Elvador spoke while touching Benard's shoulder in comfort.

"Just another hindrance removed," Zenith sneered.

"You killed her!" accused Benard.

"She died hundreds of years ago. Merely a programmed personality of her old self and nothing more," Zenith's words rung dry and emotionless.

"He's a killer. It's what he does," Elvador said drained.

With a squeeze of his fist, the dragon dashed up to smash the central globe. He was tired of hearing Zenith speak. Before he could land a punch, Benard grabbed his wrist.

Chapter 16 That White Place

The princesses paced forward through their chosen pathway. Without looking, Earrie slammed head first into a doorway. She stumbled backward and held her hand to her forehead in misery.

"I wonder why it didn't open?" the elder sister questioned through gritted teeth as she masked her pain.

"Delka. She's hurt, or . . . I just know something's wrong. She would have opened it!" Fae yelled out in sudden panic.

"Come on, Fae, let's not jump to conclusions."

The sisters stood there while trying to pry open the door. With shoving hands, the heavy door refused to give in.

"Can you get it?" Earrie asked an eyeing Fae.

Fae shook her head down as if she were embarrassed at her inability.

"Don't worry, I think I have a solution," the elder sister reached for her embers and called to them.

After a hasty transformation, she approached the door. With a deep breath and closed eyes, she touched its surface and focused all of her wind to its hinges. All the Ember Knight needed to do was wiggle its latch open so they would have an entry.

Sounds of a flicking lock fiddled in their ears. Fae stood back flabbergasted that her sister could have thought of such a solution.

With a click, the lock sprang free. "Amazing!" the youngest princess admired in a childlike manner with her hands on her cheeks.

"Sometimes the answers in life are a lot easier than we make them in our heads," she said as she smiled at Fae.

Their delightful moment was interrupted when a door of bars slowly lifted open. Sounds of shrieking dragons became evident to the sisters.

"T-The dragons!" Fae stammered.

"We can hold them off until Elvador and Ben come! Trust in your powers!" Earrie said, attempting to calm her sister.

Back in the central room, Elvador sighed at Benard's restraint, "Why?"

"What if it's useful? What if Fae could study it?" the medic asked.

"It's dangerous! Besides, it's a window for Zenith's eyes and ears!" Elvador hissed back.

"Why don't we try to get the others first?"

Elvador huffed his shoulders and went to the

doorway. He gave it a generous budge, but it remained sealed shut.

He looked startled when he pressed his ear to the door, "I can hear them. The dragons are going for them! There are more strings than my vision can even perceive."

Benard ran to his side, "We have to get to their side!"

"I'm shattering that ball! It's in control of the facility just like Delka was. Don't try to stop me," Elvador muttered as he lunged around and bolted for the mother source.

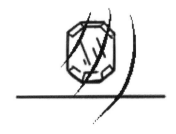

Fae flipped on her powers and morphed her boots into a thick, hardened shell around her flesh. She created duel chains of electricity in her hands. Her defense was a popular fighting technique the Inventors of Ancient.

With charged bolts, the chains danced in extended, snake slivers. The first mini beast pounced on her like a leopard. Fae choked the beast with stinging shocks and flung it into the wall.

Behind her, Earrie unsheathed her sword. It was her time to pay Zenith back for what he did to Clance, her father, and Maxwell. She flipped and struck her blade into oncoming bodies. Blood spewed her blade between each swipe.

Through the hoarding beasts, the sisters span side by side like ballerinas. Some beasts managed to break away and land rips on the two. This resulted in Fae pushing out more of her powers.

She covered herself along with her sister in a magnified shield. The zombie-like beasts ran into the heated beams only to disintegrate like dust. Fumes of burnt flesh clogged their nostrils.

"Fae, stop your field it's hurting me!" Earrie shrieked as the bolts floated into her body.

Sudden panic and self-doubt caused Fae to lose control over her powers. "I cannot!" the young princess squealed.

White, glowing text floated around the whole room. In a change of pace, dragons stood still and their relentless pursuits halted. The beasts held their hands around their necks and choked themselves blue in the face.

Earrie peered over to her sister. She noticed that her sister was absent-minded. Fae's face was just like when the Inventor seal first broke. The younger sister's color appeared bleached by illuminating, white lettering.

Just when things couldn't get worse, another door opened. Earrie held onto her sister like a lifeline unsure of what new foe would come at them. The wind knight fluttered her eyes open until she relaxed her composure at the incoming image of her friends.

Even at the death of all their attacking dragons, Fae's powers didn't let up. They grabbed a hold of Elvador and forced him to choke himself.

The unfolding situation brought Elvador back on a trip through memory lane. He thought back to a similar time his body was controlled like this.

Back during one of his many dragon revolution missions, he met Jermany the dragon-tamer. This was a time when he and Zenith were still a duo. He had been sent on a task to slay an enemy's leader.

He remembered how cocky and blindsided he was back then. He used to go around assassinating targets for Zenith without question. All in the naive name of justice.

It didn't take long for their slave rebellion to turn into an absolute holocaust. Anyone and everyone who even talked ill of the dragons was marked for death by Zenith. His x-friend loved the power and obedience murdering innocents granted.

The day Elvador went to slay the leader, he remembered being tricked into a barnyard and meeting Acadash. He ran into her sneering away with a piece of cloth from his target in her paws.

She'd set him up with a word from one of the Dwarven Elf Alliance's spies. They had carefully positioned him under Zenith's ranks.

Acadash sat there giggling with dozens of men holding up paralysis arrows all locked on to him. With a hand signal, their arrows pierced into his flesh.

It was later that day, he met Jermany the dragon tamer. Jeremy was a dwarf Inventor with the power to control dragons.

With some visits from a softhearted Acadash, his world view soon morphed. Just because the humans had done them wrong years ago did not mean that they deserved to be annihilated.

She taught him forgiveness and how justice was built on mercy and second chances. Her soft words forever loosened Elvador's heart.

It wasn't too long after, the dragon joined up with them by freewill. He spent the rest of his days doing everything in his power to stop the dragon's revolt that he helped create.

Even after Acadash's heart grew cold from her lust for power, he remained true in his intentions to bring down Zenith. His everlasting mission to stop his lost friend would end up consuming him.

Among his many thoughts of the past, Elvador twisted his fingers at his throat to fight the control.

Benard felt pressured in the situation just like he did back in the makeshift hospice. He transformed and merged two stone-arm pillars to Elvador's arms.

He used all of his power to pull and thrust the dragon's hands off his neck. With a slight inch of space, Elvador gasped mercy-filled breaths.

Earrie shook her sister and bellowed for her to stop before it was too late, but she remained unresponsive.

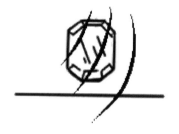

Screams of her companions echoed in her ears, but Fae couldn't ingest a word of it. The young Inventor found herself lost inside a room of light. If she were to gaze with a microscope, she would notice text inside the pixels of the walls floating every which way.

The young princess scanned downwards and failed to perceive her body.

"You will survive," a voice stirred inside her.

"We will preserve our knowledge," this time many voices were shouting in her.

Inside her head, a voice stood out, Delka's. "Fae, you must take back control, or your power will consume you!"

"Consume me?" Fae questioned with uncertainty.

"Right now, outside of this space, you are attempting to kill your friend!" Delka's consciousness shouted above the whispering multitudes.

"Kill my friend?" Fae asked.

"Fae, listen to me! The backup, emergency program took over your body. You must resist its control. I know it's easy to lay back and let it work for you, but one day you'll find yourself never able to return to your body."

Fae floated backward in shock, "How do I get back? Get control again?"

"Runaway from this pulling force, for it will suck you away from your world!"

At Delka's words, Fae skidded against the unknown dimension. She hustled her legs opposing the sucking whispers. They grabbed onto her flesh like leeches, but she didn't hesitate. She continued to run and dash until she viewed a hazy image of her surroundings.

All around her side and back was a spider web-like, white string that netted her in. Fae pressed forward not giving up instead she held onto her sister's vivid screams.

With an air-clenching gasp, she woke to a worried Earrie. To her side, a heavily breathing Elvador stood and thanked Benard for saving his life.

"You're back!" was the last thing she remembered before falling unconscious due to her excessive-power usage.

Chapter 17 More Allies

A shocking feeling bounced on Fae's flesh. She heard shouts muffling her ears and felt a warm tug. Vibrated pulsations ran up and down her spine.

In the background, doors slammed open and close. A man holding her frantically mumbled curses between his heavy breathing.

The young princess shot her eyes open to view long, draping hair in her face. She wiggled her head left and right until she could see a sweat-faced

Elvador.

Fae peeked above herself to eyeball an unimaginative flight of stairs. The case appeared hollow and pitch black.

The dragon's night vision along with Fae's light led his feet. She opened her mouth to speak out her many questions, but Elvador spoke first, "Hold onto me tightly. This base isn't going to make it. When I shattered its core, the base slowly lost all power and with that its levitation. Your sister and Ben are leading an army of willing dragons to escape. My job is getting you to safety."

Despite his calm composure, he was in a frenzy. Fae shook her head and squeezed tightly. The fall downwards didn't look easy.

"I hurt you—" Fae mumbled before falling unconscious again.

Elvador's eyes frowned at the elf's words. Fae cared about his safety, and it scared him. He wasn't used to anyone caring for him like this, and anyone who ever had betrayed him.

The dragon continued to dash up the stars hoping everyone else would make it.

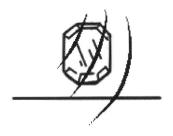

A few minutes beforehand, Earrie and the group stumbled into a dungeon of dragons. These beasts weren't hypnotized by Zenith. They were children, women, and elders. It appeared to be a throw-away stash he never bothered to control.

On their arms and legs, heavy, silver shackles weighed them down like attack dogs. In the background, lights flickered on and off until they went out.

The base started to flip around like a harpooned whale.

Rooms tipped and large objects struck prisoners. When they viewed the dragons, two females screamed, "Please, save us! We'll die if you don't!"

A hysterical, old woman in the back shouted, "It's effortless! We're all going to die!"

Elvador didn't hesitate to break them free. He ran over and snapped their constraints apart while carrying the unconscious princess.

After many screams of terror, the freed beasts agreed to come with them. None of them resisted the chance for freedom when it was offered to them, including the old lady.

Their loyalty was less for their newfound saviors and more of a desire to not be ripped apart. They'd all listened in terror as mini beasts were shred and bodies dropped.

With Fae still out of it, the group had no option but to run up and away from the melting floors. They looked beneath to witness boiling pits of lava and steam.

In front of their eyes, they viewed a powerless elevator. Before they continued upward, Benard had an idea.

"If we could just load the dragons into the elevator then we would be able to bring them up quickly. All we would have to do is hold onto the cord above them and fly upwards," he said while readying his transformation.

Earrie didn't have time to argue with him, so she kicked open its doors with Elvador's assistance. The princess then dove in and flung open the escape latch. Benard and the princess tugged together on the elevator string to ensure that his plan would work before anyone boarded.

None of the beasts had room for takeoff, but they also were never allowed to fly in their captivity. It'd been so long since they flew that they're wings were weak, and their bodies were lethargic.

With the lava now caught up to them, a mass haul would be their only refuge.

Earrie looked to Elvador right when he stepped inside. "No, you're going up the stairs. In case this fails . . . Fae can't perish," he understood nodded goodbye. The dragon obeyed and climbed up a never-ending staircase.

With just a few passing moments, Elvador heard chunks of the staircase being eaten. He could only hope that Benard's plan had prospered.

Both Benard and Earrie pulled the heavy flight

of passengers up. She channeled her wind to the underskirt of the box to give it speed.

Benard used his stone to chain a foundation against the wall, and the male knight pushed the load with all his might. Together the two sweated in their struggle to save the passengers.

The princess looked ahead and noticed the rooftop closing in. She strengthened her grip on the rope and pushed through the air.

"Almost there!" Earrie shouted in self-encouragement.

Benard shouted "Fall out! Fall out!" as they reached the door.

Right after the last dragon left, a sudden bubble of lava shot gallons of burning liquid inside the elevator. This disturbance caused Earrie to gasp and drop her hold.

Their misfortunes were as if destiny itself didn't want them to make it out of there, "The exits blocked Benard! What are we going to do?" panic clung to her tongue.

"Place our efforts into breaking through the wall!" Benard shouted.

Together they used their abilities to attack the wall. When that didn't work, Earrie struck her sword relentlessly. The wall's durability was equivalent to the unbreakable doors they'd previously encountered.

"What do we do, Benard, it's not working!" Earrie screeched in horror of her arriving fate.

Benard reached for her wrist and shoved her to the top of the ceiling, "Lay against it."

She gulped at his sudden assertion. When the buzzing lava approached their very hair string, Benard held Earrie's hand.

"If we die, I want you to know, I'm in love with you."

Earrie glanced at his hand, and her eyebrows turned up.

"Benard, now isn't—"

Right as they'd both been teased with death, a hole punched through above them. Strong hands reached for them and flung them up.

"Hurry!" Elvador shouted.

Earrie stood on shaky legs as she tried to

suppress Benard's love confession.

Benard avoided looking at the princess and ran forward.

"To the escape ship!" Elvador's voice barked orders at them.

Neither one of them had the mental strength to keep going, but Elvador's words carried them through passing walls.

Everything they passed seemed blank. All they could manage to perceive was a large ship that appeared to be made of molten rock. The ship must have been Zenith's means of transporting his subjects.

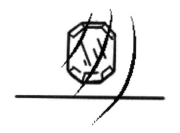

They boarded and sat down on the sides of the ship alongside seat-buckled benches. Inside the ship, they viewed dozens of dragons.

Elvador took control of the ship. With a few switches slipped on, he launched off through the magma. Benard, on the other hand, didn't bother pretending he could fly instead he sat down next to some freshly rescued dragons.

This ship moved a lot faster than the Fae's device. It must have been tested and upgraded numerous times. The pilot followed bubbles as he gained momentum on the way up from the volcano.

Earrie sat down next to her sister to avoid Benard.

The young Inventor turned in sweat as she saw images of a choking Elvador. She heard strange voices that pulled her down. The knowledge that she could permanently lose control tormented her state of mind. Fae flipped every which way as she fell into new terrors relentlessly.

Dragons discussed what they would do now with their freedom. When Earrie told them horror stories of outside of Zenith's base, they all unanimously agreed to join the Resistance Force.

Fae bounced her eyes open and flung her head up. This sudden change of elevation caused her to smack her worried sister in the face.

"Oh, Earrie, I'm so sorry!"

"Haha, it's all right. I needed that," she smiled and embraced her sister with open arms.

Fae scrunched up her face, "But, sister, I hit you right where you ran into those doors earlier."

The wind knight smiled sincerely. "Well, it smacked any sense I lost back into me so. I should be thanking you."

The young sister sighed. If Earrie was making jokes, things must have looked bad back there.

Fae asked them what happened. Her elder sister told her about her blackout and of the dragons they found. The young Inventor tried to hide her nervous shakes, but her sister knew her too well.

Benard opted to tell the young princess about Delka's death. "Fae . . . when we split up Delka she—"

"I figured as much," Fae muttered.

Her face unveiled devastation, unlike normal times when she chose to allow her emotions, the halfling held in her tears as if she was fighting them for her own sake.

Elvador to the front of the ship added his condolences, "Zenith is a merciless killer . . . I'm sorry, I couldn't save her."

"Without Delka, how were you able to get through the doors?" the Inventor questioned.

"I smashed his glass ball. I'm kind of the reason we almost all died back there," Elvador said as he scratched his head with rosy cheeks.

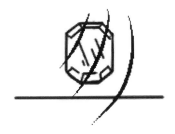

With a final surge, the ship surfaced. Everyone left to its top and waited for direction.

Elvador threw up a suggestion for the dragons to go and reinforce their defenses in Aspen Bay. Earrie agreed with him.

If the dragons wanted to assist them in the defeat of Zenith, they would need to practice their flying and battle skills. A single second loss of preparations could mean lives in battle.

Before splitting ways, they told their story to the group. Many of them were residents from a small village filled with escaped dragons.

The village Ishao was hidden in the forest. Their home consisted of dragons who had fled from their kingdoms. The beasts who didn't want to fight in the constant war instead they simply wanted to exist in peace.

Others came from Zenith's revolution but ended up getting burnt by him. Elvador had similar stories to some of them. Zenith pulled people in with his charisma only to stomp on them when he was through.

A few of the dragons were self-sufficient dragons as they lived off the land and stayed mainly in their dragon state. They'd given in to their beastly instincts and enjoyed themselves until Zenith captured them.

What stood out about their story, was the fact that every single one of them was a real dragon. They weren't mini beasts. Though they hadn't lived as long as Elvador, they were still hundreds of years old.

"He couldn't control us, so he kept those of us he deemed weak alive to . . . experiment on," the old lady from before said. Her hysterics calmed, and a twinkle of hope shimmered in her eyes at the rise of the bliss sun.

The information from the lady gave, provided Earrie with some reassurance. They had not come back empty-handed, for they knew Zenith was testing dragons. They also learned that he could control his created mini beasts, but not normal dragons.

Benard thought back to what Delka mumbled earlier about Zenith's mini beasts, growth, and the arrangement of his abilities all being linked. He tossed all of it around in his mind. This was in addition to the fact that somehow Zenith appeared to have deciphered Inventor text or knew someone who could.

"GUYS!" Benard shouted out with joy when he finally hit the answer.

They all looked at him curious to what he was on about, "His control over the dragons . . . that must be it!"

Earrie eyed him and with her usual attitude, "It?"

"Somehow someway, I just know the beasts are giving him his growth and powers. I think he's combining them with himself, or maybe it's a connection. He has to have hacked into Inventor code and found some way to link himself with them." Benard managed to say through his jumping bolts of excitement.

"Fae, if this is true then all you have to do is hack Zenith!" Earrie said with a grab to her sister's arm and bulging eyes.

"It's the only shot we have besides brute strength," Fae said honestly.

The dragon in the group didn't look too shocked. He had known for years that Zenith was obsessed with the Inventors. Back when they were friends, he would call the Inventors his god.

It was as though his search for belonging sprouted his addiction. But to master the code and rewrite it for his use, it seemed unachievable in Elvador's eyes.

If the Inventors couldn't understand the coded text, what made Zenith so special? Elvador thought.

Their newly gained allies waved goodbye and flew off to practice their flight back to Aspen Bay. The dragons promised to secure a border for the town, and fine-tune their abilities.

The group of resistors set course to a different destination. They flew in the altered ship to Soft Water Village. They decided unanimously that Fae would try and save Alice, and they would gather any willing men to fight Zenith.

Earrie and Benard both avoided all forms of contact since their near-death experience. The princess wanted to get him alone and talk about it, so they could both have clear minds during the battle with Zenith.

She needed to let him down, but his sincerity broke her heart. Earrie was in love with Maxwell and Benard was going to have to accept that.

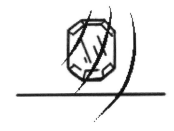

When they flew in, they were not greeted with

arrows or violence instead they were met with celebration. Clansmen brought music, and they danced around in circles.

Villagers held hands as they spun, and beads dangled on their ankles while long sleeves flowed like river streams to their palms. Women with medium, tan-skinned robes walked past and fell on their knees while fluttering leaves. Others held burnt essences up and swung them around. Some followed in front of Earrie showering her with freshly picked petals.

Earrie found herself bombarded with tribal men, "Our goddess is home!" they shouted. Smiles and laughter swooshed the village.

Fae smiled and ran to the crowd to join the party. Dancing in a mirroring fashion, Fae clapped her hands and twinkled her toes in and out, for there were no royals like in Heaven's Castle. The young princess could dance her halfling style without judgment.

She placed her feet juxtaposed with each other bent inwards. With a flip of her right leg, she hopped back her left. Her hands flew above her up and down each arm like tree branches.

Benard on the other hand, found himself drifting away from the upbeat crowd. He walked over to the miracle water to explore it for himself.

On arrival, he viewed the petrified-girl, Alice. Elvador mentioned the girl a few times since he and Earrie went to Soft Water Village, but he never informed them of how beautiful she was.

The stone knight sat down and removed his boots. Sharp, cold waters stung at his toes when he placed them in the waters for relaxation. The pain was replaced by a reviving sensation.

With Alice's inspiration in front of him, Benard took out his notepad and sketched an image of the stone woman.

The concentrated man found himself erasing his depiction of her eyes many times as he attempted to capture the fire that rested inside of them. He lightly shaded in her hair with a smudge of his thumb. Benard made ease of the delicate piece since it only took him a short time to sketch a noticeable outline.

From his right ear, bristling bushes taunted him. Benard winced at the noise as they caused him to lose trace of his concentration. He turned over to greet with whoever interrupted him only to view a twitching Earrie.

She stepped over and stood next to him. In silence, they spaced out towards the woman. With a glance down, the wind knight viewed his sketch.

The princess smiled, "I didn't know you could draw so well. You really are a jack of all trades." She stuck out one of her fingers by her cheek and smiled in a friendly tone.

Her compliment resulted in a blossoming flush under his profound gold eyes. Benard's skipping heart forced his hands to drip, and his pencil to slide down into the water.

"Look Earrie—"

She bent over and reached into the night's cold water for his writing utensil. Their hands clanked which worsened his nerves.

"I'm sorry, Benard."

Benard looked away. His heart dropped as he prepared himself for his heart to be ripped apart.

"I can't return your feelings Benard. Maxwell may be gone, but I still love him. Every night, I close my eyes and picture all my moments I had with him gringo up. I've known him since I was little, and when our relationship turned romantic, I promised myself that one day would marry that man."

The two sat silently staring at Alice's stone body. A frog croaked in the background, and the two peered into a sky of sparkling, midnight stars.

"What was your relationship like?" Benard asked to break the silence.

Earrie smiled and reached for a soft pebble to skip in the water.

"I hated him," she said smiling before bending backwards into a laugh.

The princess's eyes sparkled as the moon reflected a hazy glow in them.

Benard folded his sketch and placed it back inside his bag. "He was quite a character. It's hard to see a girl like you wanting to be with a guy like him."

"Hey, what do you mean? Girl like me?" Earrie said with a pout.

"You're so strong willed, and he seemed just as sharp. I thought you wouldn't want someone like that challenging you," Benard said smiling. He enjoyed Earrie opening up to him even if it was only a moment.

The princess felt calm around Benard as she hadn't found a moment since escaping Heaven's Castle to talk about her feelings or emotions.

"Maxwell is the only man who can tame my will," she said in a serious tone.

The two laughed and continued to chat about the world and their adventure for several hours. Earrie felt relieved to know that things were okay between the two of them. She was too prideful to admit it, but Benard had earned his spot beside her and her sister.

He saved her life, Elvador's life, and he brought them to the Inventor Trials. Benard also saved Fae's life, and helped maintain and restore Aspen Bay. She didn't believe they could have gotten this far without his help.

The princess decided that she would start treating Benard with more respect this night as she realized he earned it.

Some crickets rubbed their hands together and hopped off into the distance. Earrie stood up and picked off pieces of dead grass that stuck to her skin.

The princess stood and walked to a dirt path to begin her walk back to the village. She stopped just before some shrubs and cocked her head towards Benard.

"Elvador and Fae are readying the volunteers. As it turns out, everyone here is a trained warrior and wants to put their effort into our cause. The only ones not joining us are their kids, injured or handicap, and elders. Things are really looking up!" the determined princess spoke.

Benard waved and pretended his heart was for the battle and not lost in thoughts of her glistening, pink smile.

During his time in the water, Benard's embers were returned to a soft blue thought when he stood he felt a pain in his heart, and his embers burned a dark violet.

Just as Earrie passed through the bushes, tears ran down Benard's cheeks. He reached for his sketch and held it up, tearing it to pieces.

Panting and huffing, Benard stomped back to the village.

His body ached with rejection as thought it was stabbing him like sharp needles each second he breathed.

The group decided to rest for a night before going back to Aspen Bay as it was already night.

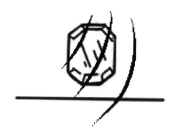

In the morning dawn, Fae expanded the ship to house all of their recruits. In the meantime, Elvador placed his will into formulating a generation of dragon riders.

He paced back and forth between the packing crew, "Since all of you have skills in precision shots, I believe all of you have the potential to be capable, dragon riders. With a proper satchel, you can ride in the air together with your dragons and target the enemy. It's a skill Zenith doesn't have. This strategy will give us the upper hand in battle."

They all looked confused. One tribal asked the question they were all banging their heads at. "Will our Goddess allow us to ride the beasts she commands?"

Elvador couldn't help but roll his eyes and mask a giggle at their naivety, "The beasts are working with us to bring down Zenith. So yes, you are going to be able to ride them."

When Fae finished her creation, she skidded off to the waters. She wanted to surprise Elvador and the rest of the group by healing Alice while they were distracted.

With turned-up cheeks and a childlike skid, she pounced off into the direction of the water. The ginger-haired lass jumped back when she viewed something startling in the pond.

Benard's red hair looked like flame-remenants dancing in the water. For a second she thought there was a fire, she sighed relieved knowing that it was only Benard.

The boy was studying the water while writing down all the potential medical remedies he could think of.

He peered over with his gold, yellow eyes and asked, "Are you here to save her?"

"I'm going to do my best!" she responded.

Fae sighed in ease, and she twiddled with her toes in the water's soft sands.

The young princess walked further in the water and summoned her powers. Familiar, white lettering floated around her and scattered into the water.

The Inventor lightly placed her hand upon the statue as she attempted to break free from the technology that imprisoned Alice.

She flinched and screamed as her powers attacked her, "Ben, help I'm losing control!" Fear was prominent in her voice along with her pale face.

Benard quickly got up and dashed through the ripples to aid her. He remembered how horrible it was back at Zenith's base when she lost control, and he grabbed her wrist wrestling it to free her grasp from the statue.

When that didn't work, he latched his right foot on the statue on the statue and propelled her back. It was that moment when Fae and Benard both fell backwards into the water, and her hand consequently landed on Benard's Blue Embers.

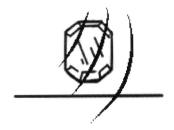

Fae woke to a room of darkness; The absent realm presented similarity to the white room she traveled to beforehand.

A dragon's roar echoed through black abyss. The Inventor shook in fright and stepped her toes in the direction of the noise.

Back when she was in the white room, Fae leaned facing away from the noise to exit. A growing curiosity of what leaked inside its depths consumed her footing.

Unlike in her world, Fae's natural glow was not present. This was something new to the girl as when she closed her eyes in Ephoreia, she could still perceive her glow inside her eyelids.

The darkness inside this realm was like a cloudy day as it masked everything in a blanket of hidden truths.

Fae picked up her pace and scampered off the sounds of a roaring dragon. Perhaps he would give her answers; Answers needed to end Zenith.

Feet carried her until she fell into long, iron bars. A type of a locked cell was before her. Before Fae could regain her composure, something clutched her foot siphoning her leg into the prison.

She screamed in panic, and chuckles rumbled from her offender.

"Please, stop! What are you doing?" the young girl pleaded with frantic squawks.

"I think the real question is, what are you doing in my cell?" a man's voice bellowed in her ears.

He pressed his teeth into her leg and bit down. Fangs grinned into dust against her prosthetic legs. The attacker fumbled back in pain giving her the second she needed to break free from his hold.

"You're Benard's ember," Fae said as she grew an understanding of her current location.

"Benard?" the beast grumbled.

The Inventor glared and held out her hand. "Don't waste my time. I need you to lend me your power!"

He scuffed and muttered, "Why would I help an Inventor like you?"

"I didn't ask!" Fae said forcing her will onto him with the help of her powers.

White lettering danced out and lit up his cell. The male dragon growled at the sight of brightness.

"ARGH!" he bellowed falling over on his knees.

"I never asked to be locked in here!" were the last words Fae heard before drifting back into reality.

His words sounded sad like a lost soul. It fiddled

with her heartstrings, and she lost herself in thoughts of how lonesome that place must be.

A lonely pit of no return; Entrapped by your memories with no future to go for. The very idea of it made her question the morality of the Blue Embers. She wasn't denying that the dragons had done wrong in their past, but was there no redemption for their wrongdoings?

When the princess flipped her eyes open, she turned upwards and reached for Alice again. Benard grabbed her hand as if to stop her from doing anything reckless.

"No, Benard, I got what I need now," she reassured him as she had the stone ember's code imprinted in her mind.

He released her forearm and stood back leaving her off to finish her business.

Something was different now; The text did not attack Fae, but alternatively, it wreaked havoc to the stone plastered on Alice's body.

Bits and pieces peeled off like shattering glass. Green, glowing skin unveiled itself under its wrapping. When plates flaked off of her head,

Alice's deep-violet hair poked through.

Benard had no idea how Fae did it, but he was amazed nonetheless. "Fae, you've gotten so strong," he complimented.

"Thank you, for believing in me, Benard, and for lending me the strength of your embers," she said smiling. With one last push, all the stone tumbled off and Alice was freed.

Chapter 18 Alice

With a deep gasp, Alice toppled down dazed, and Benard swooped in breaking her fall.

He held her head on his knees cupping her head in his hand.

"Elliot! My sweet, Elliot!" she reached leaning in to kiss Benard.

"No . . . I'm sorry. My name is Benard," the elf said, darting his head away.

Sad green eyes met golden, "Sorry, I thought . . . you were someone I knew."

Fae knelt and observed the girl. "Wow, you sure do resemble my sister," she said as she gazed with interest.

Alice's face puzzled, and she stood up and wiped imaginary dirt from her light-blue dress. The piece hung down to her ankles and opened in the back like an Ember Knight's armor. In the front, the dress cut was into a 'V' shape.

On the sleeveless gown, lace patterns of flowers swam down her sides. White, lace ribbons danced up to her elbows and tied in a finished, draped bow.

Her mannerisms were delicate and ladylike. The woman eyed Fae and Benard, "Can one of you bring me back to elven territory?"

"So, you're from before Heaven's Castle?" Benard interrogated.

"I have no idea what Heaven's Castle is. Just point me in the direction of elven territory, and I'll be off," she observed them with tapping toes.

Her impatience was never a strong quality for

the elf. Her attitude was similar to the princess she was compared to by the villagers.

Fae touched Alice's moss arm and said, "Elvador is here. Why don't you come and talk to him?"

The rescued woman relaxed at his name, "That sounds fine."

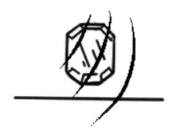

Benard and Fae escorted her back to the village. She still had yet to comprehend what period she was in. Fae motioned Alice in the direction of Elvador for him to talk some sense into her.

When they walked in the center of the village, Elvador's heart dropped at the sight of Alice. To him, she was like seeing a ghost.

With a tear bubbling in his eye, he pinched himself testing to see if he was dreaming.

The dragon ran over to his dear, old friend and tightly embraced her. Alice smiled but looked concerned at his reaction.

"What's the matter, Elvy? You're acting like I've been gone for a thousand years," Alice joked with uncertainty.

He looked at her with tear-filled, chocolate eyes, "You have."

"Come on Elvador! No jokes! Where's Elliot?"

The dragon looked at her white-faced, "He died, Alice. Over a thousand years ago, he gave his life trying to end Zenith's. . . One of the last things he ever did was bring your body here."

"No . . . No . . . I refuse to believe this!" Alice reached for her embers so she could fly and attempt to locate Elliot.

Before she transformed, Benard said, "Wait! Alice, it's not safe out there. Zenith has an army of mindless mini beasts along with an ember-fused knight in his hands, and he's obtained the power to grow a kingdom's length in size! He has hundreds of powers you cannot imagine under his control!"

Alice halted and turned. "So, you're saying, if I go out there I could die, and Zenith would continue to destroy Ephoreia?"

Elvador stood in front of her as he placed his hands on her shoulders, "Your mission still stands, Alice. Zenith must be brought down. He's found out Inventor secrets during the centuries you were frozen as stone. He isn't just an evil, lost ally anymore, he's a threat to the world and peace as we know it!"

She fiddled with her braided, purple hair, "He cannot be allowed to control Ephoreia anymore . . . I will stay and speak with your people until I am informed of the world's state."

Alice looked at the sky with her brows turned. She couldn't believe Elliot to be gone and for a thousand years at that. The elf felt a pit of emptiness inside her heart.

He sighed and smiled, "Thank you Alice, I am so glad you're okay!"

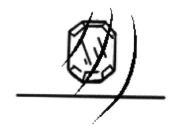

The group met in a private room to discuss their

journey and stories with Alice. They introduced each tragedy with sad faces and flailing arms.

Tears dropped and voices shattered. Alice's heart sunk and she felt a lump boiling inside her throat; It was as if the girl had been sleeping a thousand years in a world of dreams only to awake to a nightmare.

"Let me understand this, you guys are a group of elves, dwarves, halflings, dragons, and humans all working together?"

The group nodded and Alice's face turned soft.

"It's almost like the stories of old Utopia . . ." she mumbled,

"Old Utopia?" Benard questioned. He heard the name before in college, but he did not remember its origin.

"The Old United Kingdom of Ephoreia. Back when all the kingdoms lived together in a joint rule before the war or obsession over power started, we used to have a peaceful existence.

"Sure death and evil existed, but normalcy and order ruled. Ephoreians had what life is supposed to be . . . I imagine you guys must have had a similar existence in the clouds."

Earrie looked to her right to Alice's reminiscent face, "It sounds like a faraway dream what we used to have."

Elvador chimed in, "For Alice and I, it was. Our cities used Ephoreia's history to enslave us with a kind of patriotism. Convincing us to worship a fallen society and loathe the one that existed. Instead of focusing on change, everyone was focused on a past dream that never existed."

Alice turned her head, "Our people fought plenty, yet the ideals of Ephoreia united together weren't practical for our time. It only led to emperors rising up conquering nations in the name of justice while leaving a trail of blood in their path. With fewer treaties and political discussions and more war plays . . . " Before Alice could finish, she lost her trail in reminiscent thoughts.

When their discussions ended, the gang hopped inside Fae's ship. Clansmen walked by and said their goodbyes to loved ones.

A village of warriors meant that they were all prepared for this kind of sudden departure. Death and separation were nothing new to the clan of Soft Water Village.

Before they left, Earrie made one last stop to the Water of Life. She bottled up a chained vial and placed it on her neck; Close to her heart just like her where she kept the person she planned to use it for. She lifted her chest mail and threw it down under, so it wouldn't tangle with her Embers.

When the last remaining people entered the ship, Elvador took liftoff. This ship was a lot different than the others, for Fae placed her very soul into it.

The ship's colors were silver with borderlines of Inventor code except, unlike Fae's old, colorful outfit and bottom legs, the ship had only white coding. There was something about the white text that felt right to Fae as its patterns flowed from her with simplicity almost natural.

The rainbow coding seemed to give her more control over her powers, but after everything she learned, Fae discovered those colored patterns were giving the white room control and her less. She was tired of relying on that consuming force to fight for her.

It was time the Inventor created her own codes and patterns. To fight her own battles.

Fae's once black and colored suit was now transformed to an all-white as its hems were illuminating.

She felt more confident with her abilities after freeing Alice, but Fae was still unsure of how she would defeat Zenith. With everyone relying on her, the responsibility of his destruction was starting to tower on her more heavily than the others in the group.

Bonus Chapter Zenith's Uprising

Over one thousand years ago, a young man looked into a brick, cell wall that glared back at him. It taunted him with screams and clapping whip lashes.

His blue eyes darted behind raven hair to the shackles on his wrists. Behind his dull eyes, a grin steamed like hot lava. In his right hand, he held a hidden dragon-like claw.

Zenith fumbled the piece between his fingers as he inched it up to his shackles. He attempted to keep his movements subtle, so no guard would be altered.

Adrenaline pumped in his heart, and he aligned each shaking of his shackles with the lifting and releasing of a nearby guard's footsteps.

Today was not the day for hesitation; No, today was the day he would be free. A day he would see the sun with his own eyes once again.

He missed its warm light and the freeing sky that danced beside it. He wanted to fly beside it like a cloud, but he was only allowed out of his cell when under mind control.

Zenith wasn't even sure if his mind or body belonged to himself anymore, but he was determined to claim his future for himself.

He breathed in deeply and listened to each faint clicking inside his shackles that tied his hands to his prison ceiling.

Zenith was a high-risk dragon. One deemed non-compliant He was held under the highest level of security making each attempt to escape more riskful than rewarding.

His only hope was his will to gain his freewill back. He didn't care about the war or about people's ideals; All Zenith wanted was to make his own choices in life, and he didn't want anyone to get in his way.

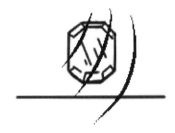

The dragon's eyes danced open as a breath of hope was released into his heart. He hung with one arm on his shackle as he shakily released his other arm.

With his feet on the ground, Zenith placed his ears to the ground. He listened to all the nearby guards as he envisioned each prison cell.

It didn't take but a few seconds for him to notice the faraway growling of his friend Elvador. Elvador was in the torturer room being reeducated to the human's ideals.

Zenith grunted, and his fists beat the ground softly as if to hide his anger. Now wasn't the time for him to lose his cover. He was sure that it was all for nothing. Escape or be terminated.

He knew if he caused the humans too much trouble, they would eliminate him in a public execution to make a scene of his disobedience.

The dragon summoned his inhuman strength and quietly broke the lock on his cell. Without the shackles on him that restrained his dragon powers, Zenith was truly a monster.

He lowered himself to the ground and walked by the wall's shadows.

Zenith stepped closely to another dragon's cell and placed a finger to his mouth in a whisper.

The dragon inside named Leyia was frightened to follow Zenith. She knew that following his antics and hoping for freedom was what got them here in the first place.

He offered her a hand through her cell, and her eyes reflected that of his own. They shined with a hope filled with a fire called vengeance.

"Trust me, and we will make it out. I'm not

going to leave a single one of you behind," Zenith said in a whisper.

As he saw the light in her eyes, he decided that his dream was not his own. It was a shared dream among the dragons, and he was the dragon who would manifest their dreams.

A guard picked up his footing at the sound causing Zenith to slam himself around her cell side wall.

"What is that door doing open?" the guard questioned as he walked with cation to the cell.

"The guards didn't lock it after they were done with me," Leyia whispered.

The guard's brows furrowed, and he smacked his head in annoyance. "Animals belong in cages. What do my men not understand?"

Zenith grunted and dashed on the man. He threw his body to the ground and covered his mouth. The caption guard looked up at Zenith with wide, brown eyes.

The dragon muffled the guard's pleas, and he

said, "You better hope your soul can save your men. I'm going to show them just what kind of animal I am."

He twisted the man's neck and stood up with his legs still shaking. "I am a dragon," Zenith said glaring at the corpse.

Leyia looked at Zenith's eyes with horror, and Zenith broke her shackles.

"They must have heard that. I'm going to use my speed and lava fist to break out everyone. You need to focus on using your water to fill the rooms with the most guards. Others will follow, and we will make it out of here."

The girl shook her head, and she followed onward.

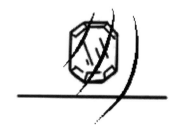

A few years after the Great Dragon Rebellion, Elvador approached his friend.

"So what do you have for me today?" Elvador

asked in a lighthearted tone.

Zenith walked with his head done and knocked into a chair.

Elvador's eyes widened, and his face hardened.

"What happened?"

"Leyia, they got her," Zenith growled.

Elvador's eyes opened. "B-But I thought that she was just on the defenses," he stuttered.

"They came after us this time, Elv. Those Ember Knight bastards are on the offense," Zenith growled.

Elvador sat down in one of Zenith's chairs with his head in his hands. He gulped and tried to hold back tears, but the cost of freedom was overwhelming him. He just wanted everyone to be free and live their own lives making their own choices. The two friends had the same dream; They both wanted to fly freely among the sky in a world where dragons could be free.

Zenith walked over and held out a piece of paper in front of Elvador. "Look at it. This is their hideout. You know what has to be done."

"Destroy everything?" Elvador said in a rhetorical phrase as he stood up and approached the door.

"We cannot hope for our dreams to exist in this world as it is now. We have to destroy it."

"Destroy the world?"

"Destroy everything. Their cities. Their inventors. Their idealistic propaganda. Everything must come down before we can rebuild the dream we both dream."

Elvador's eyes dimmed. He knew Zenith was serious. His friend's dream mirrored his own, but there was one key difference; Elvador believed that their dream could manifest in a world with the least amount of pain and suffering. A world where they could defeat all slavery over his people and rebuild learning from their mistakes.

Zenith wanted to destroy everything, but Elvador wanted restoration.

Elvador's fingers dipped down the door's frame, and he said, "The job's already done."

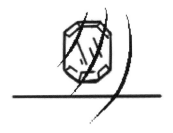

After several months of Elvador being captured by the Ember knight's, he woke one night to flames and dragon roars.

His eyes widened in horror, and he grabbed his heart. Zenith was here, and he was the only person who could stop him.

Screams filled his ears, and Elvador rushed outside. He viewed Acadash flying in the air in her dragon form.

She spewed of venom from her claws and attempted to slice at Zenith.

Zenith's dark eyes dashed to the ground where he saw Elvador. He pushed Acadash, sending her flying into many buildings.

Elvador winced knowing how many were killed by one swipe of Zenith's hand.

"Zenith!" he screamed as he transformed.

Zenith flapped his wings and laced his claws into their camp's soil.

"What's the fuss about, Elvador. It's been months. I thought when you said, 'It was already done', you meant it. But I know now! You were saying farewell!" Zenith yelled as his dragon voice caused knights to tremble behind him.

"It wasn't like that, Zenith," Elvador said faintly. He dug his claw into the ground and dived at Zenith.

"I just learned some things, and my heart opened up where I could finally see behind the clouds of my dreams, and what I saw was everyone's suffering, broken hearts hidden behind a never ending nightmare!" Elvador screamed.

Zenith Held up his dragon claws and wrestled Elvador like two elk dueling for a mate.

"Allow me to end that nightmare, Elvy!" Zenith yelled as the two took off into the air like a reverse meteor shower.

They danced in the heaven's exchanging blows filled with raw emotions.

"It doesn't have to be this way!" Elvador said as

a lump filled his throat.

"Look at us!" Elvador cried out.

Zenith glared ignoring his friend. If Elvador wasn't going to come back by choice; He would make him and convince him of his wrong doings. They were friends.

"We're flying freely in the clouds! Both of us are choosing our own actions! Isn't this the dream you fought for?" Elvador said as he dived beneath Zenith and swiped him from behind.

Zenith dashed back and grabbed Elvador's tail biting to regain his stamina. Elvador shrieked in the sky filling the knights below with terror. The beast were two high up, and their wings were causing too much turbulence for any knight to approach.

Elvador latched on Zenith and bit his side as he too rejuvenated his body.

"It's not supposed to be this way! Dragon's fighting our own! We are strong and superior to all the races of their world! We need to unite and create a new world together!"

"No, Zenith! We need to restore it!" Elvador cried, exchanging a tail wipe.

"I see now—you too are a product of this world and must be destroyed! You've been tainted, Elvador!" Zenith screamed and two continued to deck it out.

The night turned into several days of the beasts attacking each other and rejuvenating in the sky. The dragons who were allied joined in on both sides until they called it off in a stalemate.

This type of battle of clashing hearts filled with dreams of a new dawn continued for the next thousand years, and still, Elvador fought his old friend hoping to change his heart and stop the consuming madness Zenith spread like a plague.

Chapter 19 The Week Before the Battle

With soaring dragons in sight and tall walls, the ship hovered over Aspen Bay. Elvador hollered at Benard to take the wheel when he noticed an unfamiliar string in the air.

Strong feet pounded on tin metal as he ran to the back of the ship. With a signal from Fae, the dragon jumped out of the ship and transformed into his orange, scaled self.

Wind scrapped his pronounced cheeks as he flew over to the soaring dragons. Elvador leaped onto a mini beast in the sky.

He felt a sudden oddity when all the dragons surrounding him shouted, "He's one of us! Stop!"

"He's a beast of Zenith! How can you guys be so blind? He's not even a true dragon!" Elvador yelled in a growl.

"The Water of Life saved him! Zenith sent some beasts our way, and we tested the healing water on them that was stored in the village. The water healed him. He has control over himself," the old, lady dragon said as she flapped her wings staying in place.

Her scale colors were light purple and green like a flower. The lady stood out as the voice of the groups of freshly recruited dragons.

"You mean—we can cure Zenith's mind-controlled army?" Elvador asked flabbergasted.

"Zenith's mind control is an ailment. It's a beast-tamer, dragon ability. The water does no cure their dragon state though. Their forms seem to be permanent!" another floating dragon said.

In the background, Fae landed the ship, and the crew exited the ship. The new recruits stood outside with anticipating breaths as they marveled the flying beasts in the air.

In a short time after arrival, the group decided to take the fight to Zenith and end things once and for all. They sat over tea and discussed battle tactics, and it was decided that in a week, they would set their sights on ending Zenith and raise Ephoreia to stand for herself once again.

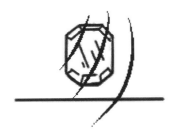

Inside Heaven's Castle, Zenith sat grumbling. "You know, if you just—"

"Silence! I will not be directed! I know soon my plan will unfold, and a certain elf will join my cause," Zenith sneered through gritted teeth.

"But, their forces aren't intact. They are all ov
the—"

Zenith lunged off his throne to Acadash an
grabbed her by the throat. With her arms danglin
he shouted, "Do not direct me! I am your God!"

He flung her body into a nearby wall, and sh
groaned on impact and falling limp. With som
twitches of her palm, it was evident that she wa
alive.

Acadash looked to Zenith with fear in her eye
"I will not speak anymore of it."

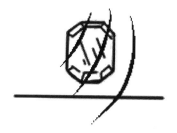

Underneath them, the Resistance Forc
reinforced battle plans and continued buildin
team morale. The resistors possessed the skil
however they needed united preparations.

They scurried off to their objectives like worke
ants. Alice and Earrie led the ground-troops whil
Elvador trained the air fighters. Fae createc

powerful weapons and melded-dragon satchels as Benard reinforced medical troops.

During a day of training, Alice and Benard rallied in the town center for a practice duel. Alice was transformed with red, orange scales on her flesh, and Benard glanced at her with a grin.

She studied Benard. For a second, Alice felt as though Elliot, her knight commander was smiling back at her with towers of smoke behind him ready to fight.

Alice remained in her delicate dress. In her days, elves didn't wear armor instead they put all of their trust into their abilities. It was an upholding of honor among the elves.

Inside of Alice's hands, she bore two white, dragon-claw daggers. She had always been a master in pure damage.

On the opposition, Benard possessed no sword. He might have been clothed in silver, knight armor from the treasury, but he still had a noticeable bond with his embers.

Crowds of onlookers on break speculated the duel. When a chime struck, they began the dancing. Alice knelt while flames of fire flickered as she flung her wrist. To her left, Benard summoned a basic bolder attack her way.

The flame knight was a trained captain of her time. Battling a rookie was nothing to her. She decided to play with him for some time while she tested her current abilities.

Benard felt pressured with a crowd roaring and clapping. Droplets of sweat poured as Alice's heat escalated. She flew behind him and shot several flamed fists his way. He dodged her attacks and covered himself in a dense dome of stone.

Alice decided to put on a show. She burnt out all of the edges of his stone wall and waited above for an opening. To her surprise, Benard tunneled underneath and snuck behind her with towering columns of stone.

She deflected his attacks with her blades but received a large, boulder shot into the dirt. Alice placed weight on her hand and wiggled upwards. If he was going to play serious, she would too.

The blaze knight grunted in annoyance when the seared ground did not birth her flames. She summoned weak, fire pellets to shower on him, but Benard easily deflected them with a stone shield.

The flame knight decided to change her battle approach to endurance. Because Benard had little stamina built up from being a medic student, she decided to drain him with her many years of built-up strength.

Alice smirked and placed him in her boiling pot of dancing flames. Coal warmed Benard's toes, and he found it difficult to breathe.

He shot a stone pillar from the ground and used his shield to dive to the sky. Benard figured the easiest way to win this battle was to use the environment to his advantage as he had the ability to fly and tunnel underground.

The flame knight shot propelling flames from her daggers and jumped into the air startling Benard. She wasn't about to be outsmarted so easily.

He shot two pillars at her only for her to dive above and kick him from behind. Benard fell over and shielded his face before landing into the ground.

Alice walked over to him and offered a hand. "You know, you're probably the best rookie I've ever seen, or I'm just rusty from being a stone woman for a thousand years."

Benard blushed and jumped up embarrassed. He bowed and scratched his head.

"You're an amazing addition to our team!" he said.

Alice smiled, and the two walked off to continue their practice.

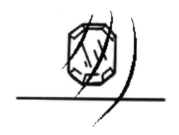

Away in a clock-shop, the young princess made herself as busy as a bee during the week. With broken-down, unsold merchandise, Fae fashioned lightning, pulsed gunnery and ballistic swords for their ground soldiers.

Fae flipped her orange hair to the right of her

ear while she summoned creations. She closed her eyes and visualized dragon armor with satchels for the riders.

The princess created reflective shields and sun-beaming spears. Belts of grenades and traps floated into her mind. With a smile, she released her inventions.

Even though she wasn't sure what she would do when they faced Zenith, the little halfling believed she would make the right choice when the time came.

A certain, friendly dragon knocked on the door. He followed Fae's tether and greeted her with a saddened expression.

Fae looked up from her work and said, "Something wrong, Pup?"

Elvador blushed at the nickname and said, "Can we talk?"

The princess sat down her creations and walked over to his side placing a sand on his shoulder. "What's wrong? You don't look too good."

Elvador paced back and forth in a frazzled state.

"It's just that I've been killing Zenith's mind-controlled beast for a thousand years—and this whole time—I could have been saving them. I'm a murder—Fae," he said with sad, puppy eyes.

The Inventor dashed to his front and embraced him tightly causing his eyes to bulge. "You did what you thought was best, and isn't that all we can do?"

Tears built in the dragon's eyes as he tried to hold in a millennium of un-cried tears.

He flew his tight arms over her shoulders and held her tightly. "I don't know if I can face him," he said, confessing.

Fae looked up and seeing Elvador's face, she felt tears building up inside her eyes too. "I don't know if anyone of us can, but we have to give it our best shot," she said.

Elvador let his hands fall to his side, and he looked up and the clock's ceiling, "That's not what I meant. This whole time—now matter how much I told myself that I hated him—I always thought I could save him, and one day—"

"I know we want to see the good in everyone—

do it myself all the time, but sometimes there isn't any good there. Sometimes—people leave their conscience and hearts behind to follow paths of evil . . ." Fae said as she thought about all of her people's oppressors.

The dragon stayed by Fae's side for a few more minutes until he composed himself enough to go back to the barracks and continue being the leader he knew he had to be.

A tempting thought crazed Fae's mind. If only she could go back to the white room then she could figure out what higher source empowered her.

With that knowledge, she could understand her purpose, and possibly save Zenith. She had never thought of saving his life before, but seeing him the way Elvador did changed her mind.

Zenith was a dragon who was sued and abused by the humans who created him. His people were suppressed and controlled like puppets. All their emotions were treated like nuisances.

His people were torched. The feeling of a lost people being oppressed gave Fae compassion for the dragon. He started his path wanting to do what was right, but he was consumed by the darkness that brewed in his heart from injustice.

Fae decided to lock the backdoor of the shop and slip into a concentrated state. She let her tiredness from working portal her to the white room.

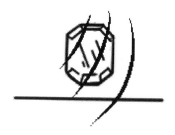

The Inventor gripped her heart and held on as she shot out lettering on top of lettering. She grinded her teeth to hold back any fear.

Codes filtered through her body and beams of color sprung forth. Fae remembered her control inside Benard's embers and decided to cling to that sense of authority.

Voices in the distance pulled at her. Fae paced past them with ease as it was time for her to discover the real source behind her powers.

Though it hurt her heart to do it, she ignored

Delka's while walking forward. Fae felt a tugging force, unlike the others. The pull was full of love, life, and peace. She didn't sense that it had anything to do with her backup systems.

Instead of a draining pull, this force spoke peacefully to her. Her footsteps led her to a glittering throne, and she couldn't perceive the presence in front of her.

Brightness over followed her as Fae fell on her knees and shielded her eyes from blinding glory.

Out of the radiating figure, a voice said, "Fae, my child, I know what you seek. I have a plan for you and all of Ephoreia. It is greater than anything you could ever imagine."

She peeked up only to see shining glares of rainbows mixed into the light, "A plan?"

"I gave Ephoreia its Inventors when I created her. I desired to give my people the ability to create whatever paths they chose. I wanted them to enjoy their world and get along peacefully. Despite my wishes, Ephoreians did not use their Inventors for good instead they used them to destroy each other. They altered the human, DNA coding that I created and changed Ephoreia's natural balance. Now when I look upon my creation, I see a show of what was intended, but I have a plan to rebirth the once great world of Ephoreia" the incandescent essence spoke.

"What is this plan, and just what are you? I need to know how I can use my powers to save Ephoreia from Zenith . . . and if I can save Zenith from himself," the young princess questioned as she held her face down.

"Zenith's rule of terror as surely as every season changes. I am the coder, writer, machinist, and compiler of your world. Every tree you see I gave root. The dragons only exist because I allow it. Death and life is in my control. I've given your world and you everything you've ever possessed, my child."

His words caused goosebumps to climb up her flesh, "Are you, God?"

"Yes, Fae, I am."

During her short life, Fae heard a few times about God. She always seemed to find herself more involved with the never-ending struggle of her everyday life to ever think much of faith o questioning her existence.

The young princess questioned her heart as to why she ever assumed that everything she achieved was her own doing. The young princess realized that every stray piece of bread she ever ate was a blessing by God.

Fae visualized flashes of him providing for her during all the times she could not go on herself. There were times when he uplifted her. When he gave her joy and filled her with a peace of mind giving her the hope to persevere through the gloomy times in the Slums.

"Fae, when you leave this place, you will inherit a blueprint that will overwrite and change Ephoreia's code. With this code, Zenith will be powerless to stop what I have planned for Ephoreia, and peace will blanket over the nations.

"In this new world, you will not have your memories, and all of Ephoreia will wake up from its dreamy state with a new chance to live."

"And what about saving Zenith? Can I save him?" she said with concerned eyes.

"You cannot save him, but I can give him a new

life."

"How can I release the code and prevent the incoming battle's bloodshed?"

"Worry not, child, when the time is right, I will release the downloaded code from your heart. You need only be a vessel for my will."

Fae's heartbeat sped to unthinkable paces as she answered in a sudden act of obedience, "Okay, I will do your will."

In a split second, Fae's consciousness slapped itself back into her being. She viewed a string of gold lettering that floated into her stomach.

The Inventor held her hand close to her heart and smiled with joy. She had a new hope. Hope in God, saving Ephoreia, and giving Zenith a second chance.

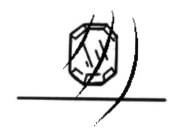

Faraway in a meeting room of Tuner Town's, King Pik held a meeting. With whispers, nobles and royals muttered out ideas of joining the Resistance Force.

King Pik was proud of Elvador's, and the princess' accomplishments. He was stricken with the booming hope that Aspen Bay marked.

The king walked back and forth and toyed with his long beard lost in thought. "We must read out troops for battle and join them," Pik said in a strong tone.

They all sat in an oval-shaped table and leaned in at his words.

"What future will we be setting for our youth if we rely on elves for help?" an ogre yelled with a slamming fist that lifted their glasses of whiskey.

"The only future they'll ever get is if we don't step in!" a brute, council member growled. Her mutterings caused silence to befall them, for it was clear the path they had to take to press onward.

"As you all know, Elvador is among them. I trust his judgment as if it were my own. Now is not the time for us to question them,"the king said.

"We must not lose out on the goofy of slaying

Zenith!" an ogre yelled.

The meeting continued on until they all reached an agreement and preparations for the impending battle took place.

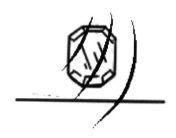

Everything was falling into place day by day. The warriors of Soft Water Village spent their time bonding with their set dragons., and they learned how their abilities worked, meshing them all up together like a mixing-pot.

The ground's soldier force learned to use Fae's weapons and followed Alice and Earrie's commands. They shot when they screamed fire and swung their blades like obedient dogs under their new commander's lead.

Benard trained his medical staff to be ground medics. They gathered herbs and remedies, and the trainees brewed up ointments for battle. With cotton and stitches, they stuffed up their bags. He advised them to hide in the shadows and pull injured behind walls.

In the meantime, Elvador invested himself in mentoring the dragons and their riders. He took no rider since he planned to take Fae to Zenith. The young princess was their secret weapon. But since Zenith already knew about her, she needed the best protection available, Elvador.

The princesses shared a room with Alice with three makeshift cots out of hay and blankets in a stone-created inn. Benard crafted the building for the massive amount of volunteers to rest in. Every night they would talk for hours and giggle together like they had a new sister.

Alice discussed her powers with Earrie. They planned to harmonize their abilities as Alice told them of her many power combinations with Elliot.

"The two of us would smoke out and sear up enemy forces. We could take out entire fleets by ourselves. He respected my power and never looked down on me.

"We were equals. Two commanders working for

a common goal. I trusted him with my men's lives, and he did the same. Oftentimes, he would make risky plays because he knew I would come through every . . . " her words softened until they quietly disappeared. Alice's eyes trialed out a star-cluttered window.

The flame knight sighed and leaned into her pillow. Fae couldn't help but continue to ask her a plethora of questions. Things got more intense when the young princess asked her about the halflings of her time.

Alice's face appeared disheartened, "In my days, there were many droughts. Our people were property stricken from war and lack of trade. So when we lost our food sources, the halflings stepped in and saved our lives. They traded with us, providing us food and freshwater.

"If they hadn't stepped in, we would have all died of starvation or dehydration. The halflings in our times were royalty while elves were merely their humble subjects. We lived because they aided us in our time of suffering. To think, we repaired them by enslaving them and all their ancestors. I—

I just can't bear it."

Earrie's heart throbbed at her words.

"In Heaven's Castle, we were taught that we saved them. Isn't that ironic? The only reason our people lived was because of them and we go and enslave them as if we didn't owe them our people's lives," Earrie's words sounded like bitter tea.

The princess's naive view on Ephoreia and her kingdom was shattering bit by bit from the reality that stood before her. No one in Ephoreia was perfect even her father failed to reach that standard of goodness.

"Sister," Fae whispered in Earrie's way.

"What's wrong, Fae?" Earrie questioned her sister.

"I know this sounds odd, but I met God today."

Earrie flung up from under her covers and wiggled her eyebrows at her sister, "Fae, be serious what are you talking about. What God?"

"I went into the white room again," the halfling mumbled under her tan pillow.

Alice stayed out of it and listened. She knew

next to nothing about Fae's powers, but she knew that they weren't like embers or dragons. They were the source of everything powerful in Ephoreia, for it was almost as though their creations were beyond tangible.

"You did what? You told me Delka warned you to leave that place, or you would lose control over your powers!" The elder princess ran to her sister's cot and shook her violently.

Fae turned over to face the wall in embarrassment. With a pull of her green, blue sheet above her face she spoke out in defense, "I needed to know how to stop Zenith."

Alice finely clocked in, "So, what did you find out?"

Her curiosity brought out Fae's childlike faith, "I learned that God sent us the Inventors to aid us, but they're choices weren't what he indeed. Death and war, all of it isn't what he intended. We were supposed to live in peace and enjoy our world instead of fighting among ourselves like what our world has become. He wants to change Ephoreia."

"Change Ephoreia? How?" Earrie said

intrigued.

"He wants to do something that will rebirth the nations and give us a blank page. A sort of redemption plan. A second chance to do good with what he has given us," Fae's eyes twinkled with glittering hope.

"So . . . the Inventors . . . they come from God?" Earrie asked as though she was taking it all in one breath at a time.

She turned her head around to hide the tears that grew from a blossoming belief in something bigger than herself. Just like the rest of the group, Earrie thought they were alone on their journey, but now she knew there was a higher force directing their path.

"Everything comes from him. He created all of it. But we molded those blessings into something dark. I'm starting to understand the power of knowledge now. Like what Delka said about harvesting it. Nothing truly ever comes into existence by us. We just go around shaping the things we already have. It's like we are part of a play, and we only have the tools on stage to utilize .

. ." Fae mumbled off, gripping her sheets in enthusiasm.

With her newfound spark of faith and hope in God, Fae did not own the same doubts as before. The fate of the world was not on was not on her shoulders anymore.

The sheer power that sprouted from this idea of change brought forth shivers to Alice. If there was a God then there was so much more to life than battles and death.

If heaven was real, unlike the counterfeit in the clouds, maybe she could be with Elliot again one day. Alice had faith now that together they could bring back the Utopia Kingdom, or at least, a new one formed by the almighty hand of God.

The three chatted all night long of their many fascinations of God and of their ideas of what a changed Ephoreia would be like.

They didn't question anything Fae told them. Everything seemed to make more sense the longer they spoke.

Fae had not been entirely open with them, she didn't want to tell Earrie that she would lose her memories, or the depths of the changes planned. An entire world reborn to live its days without the damage caused by Ephoreia's corrupted state. She also had no intentions of telling her she planned to save Zenith if possible. It would only worry her sister.

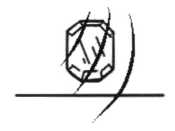

In the barracks the following day, the dragons pressured their wings and tuned into their instincts. If Zenith were to be brought down, everyone would have to give their all.

Elvador walked back and forth in the training camps. "You must move with them, duck when they duck, and dodge when they dodge. Also, take into account the air pressure. When they are flying, you shoot your arrows and throw your javelins. Always pay attention to your surroundings at"—he walked in front of a smiling tribal—"all times. The last thing we need is collateral damage."

Some men scuffed and turned their noses up at his words. They did not believe themselves to be unskilled enough to hit one of their own. Elvador eyed their attitude and challenged it with a smirk.

"When you're up that high in the air, the last thing you want is to be dropped. Am I right?" His smirk transmuted into a beaming smile.

The color on the men's faces faded. They were not amused by his words. Now was the time to take things more seriously.

The next six days were built of sweat and heart as everyone gave their all to their preparations. They brought their strongest punches, highest kicks, and best swings to training. The army of resistors looked like a force to be reckoned with as they scurried around with one mission in their minds.

Chapter 20 The Feast Before the Battle

On the morning before the battle, a messenger bird flew in with a word of Tuner Town's alliance to join the Resistance Force.

At dawn, they would bring their copper airships to meet them at Heaven's Castle. The message said, they would bring group troops of dwarven knights, ogres, and brutes. It also mentioned their strong, air defense of missiles and dwarven technologies.

The final moment before the war, a feast was scheduled to send the troops off. It was a sending away party for those to leave as many knew they would never see their loved ones again. Everyone put their into this festival with decorations of cultural themes, dancing shows of lights, and games of gambling and duels.

Elves clothed stone benches with silk and white, laced bouquets. They spurred glitter dust and diamond, napkin holders. Feathers of every color were glued into headdresses for their kind.

The humans of Aspen Bay decorated with their finest pieces. Black portraits of soldiers' faces were painted professionally on their wooded plates. They placed down cotton, deep-green tablecloths.

On the tribal tables, they dressed them with thin, beaded coverings. They placed multicolored napkins down and red-painted, clay dishes.

Some halflings made tables as well. Without much culture of their own to rely on, Fae created small, decorative pieces for them. They consisted of robotic, halfling dolls that danced in and out of small homes. With claps and twirls, they released a fine tune of music to the festival.

On the tables, she placed humble coverings. Smells of fresh-baked, blueberry pies filled onlookers noses, and arrangements of fruits were shelved on the tables.

The halflings enjoyed a fresh multitude of warm loaves of bread along with other homemade items. Their tables were cluttered with cheesy slices of bread and melted-butter dips.

The clan members, on the other hand, loved to cook their game. They left out roasted wild boar on display for all to gawk at.

Local humans of Aspen Bay enjoyed lots of fresh fish and seaweed because of their harbor taste. They placed down sushi and fish salads.

A soft melody rumbled the skies as it molded with the laughter and joyous shouting of the party. A cloud of peace and contentment left them over bloated.

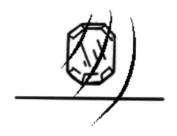

Earrie peeked into a wardrobe mirror inside her inn room and moved her necklace slightly to the left. She shrugged her shoulders upwards and offered a shy smile. With a feminine twist, she marveled her elven garb.

Her outfit was a silk, glittering slip, and its color was as white. The piece sparkled out rainbow glimmers hanging to her ankles. It accented her hot-pink heels.

"You know, you've got to be the most beautiful elf I've ever seen," Alice said as she gawked at the princess.

Earrie threw her hands up to her cheeks in embarrassment. "Y-You're joking. If anyone here was the prettiest elf, it would be you!" she folded her arms in stubbornness and huffed.

Alice's cheeks beamed, "Come on now, you're reminding me of Elliot," she waved her hands as she refused to accept the compliment.

The flame knight wore a black, thin covering that fell on her like a bathrobe. Underneath it, a red, laced skirt peeked through guided by her tan top.

Her style bore much difference to that of the modern-day elves as she dressed more modestly. The elves of nowadays opted for more the more revealing appeal. During Alice's time, they preferred to veil their beauty.

Earrie faced Alice. Her face didn't appear to be lighthearted. Whatever was troubling her, it was something serious.

"You okay?" Alice asked.

"I have something I must inform you of."

She raised an eyebrow and said, "It's alright. You can tell me anything." Alice smiled and approached Earrie.

"When this is all over . . . I want you to take my place as queen of Heaven's Castle or um . . . Utopia."

Her words caused Alice to step back, "What are

you talking about? You're a great princess!"

"The things you told me about the halflings and what people did to them, they are just not right. I can't continue that rule of handed-down oppression. Our people don't deserve to be ruled by such corruption," the princess said as she turned to cloak herself from any potential rejection.

Alice placed her hand on Earrie's soldier, "Your people can't go forward if you're dwelling on the past. It's kind of like what Elvador said. I think, you're just the kind of princess our people need, and you need to trust yourself to be capable of shaping the future."

Earrie looked around with wide eyes. "I'm a knight. I'm no leader, and without my father . . ."

"They are still *your* people, Earrie. They believe in you. Just looked around at all the survivors of your kingdom. They're counting on you, and I am too," Alice said.

"Maybe you're right," Earrie said in a sigh.

Fae left for the gathering. She didn't go for elf fashion instead she wore a gifted, tribal dress. Fae loved their style and found it freeing to make her own choice of clothing.

She sat next to some halflings and sang songs of love and victory. With taps of her fingers, others joined her chanting, and not too long after, they all found themselves in a circle of arms kicking their feet back and forth in celebration.

Elvador wore a brown tuxedo he purchased from the town. The suit's sleeves rang a few inches too long so he folded them in. With a pinch to his neck, the dragon adjusted his tie. Tonight was a night of relaxation, yet he couldn't help but dwell on the impending battle.

He turned his head when a thump tapped on his door. With a nudge to the door, Benard peeked in smiling.

Elvador couldn't help but mask a giggle. The dragon had to turn his head to the right to clothe his snickering.

Before him, Benard wore a skin-tight, male dress. The covering danced with long sleeves under a slip of opal covering. On his waist, a braided, gold cord rested.

"Wow, if I didn't know better . . . I'd think you were getting married," Elvador teased and poked him on the shoulder.

Benard pushed back his fiery locks and eyed him back, "This is just customary for the elves of Heaven's Castle."

"It's . . . fancy."

The two walked by the girls' rooms as they were ready to escort their friends to the party. Together they both dove for a knock, but at the same time they held back their wrist in neutral hesitation.

Earrie opened the door with a bright smile, and Benard bundled up his fingers in noticeable distaste as one canister of liquid showed her intentions, Maxwell.

The princess would save Maxwell and live the rest of her days happily ever after, but Benard didn't want that happening. He needed to get that water from her.

Elvador peeked around and looked confused.

"Where's Fae?" he asked.

"Fae's already at the festival," Earrie said with a grin. It appeared the dragon was out to swoon her sister tonight.

"Oh," Elvador said looking down.

"Don't sound so depressed," Alice said with a laugh. "You can take me."

Elvador flushed, and he lent out his hand with a bow to Alice. She smiled and reached for it.

"I don't remember you being such a gentleman before," she teased.

"Well, a thousand years changes a person," he gleamed.

Earrie waltzed over to Benard with her arms crossed, "Aren't you going to escort me, Ben?"

He looked with cheeks that matched his hair, "Well, of course."

With a bend to his knee, he copied Elvador's style and offered her a hand. The princess rolled her eyes and accepted the palm. The two pairs went off to join the festival.

Soft crickets chirped as they walked through the moonlit night. Earrie sped up when she viewed her sister dancing. A little fire in her spirit arose as she let go of Benard and ran off to join the dance.

Through the night, people danced and stuffed themselves till their stomachs grew nauseous. Loved ones held back tears and made the best of the time they had left. It was after dessert was passed around that drums sounded for a show.

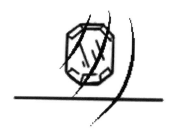

Alice stood upon a stone-paved stage and covered her front with wings. Tribal men behind her beat on their drums while violin players from Aspen Bay played sharp speeds.

The knight thought for a second that their

strings may burn off from the friction of their tune. She wasn't used to such vibrate music. Her age had softer, delicate tones of artistic dances.

The crowd watched in silence as they anticipated the show. Men marched behind the performer. With a loud bang, Alice flung her wings. Feathers fell in dramatics behind her body.

As the music played, she tapped her toes to a matching pace with the fiddle. Men behind her held up sticks to which she lit through her embers. When the music rose as did her flames.

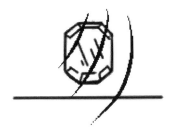

During this time of entertainment, Benard noticed Earrie slip away from the crowd. The princess walked back to her room exhausted from the week of preparations.

Benard had listened in to her conversation with Fae. She indicated to her sister that she would be heading off to bathe. He decided if he was going to go through with his plans to demolish her vile of water, this would be his last chance.

He gulped nervously and stumbled off in pursuit.

Benard followed her into the woman's bathing area. With sneaky ducks, he awaited her disrobing.

His ears pressed to a thin door, and he heard her fumbling with her armor. Benard remained close masking his breaths. He perked up to her, closing the door to the changing room and entering the communal bath.

Benard creaked open the room, and he spotted her clothing. With patience, he lifted each piece and canvassed for the vial. His heart pounded as he spotted the water.

His hands shook violently, and he unscrewed the lid. He dumped its continents and replaced it with a dud. When his mission was complete, he set the vial down and wiped his brow sighing heavily.

A sudden opening of a door caused Benard to jump.

"Benard?" the princess questioned.

The princess scanned Benard, and her eyes

leaped at the sight of his embers glowing a dark violet. They appeared black in color with flames of purple.

"This is the women's bath, Benard," Earrie said with a gulp noticing Benard's flushed cheeks.

Earrie remembered her appearance and jumped back with her hands. She was merely in a towel.

"I'm sorry," Benard said, and he turned around embarrassed.

The man's heart fell into a pit of guilt. He reached for the door only for Earrie to grab his arm from behind.

"Benard, give me your embers," she said.

His eyes lit up, and he looked down to the embers.

"My embers, it's black!" he shouted pulling off his embers and throwing it down in a panic.

Earrie picked up the embers, and their color turned to a slight purple. She looked sad and said, "This is my fault, Benard. Part of being an ember knight is learning to control the dark heart of the sealed dragon inside."

She looked away frowning. "I think it's best that you don't use these tomorrow. I don't want you turning into another Maxwell."

Earrie tried to hold back tears. She knew that if the water didn't work on Maxwell, she would have to end his life. There were no hesitations in her mind.

Benard still facing the wall broke into a fit of uncontrollable tears. Before Earrie could ask him what was wrong, He burst out of the room and ran through the hallway.

She yelled for him to stop, but he didn't listen.

"What have I done?" Benard sobbed as he dashed past the festival into nearby woods.

"I must leave and never return. I cannot face her ever again. Earrie trusted me, and I betrayed her . . ." he tripped over a broken tree and hid his face defeated in the ground.

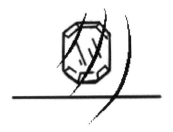

Fae finished eating and clapped for Alice's performance. She wiped her mouth with a napkin and spaced her green eyes into the crowd.

For a second, the dancing bodies led her thoughts back to the Honor Ball; The last night she was in Heaven's Castle.

The young elf remembered all the men begging for her hand simply because she was a royal and giggled to herself, for not a single young man had asked her to dance this night.

Status was everything back in Heaven's Castle. Being a part of this world underneath her, once sheltered life, opened the elf's eyes.

Not everyone's life was shaped by the ideals of superior bloodlines and wealth. Just like the halflings in the Slums, people had different views of life. They all walked different paths that lead to perspective filled with individuals and diverse futures.

There was a freedom in this world without status. It was as if anyone could be the person they were created to be.

She closed her eyes and imagined how the world could be without Zenith and smiled softly.

Fae pictured herself dancing freely and cooking in a bakery. She eyed her sister in her imagination and couldn't see her without her armor on leading a force of troops behind her.

Closing her eyes tighter, she was able to see her sister in a soft dress leading a kingdom of elves.

"You okay?" a husky voice asked from behind.

Fae leaped in her seat and spotted Elvador.

"Oh, it's you," she relaxed.

"Care to give a dragon a dance" he asked with an offering hand causing Fae to blush.

She nodded and grabbed the hand with a delicate grip.

Elvador escorted Fae to the other couples, and the two turned their footing to a slow beat.

The dragon held Fae close by her waist and

gazed softly into her eyes. The princess smiled brightly back and laughed.

"I thought—no one would ask me to dance!" she said with enthusiasm.

Elvador's eyes darkened, "And why is that?"

"I'm not a royal here or noble. I know it's silly, but I didn't think anyone would notice me," she said blushing.

"I noticed you," Elvador said softly.

They continued to dance until the dance finished and Elvador walked with Fae off into a distant, garden bench.

"Thanks for dancing with me, Fae," the dragon said.

"Uhh—thanks for asking me," Fae replied blushing as she fumbled with her dress nervously.

"You know, I really like you," Elvador said looking into Fae's green eyes. "You're an amazing person, and I don't think I have ever met someone with a heart as big as yours even in a thousand years . . ."

Fae grabbed her red cheeks and turned away from him. Her hand danced across the bench as she moved it tracing invisible circles.

Elvador looked at the stars and set a hand on Fae's shoulder. She leaned in softly and followed his brown eyes to the distant stars.

"This new world you told me about, a reborn Ephoreia, I want to find you in it and live my days with you," Elvador said.

Fae's eyes shot wide open, and she turned her head to him dramatically throwing her hands around him and embracing him tightly.

"Elvador, I . . ." her words drifted off, and tears fell from her cheeks.

"What's wrong?" he held her and lifted her crying face.

"There's something that I didn't tell everyone," she said.

Elvador's eyes widened, and he asked, "What do you mean?" in a pancaked tone.

Fae removed her hands and wiped her tears. "I'm going to lose my memories," she said.

Elvador's eyes relaxed, and he waited a few

minutes for Fae's heart to clam as he listened to its beat.

"I'll find you whether you have memories or not," he declared.

The Inventor turned her gaze up to meet his eyes. "How are you going to do that?"

"I'm a tracker dragon," he said with one of his hands out dramatically in a jest.

Fae tilted her head back and let out relaxing laughter. "I guess, when we met, you didn't have your memories, and we still . . ."

The princess wasn't sure how to phrase her words. She knew that from the moment she met Elvador, she felt a connection, but she wasn't sure what it was till now. Love.

"Come find me in this new world," Fae said while she placed her hand inside Elvador's.

The dragon leaned over to Fae's forehead and planted a kiss. "I promise," he vowed.

The princess felt revealed to have confided in someone of the true sacrifice behind reinventing the world. She didn't need to carry all of her burdens alone anymore.

Fae was reluctant to tell Elvador that she wanted to save Zenith because she didn't want to hurt him if it didn't work out. She could tell he had tried too many times to save his lost friend, and she didn't want him to be hurt anymore.

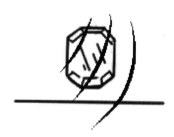

Earrie ran into the festival with her armor back on and looked for Benard. She spotted Alice eating a slice of white cake and ran to her side.

"Alice, Benard ran away," she said in a worry.

The flame knight dropped her fork and stood up. "Where did he go, and why did he run off?"

"His embers," Earrie held up the stone embers from her right hand.

Alice's eyes bounced at the sight of violet embers. "What on Ephoreia?"

"He wasn't trying to restrain the dragon's heart so the embers started controlling his heart," she looked around worried.

"Control him? I haven't ever heard of that," Alice said.

"That's because when the embers were first created their seal was strong enough that the soul had no power, but through the centuries, the seals grew weaker giving dragons the ability to overpower a weak-willed host.

"This is the first time that I have ever seen someone's embers so dark. I'm worried that Clance's hatred gave the dragon a weaker seal. In training, if anyone's embers turned even the slightest shades of purple, they would be banned from becoming a knight. The rules of the knights were always so serious, I should have been a better leader like my father and . . ." Earrie's words drifted.

"Learn from this," Alice said as she grabbed Earrie's wrist.

"Let's go and look for him," she said, pulling Earrie through the festival.

"Alight! I already checked his room, the hospital, and even the library. I think—he ran to the woods!" she said defeated. She looked arour for a certain tracker dragon with her eyes but didr see him.

"Elvador can track him!" Earrie stated and Ali nodded.

"Let's look for both Elvador and Benard. If yc find Elvador first and Benard is far away, come ar get me," Earrie said, and the two split off.

Benard heart trees bristling, and he looked up t see three minions surrounding him. The defeate man scooted to his legs and noticed a familia fright returning to him.

"Back away!" Benard yelled.

The beasts laughed and circled him. He reache a shaking hand for a stick near him.

"Get away!" he screamed, shaking the stick.

"Zenith sent us," a minion said.

"Zenith?" Benard questioned trying to remai

calm.

"He wants to offer you a deal; Join us, and he will give you what your heart desires most."

"What my heart desires?" Benard stepped back and a picture of Earrie popped into his mind. He shook his head and lifted the stick in his hands back.

"No!" he shouted.

"Wrong answer!" a minion growled.

The beasts shot webbing at him, and another lit the netting with lighting. Its circuit shocked Benard, and he screamed in agony.

Trees bristled above, and Elvador along with the rest of the group flew down beside Benard.

Fae used her chains of lighting to carefully remove the webbing from Benard and Alice and Earrie jumped the beast, but before the group was able to subdue the three minions, they dove away into the air.

"You alright, Benard?" Earrie asked gilding him up while the others surrounded him with concerned looks.

He looked at all of their worried eyes and felt guilt stirring in his stomach. "No! I'm not alright!" he yelled as tears fell down his cheek once more.

"Earrie! I betrayed you!" his confession caused everyone to gasp, and Earrie's eyes widened.

"What did you do, Benard?"

He looked in her innocent eyes and stood on his legs. Without facing anyone, he shamefully admitted his actions. "Earrie, I didn't walk into the wrong bathroom earlier. I-I followed you there because I wanted to sabotage your water."

Fae and Elvador stepped closer to Earrie to ensure she didn't make any sudden actions. She wasn't the type to hold back her anger.

Earrie surprised the group as her face relaxed. "It's okay, Benard, I forgive you. Your embers were tainted—I should have paid more attention to your training. Zenith used my father's embers against me to poison you. I see it now," she said.

Benard kept his back from the group as he was too ashamed to face them. "Earrie, I'm the one who did that to you. You need to replace your vial with the healing water. And save Maxwell. Don't blame Zenith for what I did. I'm a horrible person," he said as he tried to hold back tears.

Elvador approached Benard from behind, "You're not a horrible person, so you made a mistake, what matters is your choices moving forward."

Fae walked to him from the other side and beneath in front of his face. "I'm the fool who let Zenith into our castle and started this mess in the first place.

"Look at me now, I'm helping lead the army to defeat him, and I'm going to do everything I can to rebirth the world with the code God gave me. If God chose me to do this knowing that I made a mistake that cost so man their lives then it's obvious that all mistakes can be forgiven."

Alice walked in front of Benard, "If Earrie has the heart to forgive you, I can too." She smiled a friendly smile.

"Guys—I'm so grateful for your kind words," Benard said.

After some time, the group flew back to Aspen

Bay and headed off to their beds to sleep.

Benard went to the hospital and spent the rest of the night creating as many medicines and sterile bandages as he could since he wouldn't be much help without the stone embers.

"Benard didn't join us," Acadash said, informing a preoccupied Zenith.

She fumbled with her right arm while looking into a dusty window. Acadash avoided confronting Zenith on any topic in the past week as his anger was boiling.

Zenith knocked over his set of chest pieces he was using in the castle's study. "I know he didn't!"

"B-But you said—"

"I know what I said!" Zenith shouted as he slammed the desk in front of him into a nearby bookshelf causing its continents to fall on Acadash.

"Sometimes—changes happen! I have

everything under control!" he shouted.

Zenith glared at Maxwell's weak body. He had been taking his anger out on Acadash's host body too many times. The body was bruised and weak.

"Get up!" Zenith yelled.

Acadash tried to lift herself up but the bookshelf felt overwhelming.

He glared and reached for her limp body. "You've run out of use to me."

He held up Maxwell's body, and Acadash screamed, "Don't!"

Zenith smiles, "What are pawns for if you never use them? It's time I upgrade to a knight!"

"No . . ." were the last words from Acadash as her hands fell from Zenith's grip.

The inventor technology on Zenith's arm glowed, and a blue color left Maxwell's body.

"There, you're more useful to me as leverage anyway. The princess's eyes seem . . . so fixated on you," Zenith sneered before exiting the door.

Zenith was no fool to playing with people's emotions. He knew he could weaken the princess with her love.

The dragon walked around the castle and into a locked safe room while an unconsciousness Maxwell laid frozen on the study room's floor.

His body regained its natural, elven state. All of his scales disappeared, and his wings left his back.

It was time that the beast brought another piece to his game.

Chapter 21 Take Down

On a cold morning, the dawn of the battle rose. Troops readied themselves out in a lined fashion in front of all of Fae's silver ships.

Earrie opened her eyes and with a deep breath, she gathered herself and all of her determination before getting out of her bed.

The others finished their assignments, and everyone met by the ship. All of them wore sparkling battle gear while Elvador wore a long scarf. This time he would be prepared for his transformation.

Sad goodbyes were tossed around as troops boarded the ship, and townspeople laid in wait with dripping tears for the departure of their loved ones.

After an hour, everyone finished loading the ship, and they were ready for takeoff. Elvador manned the ship to give Fae some rest before the upcoming battle.

Deep inside the halfling's heart, she knew how she would play her part in saving Ephoreia. Fae would release onto Ephoreia a new birth while giving the nations another chance for all those lost souls bound to a never-ending war.

Shortly after the dip into the sky, Earrie met her men inside the ship's auditorium. She prepared herself for a long thought out speech.

"As you all know, we've made a god our target An unstoppable man who's been driven to insanity In his conquest to end his kind's slavery, he's enslaved us all. We live our lives in shackles to his will. Death and destruction are normal to us, for we were birthed into it. I'm here to tell you that it doesn't have to be that way.

"Zenith is pure evil. He is a captor, oppressor, and slave driver; Nothing good resides in this man. Today we will bring an end to this man, and a new Ephoreia will be created without oppression!

"This is a day that we shall mark in history. A day marked with resistance! A day where halflings, elves, dragons, dwarves, brutes, ogres, and humans all join together to end this chapter of tyranny in history!

"Though we may call him a god, I'll let you know he is not the God of all creation. For my sister, Fae, met God! Our true God gave her the power to change all of Ephoreia. We are not alone in this battle! For if our God is for us, who can stand against?

Zenith will fall today, and liberty will reign over Ephoreia!"

Her strong words caused whispers and goosebumps to befall the crowd before her. Some questioned her sanity while others rallied in her defense. A few elves walked out to the dock in their disapproval of her faith, but their actions didn't stop her.

Crowd listeners toasted on her words, "Liberty!"

A sudden stop to their flight alerted all attention to the deck. They made contact with Tuner Town. A few exchanges over the intercom let word pass of battle plans and strategies.

Tuner's airship was bright copper like Elvador's previous aircraft, but the ship was ten times the size of his. Sun beat off its edges and blinded the on looking crew.

Pik marveled at the technologies of Fae's mighty airship. The ship suited steam engines and hard, metal bunkers. He admired the girl's taste.

The battleships pierced through Ephoreia's open-air like a knife into soft butter.

The fleets hovered a slow ascension to Heaven'

Castle. As they floated, Dragons along with their riders fell into the city. Like hail, they plummet down without hesitation.

They were met face to face with Zenith's triple-numbered army though the dragons were not unprepared. Due to Elvador's precautions, all of them were loaded with miracle-water, syringe shots. Sharp, metal needles pierced through the sky with wind whistling streaks.

Dragons jumped onto mini beasts as they wrestled mid-air. Roars of beasts rumbled through the streets of Heaven's Castle. Dragons against dragons covered the sun from the ground eye's view. After their airship was cleared out, Elvador awaited Fae.

With a joint agreement, he jumped into the open skies. The beasts pinched at his flowing scarf and loosened its restraint while he grew in size.

The wind brushed his cheeks as he awaited Fae's jump.

Crunching sounds cringed Elvador's sharp ears when Fae condensed her ship into an armor covering for herself and a slip-on saddle for

Elvador's back.

She fell and landed onto him. The two went whipped through the air as they provided support to the resistors. The young princess decorated the sky with sensory cannons and fire ballistics for the ground.

Many beasts turned docile from the water's remedy. And after their freedom was given to them, they gladly joined the battle against Zenith.

The new supporting dragons possessed many memories of Zenith's control. They remembered his cold touch all too well and the lengths he would go through to traumatize those against him. They jumped at this opportunity to end him once and for all.

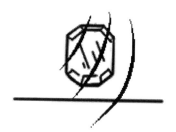

Elvador looked to his left, and he noticed a familiar, orange tether. The dangling string was far away from the battle like bait for a hungry fish.

"Fae, Maxwell is in the Slums. I don't know why, but his tether looks different."

"A trap!" Fae yelled. She looked around and spotted her sister in the crowd. "Go and check it out, but be careful. I don't want Earrie to fall for any of Zenith's tricks."

The dragon nodded, and Fae slipped into her hovering boots remaining in the air. Most of the enemy's dragons were already taken care of, so she was safe for the moment.

Elvador followed the string into the Slums where Heaven's Castle rundown machinery laid.

He bit his lip knowing that this was the place Fae grew up in. The oppression hit close to heart. Treating people like machines was never ago. People were not meant to be weapons or robots.

The orange cord ducked into a clothing factory. He transformed into his human self and wrapped his scarf around his body in a robe-like fashion. He squinted in confusion and stepped in.

Maxwell stood in the middle of the abandoned

workplace. There was no light except a small window above them that seemed to beam a spotlight directly on his pale skin.

In his hands, he held up Nefewra. His eyes glistened, and he ran at Elvador. Maxwell used his spare arm to fling Elvador backward.

Feet clawed into the barren dirt beneath them. The struggle didn't last long as Maxwell pushed his body into a broken pipe.

Elvador coughed up blood and wiped it from his mouth, "Zenith's controlling you, isn't he?"

He stood up on shaky legs and walked over to Maxwell with raised hands, "Resist him, Maxwell, I don't want to hurt you."

Maxwell shifted his fist to his gut, but Elvador pressed his legs into the ground and stood his ground. The dragon grabbed his fist and clenched them together.

"Acadash's tether is gone. You're a minion now aren't you?" Elvador shouted between blows.

"I'm going to save you, Maxwell,"just as Elvador's words left his mouth, he felt himsel replaying history. He remembered all the times ir the past when he had said the same words to Zenith.

Maxwell remained speechless. It was like he was a zombie. With an overpowering grip, he clenched onto Elvador's ankle and threw him down.

Earrie noticed rumbling in a faraway building in the Slums, and she remembered beforehand watching Elvador fly off in that direction.

Benard not too far behind the charge approached a concerned Earrie. "What's wrong?" he said.

"I think something is going on in the Slums— I'm going to go check on it. You stay here with Alice and lead the men."

The red hair-ed man eyed around with freight in his eyes. "Lead the men?"

The princess placed her hand on Benard's right

shoulder. "You can do this. I wouldn't leave you in charge if I didn't believe in you."

Benard nodded his head and glanced at the front where Alice was. "Be safe, and save Maxwell," he said before walking towards the charge.

Earrie smiled and dashed to the Slums.

Fae eyed her sister leaving, but she couldn't follow. Fae knew she was needed here. The Inventor gulped and hoped Earrie, Elvador, and Maxwell would be okay.

The young princess continued in her best efforts to shield the ground force while maintaining her air support.

Fae ducked as arrows were shot at her low flight. She was the target of many of Zenith's attacks. He must have seen the others leaving and took the opportunity to focus on a vulnerable Fae.

But Fae wasn't about to give up, she set robot underlings on her front to shield her, and continued to focus on her war plays.

She was the support the troops needed to push through Zenith's front, and without her shields and weaponry they would have been demolished.

Ducking and divining her way past several more attacks, Fae sighed as she made a close call with an icicle. She held her heart and wondered what was taking the others so long.

Underneath her, Alice burned herself out a crisp pathway to the royal courtyard. She peered over the shrubs and discovered green grasses filled with flowers of every kind. A tug of memories lifted inside her heart.

She visualized herself planting some roses in her garden. Toes scrunched into the grass as they stepped to her side. She looked up to see Elliot smiling at her in white armor.

With long red hair that flew in the wind, he knelt beside her. In a kneeling position, he pulled out from his side pocket a white case. With a pop, he opened it to reveal the most magnificent sapphire, diamond-cut ring.

She remembered herself squealing and flipping around to hide her flushing. With hands to her soft green cheeks, she jumped up and down.

Alice ran past the scene and blinked hard to

suppress the memories weighing her down. Her legs continued to march to the castle walls for her. She raised her daggers and directed her men to siege the towering structure before her.

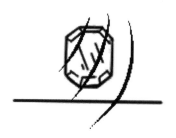

Overhead, Fae brought her eyes to Zenith. He stood casually on the steps outside of the castle's front door with his hands laying calmly behind his back. She squinted vigorously as she noticed that his lips appeared to be whistling.

He leaned back onto a while pillar and flung his head to the clouds to glare back at the Inventor. The young princess jumped in shock and shook her head. She wasn't going to let fear hold her back from her destiny.

Inside the clothing factory, Elvador reached for Maxwell, "You've got to fight for control, Max!" He shook his shoulders.

Maxwell's body moved like an empty doll..

The lost Maxwell swung at Elvador, and he dodged the swipe with haste.

The rundown factory door flung open and Earrie stood there with a shocked look.

"Be careful, Earrie, Zenith is controlling him. He's a minion now," Elvador warned.

"It's okay, I have miracle water!" she yelled while running to his side. "Subdue him for a second!"

Elvador obeyed, and he smacked Nefewra across the wooden floor. The dragon placed his weight on top of a wobbling Maxwell, and he set his knees over his arms.

Earrie managed to get a drop of the Water of Life into his man causing Maxwell to fall limp.

"What's wrong with his body, it's limp," Earrie muttered.

Elvador scanned his tether and held it in his hands to connect to Maxwell. "I have never seen anything like this. I think his soul is gone. It's like his tether is barely hanging on being controlled by Zenith like a puppet string."

"No!" Earrie screamed tugging tightly to Maxwell with tears falling down her eyes.

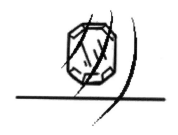

With loud grunts and a slammed door, Alice's men managed to bring down the royal gate's entry She remained ground level in the front line of her men.

"For Ephoreia!" Alice screeched holding up one of her daggers.

Men behind her echoed back her call like

wolves. Together they rushed into the castle's front.

Benard followed in awe. He motioned for medics to remain past fallen structures and pull wounded to safety.

To the men's surprise, Zenith stood in front of the castle doors like a statue.

Wind swooshed around Alice as it grazed her knuckles, and she peered to her left and then to her side as her men fell one by one like flies as Zenith remained still.

In a panic, Alice rose up a wall of fire around herself and her army to cloak them from the unknown attack. The violet-haired knight continued listing in horror as her men dropped. Her heart raced like a running stallion.

Benard stayed back and his eyes lit up in a familiar fear. He grunted and shook his head. He wasn't going to let fear control him any longer.

"Tsk Tsk Tsk . . . Lava beats fire. MwahaHAHA!" Zenith teased in a whisper that evolved into a hysterical scream.

The dragon flung his finger back and forth in a mocking mannerism. With a deep, bird-calling howl, Zenith walked down the castles' stairs morphing into his dragon form.

"Don't let him transform!" Alice yelled out, but it was of no use; She knew they were out of time.

Benard reached for a fallen weapon with a lightning discharge and ran towards the beast. He held the weapon out and attacked Zenith from his side.

The dragon growled and turned his head to Benard. "Wasted potential," he said.

The beast kept his lava around the enemies and approached a shaking Benard.

Benard held the weapon out and noticed the Inventor technology on Zenith's hand. His brain flashed with an idea, and he diverted his attacks to Zenith's wrists.

The technology glowed a multitude of colors before it shattered with a spark. Its color left, and thousands of trapped consciousness and souls pierced through the sky like dazzling lights.

Zenith dashed to Benard and grabbed his neck

"What have you done?" the beast shouted before snapping Bernard's neck.

He threw Benard's body underneath him and walked over it to a hesitant Alice.

Alice watched the scene without being able to do anything. "Benard . . ." she muttered, feeling a piece of her soul crack.

Zenith's body collided into the courtyard's wall making wreckage in his shadow. The tyrant's scales glistened a fuming red while his flesh darkened to coal black while he wailed and yelled historically.

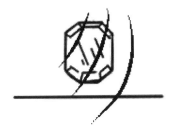

From above, Fae scanned the scene. She noticed all of Zenith's beasts' souls and consciousness were floating back into them like white lights similar to the glow of her powers.

One bright light dashed beside her cheek and made its way to the Slums.

She used a created telescope to scan heat signals between the flames around the palace.

Fae saw limp bodies, and a dash of heat knocked over other bodies.

The princess gulped in fear, and she made her descent to the scene.

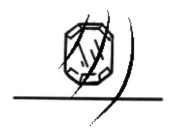

A light shot past the mourning princess and Elvador and into Maxwell's body.

Maxwell turned and regained a lifelike light. He reached for Earrie's soft cheeks and said, "What's wrong, fairies aren't supposed to cry."

"Maxwell!" Earrie shouted, flinging her arms around him.

Elvador watched the two embraced and turned running out the doors. He saw lights and tethers all around the sky.

"Something is happening outside. Tethers are everywhere," Elvador yelled to Earrie and Maxwell.

The princess lifted Maxwell on her side, but he shook his head. "Zenith changed me. He made me a minion. I'm okay. I feel strong," he said.

Earrie looked at him with concerned, green eyes. "There's a battle outside. All of Ephoreia's capable fighters came to Heaven's Castle to take down Zenith."

Maxwell eyed her intensely, "I-I know Earrie. My memories are all back. All the things Acadash did in my body—I remember everything."

The princess reached for Nefewra, and she motioned for the group to exit.

Outside Elvador transformed back into his dragon form. Earrie released her embers, and Maxwell changed into his minion form.

Fae approached fallen men in a suit of full armor. She kept her ground firm as she walked into flames.

In her front, Alice stood in a wall or flames. The knight danced into the air dodging a flaming rock from Zenith while breathing heavily.

Alice was able to withstand the heat and air quality due to her years as a knight. She retained all of her knowledge and skills while she was frozen those thousand years.

Fae summoned a glowing shield out of the weapons from men around Alice. She looked for Benard and frozen in pace at a pale-colored elf.

The princess screamed in terror causing a distant Elvador to pick up his pace.

"Benard!" she shrieked as her hands trembled in front of her lips.

Zenith laughed at the Inventor and dashed in the air behind Alice's flame to confront her.

The princess pulled out her chains of lighting and slapped at the incoming beast. He danced back dodging her blow and licked his lips.

Goosebumps crawled on her flesh, and she glared at the man. "You killed Benard, my father and destroyed my kingdom. You poisoned Clance and toyed with Maxwell."

The princess shot her chains out and dived in the air while Alice managed to escape her trapped position.

"You will be stopped!" Fae yelled.

Elvador along with the others arrived to witness the face off with Zenith.

Earrie noticed the source of Fae's screams as she eyes a unlit Benard. "N-No," she said faintly.

Alice ran to the princess's side. "He died releasing those souls from Zenith. He died a hero," she said.

The princess resisted tears, and grabbed her heart.

Benard's last action on Ephoreia was helping her save Maxwell. She silently thanked him and held up her sword.

Zenith's massive wings puckered sucking in everyone beneath pouring lava. The group dug their swords and claws into the ground to keep from falling into his lava.

Fae jumped on Elvador's back, and Earrie followed, bringing a typhoon of wind. Maxwell dashed to Zenith's side while Alice propelled herself into the air.

Zenith was surrounded, and all of his mind-controlled minions were free. He had no one to hide behind him any longer. The fight was on.

Earrie followed Zenith in the air and sucked his wind into a circle. She flew around holding Nefewra gathering as much friction as possible into her wind cycle. Maxwell eyed her and understood what the princess was planning.

He followed in the typhoon of wind and grabbed Alice. He noticed her flame powers earlier and could see the pieces to Earrie's plan.

All his years studying her were not in vain. The two had a silence method of understanding each other in battle, and it was about to pay off.

"At the right time, right before Earrie channels her wind, I want you to shoot as many flames as you can alongside her," he said.

Alice nodded, focusing her flames alongside the princess.

Fae held Elvador's neck above the others as he was the only one quick enough to match the beast in speed.

He dodged lava and hard rocks with hard turns of his wings. Fae secured herself with a tighter belt and breathed in deeply to focus on the code she needed to release.

The Inventor was certain that the time to release the code was upon her. She clenched Elvador's neck and yelled, "It's time!"

Behind them, a cycle of wind pulled Zenith into a sucking siphon.

Alice's fire exploded into dozens of continuing attacks. Bangs went off, and the attack sent the others back.

Zenith's dragon shrieks filled the air, and blood-spattered scales flew off into the air.

Elvador dove down on top of Zenith. He dug his dragon claws into Zenith's large neck sending his broken body into a smack down on top of Heaven's Castle.

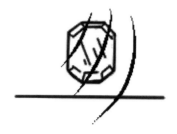

A silence followed as smoke cleared, and Zenith's growls went weak. The group looked at each other with shocked faces as they attempted to grasp their victory.

A light blinded the group from above, and Elvador reached his head up to study the light.

He noticed Fae wasn't on his back anymore. The Inventor floated in the air, and her body turned golden. Out of her stomach, a gold, Inventor code shot like bodies of water.

The sky around them changed into a pure blue as smog cleared from the Slums, and pieces of gold dust shattered around them like broken glass.

Elvador transformed and ran to the others Together they all starred at the young Inventor as she lit up Ephoreia like a fallen star.

"Is this the code she was given?" Earrie yelled holding Maxwell's hand.

Elvador shouted back, "It has to be!"

Alice fumbled with her hands trying to cover her eyes, so she wouldn't be blinded.

They felt a tug. Suddenly, they looked around, and all of Ephoreia was white with glowing, gold lettering dancing left and right.

"What's happening?" Elvador yelled.

"The rebirth of Ephoreia!" Alice shouted.

The princess released her hand from Maxwell and turned to give him the kingdom's blade only for it to shatter into golden ashes in her hands.

Her brows turned at its deconstruction, and she ran to her sister in a panic. As the knight ran, her embers disappeared, and her wings dissipated. She tried to jump on invisible steps to reach her sister, and she screamed out her name.

"Fae!" Earrie yelled with her hand out before the princess was sucked into a portal of pure white.

Chapter 22 Born Again

On the day of the Battle of Heaven's Castle, Ephoreia was reborn into a new world called earth. Everyone was given a new chance to live their lives without the taint of what one was.

As Ephoreia was reset, souls lived out their lives progressing at a faster speed without relying on Inventor code. Everyone was transformed into humans as the first Ephoreians had been before their DNA was altered by Inventors.

Fae was not alone in losing her memory. Everyone in all of Ephoreia was born again to live new lives with a second chance at living.

The story between the heroes of Ephoreia did not end there, but it began a chapter as they continued to live out their lives.

Leading into an era of arcade games, economic prosperity, and disco parties, the lives of the girls continued.

Far away inside a three bedroom city house, Fae munched on her favorite, salty chips. She reached for a remote and changed her TV station to a comedy show.

She giggled flinging her body back on the family room couch.

"Stop being so lazy, Fae!" Earrie yelled from behind.

She wore a blank skirt and a pink, ruffled top. Earrie flung her light, brown hair and glared at Fae's back.

"Are you coming to the game tonight?" she asked.

Fae sat up with an annoyed look and eyed her half-sister. "Yes, but I'm going with Alice and Acadash."

Earrie huffed and walked into the kitchen. "You know those two are only trouble makers," she said waving her finger in disapproval.

"They're my best friends! What do you know?" Fae said angrily.

"I know you only hang out with them because you like the boys they talk too," she said with a grin.

"Who doesn't like Elvador?" Fae said annoyed as she threw her face into a couch pillow.

She poured herself a bowl of cereal and sat a the dinner table.

"Put down your chips, and come and eat some breakfast!" she commanded folding her legs.

Footsteps entered from the hallway, and a tal

man with brown haired sighed.

"When are you going to stop bossing around your sister like that. You know, she's a freshman now she doesn't need you directing her every step," Richard said smiling.

Earrie's eyebrow twitch. "Don't remind me, she goes to my high school now! And if she didn't need me, she would get her act together!" Earrie muttered between gulps of cereal.

"Don't be like that—Earrie—she's your sister, and she'll always be by your side. You two need to cherish that bond. Why don't you all go to the game together?" Richard said endearingly with his arm on Earrie's shoulder.

Fae shot up and laughed with her arms folded. "She doesn't want me going because she's going to the arcade first to see her crush, Maxwell!"

Earrie's face burned pink, and she yelled, "He's not my crush! I cannot stand that fool! Always trying to one up me! I swear it!"

Richard laughed and Stella walked into the room "Look at all of you—eating breakfast without waiting for me to fix us a proper meal! I had bacon and eggs planned!" she said with a smile.

Richard walked over to her and placed his hands behind her back. "I've got room for more," he teased.

Stella smiled and turned to Earrie. "Want me to drop you off at Clance's tonight after the game?"

Earrie sighed and stood. "You don't have to—my mother is going to pick me up."

After some more disputes, the two girls were dropped off at the arcade several blocks form school.

Fae ran inside and grabbed out her coins throwing them into her favorite machine. She pressed each button while licking her lips and raising her eyebrow.

Earrie walked behind her sister up to her favorite fighting machine and started a tournament. She picked her main to fight with; A girl with a sword and wind powers.

She started match one with a calm composer no wanting to overthink herself into an early defeat.

Earrie sighed as she passed the first two

matches. She needed to get ten thousand points to beat Maxwell's score, and she needed to do it while he wasn't around either. Whenever he was at the arcade, Earrie couldn't get her game on.

Her thumbs sweat, and she nearly missed a button smash. Behind her an annoying voice sung out, "Trying to beat my score again? Oh—Earrie—you never learn."

Earrie shouted in annoyance as she missed her attack losing her third match. She grabbed for her hair pulling at its strings.

"Relax, Earrie, it's not that big of a deal," Maxwell said.

"Come on, get up, and I'll show you how it's done," he said smiling.

Earrie glared and said, "Don't you have a game to get ready for?"

Maxwell looked down at the girl and leaned his arm behind her.

"Well, class-rep, don't you have some cheerleader stuff to do?"

Earrie's face shot red, and she fumbled out of

her seat in a fluster.

"I-I don't have to be there for another half hour!" she insisted.

Maxwell laughed and sat down in the arcade seat choosing his fighter.

"Actually, I'm out for the rest of this season. I twisted my ankle, and coach Pik is pissed at me. I'm just hiding out here, so he will get off my back,' Maxwell said.

"You hurt your ankle?" Earrie said as she bent over to get a look. She noticed some wrapping, and she glared at Maxwell.

"Shouldn't you not be walking on it?" she said in a motherly tone.

Maxwell waved one of his hands dismissing her. "Nah—It's not that big of a deal, really."

Earrie relaxed her shoulders and stood beside him. "That's too bad, I wanted to watch you play."

Her words left a faint blush on Maxwell's cheeks that he tried dismissing with a shake of his head.

"You can watch me play arcade," he joked and Earrie laughed.

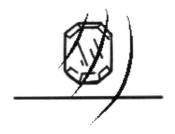

At the game, Fae spotted Acadash and Alice. She waved and ran ecstatically to their side.

The girls giggled making jokes about the cheerleaders as they walked over to a spot close on the bench.

Benard waved, and the group sat next to his side.

"Hey Benard, I see you're eyeing my sister again," Fae said laughing.

The boy's cheeks ran hot, and he stuttered, "N-No, I just think she's got some great moves! Look at her flip like that, isn't she amazing."

"Yeah, she's something alright," Fae muttered.

Alice looked over at the boys getting ready to start the game. "My boyfriend has got to be the cutest boy on the team," she muttered.

"Elliot is cute, but I think Zenith is way cuter,"

Acadash said.

"Zenith? Isn't that the other team's quarterback?" Fae said with wide eyes.

"Yeah, sure is," Acadash said with a grin.

"Why you little betrayer!" Fae giggled as she nudged Acadash with her arm.

The four watched as the match began, and Fae smiled when her favorite quarterback made a play.

"Elvador, he's the best one on the team," she said in a dreamy tone.

Acadash turned at Fae's words. "I almost forgot, Fae. Elvador asked me during chemistry class if you were single!"

Fae covered her mouth in a gasp. "A-Are you tricking me?"

Acadash leaned in with a glare behind raven hair. "Why would I trick you?"

Fae held her hands on her cheeks and stared at her thighs. She flicked one of her stray pieces of red hair behind her right ear while fiddling with her hands.

"And—I told him you were. He said he's going to ask you out after the game," Acadash said.

Fae jumped in a squeal before others yelled at her to sit down. "I can't believe you told him that!" she yelled, throwing her face in her legs.

"He's bold, isn't he?" Acadash laughed.

The four watched the rest of the game while Fae continued to hide her blush and muttered to herself.

A finger pressed at Fae's side causing her to yell once again.

"Stop being a spaz," Earrie said from behind. To her side was Maxwell.

Normally, Maxwell would be out on the field. Since he didn't have any buddies to sit by, he followed Earrie.

Benard blushed and motioned for her Earrie to sit next to his side, and Earrie shrugged sitting behind the group on open benches.

"If our team wins then we'll make it to layoffs!" Earrie said, smiling.

Maxwell sat to her side and smiled. "Come on everyone, let's all shout together!" he said.

Benard scuffed at Maxwell and rolled his eyes.

"Come on!" Earrie said.

The five raised their hands and shouted, "Go Ember Knights!"

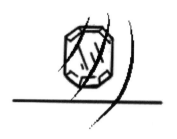

The group of cheering children were ecstatic as their team won. They could barely contain their excitement, and Benard split his soda over during the commotion.

Everyone around the group began to leave the benches while the six of them stayed in their seats talking.

"Alright, my that's my mom's car. I'm heading off!" Earrie said before waving goodbye.

They stayed on the benches talking until a janitor ushered them off.

Alice split from the group and ran into a hugging kiss with Elliot. Benard said his goodbyes and walked off to his car.

Maxwell and Acadash looked at each othe

oddly, and Acadash pulled him aside.

She whispered something in his ear and told Fae, "I need to borrow Maxwell. Let's all meet up sometime this weekend, okay?"

"Okay," Fae mumbled. She walked over to the parking lot and waited for her dad to pick her up.

Her face sunk as she was somewhat upset that Elvador didn't ask her out. She thought back to Acadash's jesters to try and place if she was joking.

When her hope was lost, a boy walked up behind her startling her. She turned to see brown, puppy eyes.

Her cheeks instantaneously, lit-up pink and she looked around pretending that she didn't notice the eye contact.

The boy continued walking up to her. His footsteps caused her nerves to run high.

The crow dwindled, and the two of them were some of the last high school students left at the school.

"Fae," Elvador said.

"Oh, hello," she said in a panic while turning to

meet his look.

"I've been looking everywhere for you, Fae. I wanted to ask you if you wanted to go to the movies with me tomorrow?"

Fae's cheeks went from pink to red, and her heart skipped a beat. "I would love too," she said with a surprising amount of confidence.

Elvador turned and threw his hands up in the air while shouting a 'YES'. His enthusiasm caused Fae to lean in with covered chuckles.

The pair stood there continuing to make their Saturday plans, and both of them felt a familiar bond between them as if they already knew each other in a life long ago.

In that moment, Elvador kept a promise he had forgotten from another world.

This was not the last time that fated promises or vows unfolded as the group of once heroes and villains were all tied together by a string of fate They all continued to live their lives in a peaceful contentment having never remembered the land that was once called Ephoreia.

Thank you for reading this book. I hope you appreciate it, and that it brought some joy to your heart.

As a self-published and beginning author, I would greatly appreciate your review. Everyone's thoughts matter. Please share what you like or things you wish may have happened, so I can have instructive and positive criticism as well as see what you, my reader, likes. Thank you for the support during this journey, and I hope you will continue to read my latest books!

Made in the USA
Middletown, DE
11 November 2022

14534056R00272